The Girl from Far Away

Dedicated to my mother, who taught me that if you fall down

five times, stand up six.

The Girl from Far Away

Jennifer Austin

Prologue

Jess

When I was five years old, I fell off my bike.

It was this new model my parents had saved up for over many months. My dad, David, had worked odd jobs, from painting garage doors to building flat-pack furniture, to earn the extra cash. They had this old jam jar they collected the money in. It was kept on a high shelf next to the wine glasses, which would disrupt layers of dust whenever moved. My brother, Everett, told me it was money they were hiding from the tax-man, something he'd learned about from kids at school.

When a new family moved into our street and one of their kids proudly proclaimed their dad was a taxman, I tried to move the jar to a better spot. But I ended up knocking down the entire shelf as I balanced on a kitchen chair. My parents were more worried than angry, and I even got to keep the scar on my foot from stepping on broken glass. I remember that night—drifting off to sleep in my mum's arms as my dad swept up the mess I'd made.

"'Sup, buttercup?" my dad whispered to my mum. "Fine day for a great escape."

"Hey, May. Shame this winter will never end," she whispered back.

A few days later, I came home to the bike. It was coated in mint green, with cream wheels—perhaps in hindsight a poor wheel colour choice—a pleather seat and handlebars, a *Teenage Mutant Ninja Turtles* bell and this woven basket on the front that was just big enough to fit my *Postman Pat* toy. My dad attached stabiliser training wheels to the back, and off Everett and I went around our town, Fairwater.

He was so excited to show me around this town he'd already started to discover. We went to all the places he'd been to with his friends, and he even spent all his pocket money on sweets for us. And as we cycled up and down the streets, he'd always be turning around to check I was okay, holding himself back so he never strayed too far. He was always looking after me.

But I was too brave. At five years old, I thought I could conquer anything. As we neared the top of the big hill overlooking our town, I pulled out a hidden screwdriver from my basket and convinced Everett to remove my stabilisers. I'd dreamed of the rush I'd feel as gravity and wind teamed up to carry me home. But dreams aren't real, because instead of carrying me home, they knocked me flying.

After checking I wasn't badly hurt, Everett cycled home as fast as he could to get our parents. I cried all alone at the top of the hill for what felt like forever, until this woman appeared. I can't picture her face or anything about her. She's just this taller blob in my memories now. But she saved me.

She said, "I have a daughter your age, and this is exactly something she'd do, because she's just as brave as you." She picked me up and rocked me. "But I do worry about her, to be that brave and hopeful. What happens when she fails for the first time?"

My tears started to fade as the sobs softened.

"If I could wish anything for her, it'd be that one day she'll be able to pick herself up when she falls, to not need saving."

The woman was long gone by the time Everett returned with my parents to rescue me. My mother frantically cried about her baby while my dad carried me the whole way home. Everett promised to fix my bike as he dragged it behind us.

But there's one part of this memory I can't rationalise, so instead I brush it off as my childhood imagination. Because Everett's never mentioned it and if it had happened, he would've definitely seen it. You don't miss something like that. But I swear, just before I fell, my veins had been glowing black.

Maybe it didn't happen; maybe I'm making it up. But this memory will always stick out in my mind, because that was the first night I dreamt of Biack.

Chapter One

Jess

"I had another dream last night. About the other world," I whisper in Chris's ear, to which he mumbles an incoherent response. "She threw him across the room."

He manages a groan. "Who threw who?"

"The Girl, she threw Fire Boy. He wasn't very pleased, but she didn't really have a choice," I say.

"Who's Fire Boy again?"

"Aiden," I answer, watching as he tries to open his eyes.

I trace the familiar scars on his arm until his deep breathing irritates my skin. A swift kick, and he jumps to life.

He mumbles, "Okay, cool dream. What time is it? Do I have to leave?"

I wasn't finished. There's more to my story. "You should go now." Pulling myself out of the bed, I push the blinds open to peer out the window at my brother below. "Everett's already packing his car."

He seems to have fully regained consciousness as he gathers

yesterday's crumpled attire off the floor. "Do you, like, need me to stay with you or something?"

"No." The window struggles open after a serious amount of force; I gesture to his exit.

"You know, I'm sure your parents won't mind me being here, Jess. We've been dating for a while now. Your mum smiles at me sometimes, and your stepdad gave me a pat on the back that time, and I'm friends with Everett. Maybe they'll invite me to breakfast."

My brother can't stand any of my friends.

"Go out the window," I reply.

I hope he doesn't think I'm cold, kicking him out so quickly. Because he's wrong, my parents would mind him being here. My stepdad would mind.

After yanking on oddly damp sweat shorts, I rummage around my desk; it's a mess of unfinished—or started—homework and uninterpretable sketches. I manage to find what I'm looking for beneath a half-empty beer bottle from last night.

Moments later, his lips attack my neck, a sloppy but much-needed gesture of affection. It melts me. Turning around, I give in before gesturing at the window a final time. I'll tell him about the rest of my dream later.

I hand him the beer. "Here, take this with you. If my stepdad found out…"

"I know," he replies.

He drinks what's left in the bottle without frowning at its warmth or lack of fizz. My eyes are drawn to his lips as he licks the last drops away. I fight the urge to kiss him; I don't want to seem clingy. Boys don't like that.

"I'm coming to yours later, right?" I ask. "You haven't forgotten?"

Sat on the window ledge, his blond hair an utter mess and garments creased to hell, his attention has already left me. "Yeah, sure."

"Hey." As I speak, he turns around. I continue, "I love you, Christopher."

The edge of his mouth twitches as he says, "Back at ya, Jessica."

He struggles onto the roof of the porch before falling onto the grass below, quickly vanishing down the bleak streets of Fairwater into the known of another predictable English town.

For seventeen years now I've been trapped under the familiar chill of the sun and the harsh borders of the sea. The challenge of finding purpose in such an average place has only become more and more apparent, and it wouldn't be a lie to say Fairwater is a place where ambition comes to die.

To obnoxiously quote Shakespeare, nothing will come of nothing.

Below my brother walks out of the house, box in hand, towards his crappy red car, where the rest of his few possessions wait. My eyes trace his movements until they result in an interlocking gaze. He musters up an empty smile. Grabbing my find from the desk, I rush to my bedroom door to discover a lukewarm mug of tea lying in wait on the frayed hallway carpet.

I race down the stairs as fast as I can without spilling the tea. Once outside, my pace turns to a shuffle.

"'Sup, buttercup? Fine day for a great escape." Everett recites. Tall and broad-shouldered, brave and smart—the traits he stole from him.

"Hey, May. Shame this winter will never end," I reply. "Thanks for the tea."

"You should get an IV drip full of English Breakfast. To think of the hours I've slaved over the kettle."

"I doubt it'd taste the same without the blood and sweat." I fidget with the paper in my hand. "I had some spare time yesterday." I pass him the paper, a drawing. "And Fire Boy had another literally bright idea."

"That guy does not look impressed." He laughs.

"Yep. But he definitely deserved it," I say.

His fingers trace the lines. "Have you ever given any thought to writing about this?"

Yes. "No. It's a stupid childhood dream that makes no sense. Why would five random teenagers have special powers as opposed to a world of experienced adults? It's silly. There's a reason I don't show other people these drawings."

"Shame. I'd read it." He shrugs.

"If you didn't, I'd have to disown you."

"Ha. I doubt that. What would your life be without your older brother?"

"Easier?"

"Oh, come on." The car boot slams with light pressure. "I've met your friends. How would you have survived if your older brother wasn't looking out for you?" It only takes a moment for his tone to change and his arms to wrap around me.

"Oh, Jess, I promise I'm coming back."

"I'll be surprised if that car survives the journey, let alone a return."

"Jess." He sighs and moves away. "If I had a choice, I'd stay."

I know.

He continues, "You be careful, okay? Tread lightly until I'm back. I don't want to return to find you gone."

"Hey, where would I even go?" How would I even go?

"Okay." A forced smile. "Just don't do anything reckless." He removes his jacket—his favourite, a plain grey body with green sleeves and hood. "Here." He hands it to me. "Have this. Maybe it'll keep you safe." A shadow slowly creeps over our conversation. "Or at least warm."

The hairs of my skin stand to attention, although little difference they'll make. A waste of atoms, he appears only in the doorway, but his shadow has spread across the entire house; the stench of hatred will do that.

"I don't expect to see you back here again." Sam, our stepfather, stares Everett down. Maybe he thinks he can move him with his eyes.

I want Everett to say, *I didn't know you owned the town.*

"I'm packed," he actually says. As we walk, I feel daggers piercing my back, so real I can almost smell the hot blood running down me. If looks could kill. A final embrace before the last words. "I'm coming back, I promise."

I had another dream last night. I want to tell him, but it's too late. He's already in his crappy red car, and all I can do is grip my cup of tea and watch as he makes his great escape.

❖❖❖

I sit at the back of the classroom, stroking the tattered cuffs of Everett's hoodie. I think I've figured school out—trying too hard draws attention, but a lack of trying also draws attention. But there's this sweet spot of mediocrity where the teachers forget your existence. I thrive in that spot. It's a shame it doesn't work on the other students.

Near the front, Scarlett sits next to my Chris. The two of them pass notes. Scarlett's a pretty girl; some would argue unfairly pretty. How can someone be born with pure gold locks and move through puberty with an untainted complexion? But if she looked any different, maybe she wouldn't be so popular. I wonder, if we weren't friends, would I like her?

We met at the start of primary school. I forget how we became friends. I just know we were. It was always Jess and Scar and then everyone else. The late-night movie marathons, long rides in the back of boys' cars and shared collections of expensive lipsticks have been long-running trends in what appears like a perfect friendship.

But I heard a rumour that best friends can tell each other anything.

As usual during lessons, my mind drifts to my fantasy world, this time to last night's dream. Fire Boy was running across the room and he didn't see them, so The Girl had to throw him out the way. I know it doesn't sound that special or out of the ordinary—it probably sounds more like a particularly strong girl pushing her friend out the way of something. But she did it without touching him. She did it with her mind.

If you could define perfect in a person, it'd be The Girl, Ella, the centre of my dreams. Every word is spoken with complete confidence, and every choice is always right. She's a being I could only dream of becoming, and that's what she is: a being I dream of.

We may be the same age, but we live two very different lives; we're nothing alike. She's not real.

Besides Chris, I've only told Everett and my father about the dreams. I can't imagine telling Scarlett. Everett used to ask me on our way to school to tell him the stories; he was especially fond of The Unbreakable Boy. My father once caught me drawing The Girl, and when I explained her origin, he encouraged me to make it a permanent habit: to draw what I dream. And so somewhere in the attic is the history of another life.

"Did you see Clara's hair today?" Scarlett steals the seat next to me.

I'm stuffing my notes into my backpack. "No, what did she do?"

"What, or more like who, hasn't that girl done?" She laughs at her own joke. "No, but it's, like, the highest ponytail ever, and you know what they say—the higher the ponytail, the bigger the slut." I find my hands reaching to my own ponytail. "Oh, don't worry, yours is fine. I mean, I wouldn't have gone that high, but it's fine." I sling my bag over one shoulder. "Anyway, I was just talking with Chris, and apparently she drunk texted him last night." I was with him last night. "He's so done there. I mean she was crazy and like clearly because she's still trying to get him back when he's so moved on with you, Jess." That bitch. "But don't worry, babe, I have your back. I asked Kate to sit with us a lunch so Clara will be all on her own. I've got you." She gives me a quick hug before we part ways for our next class.

I pull my hair down.

The rest of the day soon drifts past, leaving me feeling like a passenger to my own existence, simply watching as it goes by, trapped in this state of blissful ignorance. At least until lunch.

"Where's he going then? London?" Kate asks. "When my older sister moved out, she went to London. That's where all the jobs are." Kate's older sister moved to London for a boy.

"I think he's staying with a friend in the north." I answer.

We're sat in the middle of the canteen, a coveted spot despite being the most difficult to get to. If it wasn't for Scarlett, would I be sitting here? I think I'm only popular by association.

"Why'd he go up there? There's nothing there, there are no jobs, and you have to drive so far to get anywhere. I mean, sure, it's probably pretty, but no one moves up north." Kate reports an opinion I'm sure I heard from Scarlett.

"Maybe he wants to get his money's worth out of the car." She doesn't laugh. "One of his friends from school lives up there now. I think he went to Newcastle University." Everett's friends were all smart. When they finished their A Levels last year, they disappeared to universities around the country. Everett should have too.

"I guess that's a city. I'm sure he'll find a job there. But he should've moved to London. That's where I'm going as soon as I'm done in this hell hole." I wouldn't have said hell hole. Maybe bland abyss? "Where are you going, Jess? When we finish next year?"

"Good question," I reply with no intention of answering it.

Because I don't know where I'm going. I don't have any plans; I haven't thought about university or a job. Luckily, my grades are enough to get me far away, but I haven't given much thought to where far away is.

"Where do you think everyone else will go?" Kate asks.

I reply, "I know Chris has plans to join his older brother at Manchester and do some engineering course." I always thought he was good at fixing things. "Scarlett will probably enter the workforce, maybe in London. She'll start as a sales assistant, work her way up to manager. Then she'll meet a guy who has it all figured out, she'll fall madly in love with the safety of it all and they'll marry and have several kids."

Kate says, "That sounds perfect." Does it?

I wonder what Ella wants to do. I know what she's going to do. I mean, if she was real.

Speaking of Scarlett and Chris, where are they? They haven't shown up after their last lesson. The class probably got held back over lunch for some reason. I think they had geography.

"What do you want to do in London?" I ask.

Kate replies, "I don't know, maybe go to university? It's the best way to get the good jobs, and I want to be rich." So does everyone. "I think I'll be a manager. It's the easy option, anyway—you just boss people around all day and get paid the big bucks for it." She's rambling on about how easy it is to be a manager when Clara enters the Canteen.

The whole room stops to stare at her; our eyes lock.

The awkward silence lasts far too long before she finally walks out.

Kate flings her arms around me. "I'm so sorry, Jess. I heard about what she said to Chris. God, to think I was ever her friend. She's so fake."

Everyone is fake. "I need to pee." I excuse myself while she's still talking.

Our school's pretty big; I think it has around a thousand students. Although, the buildings can cater for several thousand, as our head teacher likes to proudly remind us. It feels like an attempt to make us understand our own insignificance.

On the outskirts of the grounds lies an old classroom block. Sometimes lessons are still held there, but there's no heating, so on this icy January day I know it'll be empty.

There's a chilly breeze as I sit in the girl's toilet. Even though the windows are jammed shut, a fly has still managed to navigate its way through the cracks. I can hear its hissy melody fly past my ear, frantically trying to find the exit but oblivious to the exit from which it entered. My gaze follows its futile attempts to leave until it becomes too depressing.

"You're not the only one trapped," I say as I scratch my name into the back of the toilet door with a spare coin.

Jessica Durand.

I return to the events of last night. It started out so ordinary.

To any onlooker, we were just another happy family eating dinner at the dining room table, passing condiments in silence.

It was my fault. I shouldn't have asked Everett about the job interview. I should've known any failure would send Sam into a rage that would flip the table, spilling the food and breaking the plates.

But this time was different. This time when Sam threw the first punch, Everett fought back. Maybe that was the mistake, because it's Sam's house we live in. Lived in.

Sam gave Everett until nine a.m. to pack up his car and leave.

I hide the sadness deep down inside me because I need to be happy for him—he got away. And one day soon he'll come back and save me.

But I wish he hadn't asked to be alone while he packed. I wish we could've spent one last night together. At least I had my Chris to keep me company, to take care of me. If only he could be there all the time, but I can't scare him off by being needy.

What would Ella do? Well, she wouldn't have to worry about this. She has her friends.

I need an Unbreakable Boy I can crawl into bed and sit with in a comfortable silence. I need a Girl of Oceans who'll dress up in weird outfits and dance around the room with me till our feet hurt. I need an Invisible Boy who'll build me overly complicated toy rockets to shoot into the lake. I need a Fire Boy who'll steal us snacks from the cafe and then sit in the stairwell trying trick shots.

I came up with their nicknames when I was very young.

Abruptly the sound of voices enters the hallway outside; I quickly press myself against the cubicle door to conceal my presence, even though I know there's nothing wrong with being here. Despite that, I still feel the need to hide. Maybe it's the social suicide of being found in your own company.

"I'm fixing my lipstick." Scarlett enters, her hair gently blowing in the breeze, like something out of a hair dye advert.

"It's almost the end of lunch. Is it really that important?" Chris mutters from outside; he has no care for the effort girls put into their appearance—although he's a great admirer of it.

"Yes," Scarlett replies. "You can come in, you know, instead of shouting from outside."

He enters. "Do you want to come over later?"

Has he really forgotten our plans?

She answers, "Okay. But I have dance in the evening."

"That's cool. We won't need long," he states.

Won't need long for what?

"That's not something to be proud of." She sounds disapproving. Won't need long for what?

Through the gaps I can see him moving closer to her as he says, "It's long enough for Jess."

What?

"Maybe I'm not as easy as Jess?" She laughs.

I'm not easy.

"Maybe I like a challenge," he says before grabbing her face and kissing her.

No.

"You're ruining my lipstick." She laughs.

No.

"I don't care." He kisses her again.

No.

I've felt rage before. I've felt rage many times but never like this. It's like I'm no longer in control. I'm watching from the sidelines shouting advice that falls on deaf ears, because if I could be heard, if I had some control, I wouldn't be doing this —this isn't me.

The mirror shatters as I push her head into it. Chris runs out the room. Her hands scratch my face. It stings. I pull her hair. She pulls mine. I try to stop her. She knees me in the stomach. I keel over. She runs out. I find the sink basin and cling to it. I can't look in the mirror.

It would've been that quick.

But it didn't happen. Instead I emerge from the cubicle long after they're gone.

❖❖❖

I have no one.

It's hard to describe this feeling; it's not empty. It's like a million wasps have flown down my throat and are begging me to throw them up. It's like my heart's running a marathon and I fear it'll die before the finish. It's like waiting for your bones to crumble to dust but finding time won't do you the justice.

But then, it's also...quiet?

No. What's wrong with me? Why am I not good enough? Why am I not enough? I'm not enough. I'm not Scarlett. She's prettier, more interesting, and more attractive. She's everything I'm not.

But I don't want to be like that.

No. Did he ever care about me? Was it always Scarlett? Maybe I was just an excuse to get close to her. All those times we hung out as a three, was I the outsider? Did he ever love me?

She was my best friend. It's like we're little kids again and she just stole my toy, although Chris isn't my toy, he's my boyfriend. Was my boyfriend. Did she ever learn not to steal?

But maybe I let her? I never refused her taking my lipstick and adding it to her collection; it was never shared. And the movie marathons, did I ever get to pick the choice? What purpose did the long rides in boys' cars serve other than to let her get closer to them? Maybe I was always her pawn. Maybe I wanted to be.

Maybe this is my life. Maybe I'm not the leading lady. Maybe I'm just a minor character. The cameras have already moved past me.

I feel sick. My legs start to crumble beneath me like ancient columns finally giving in, and it's a bliss I find myself craving, I mean, what else is there for me now?

I can't breathe. I'm gasping for air, but my lungs are drying up. My whole body is quitting. Pain surges through my nerves, triggering my fight or flight, but it's too late to fight. Around the room, everything's spinning. I try to focus my gaze somewhere, anywhere. The toilets are multiplying. The taps are moving. My skin is turning to ash.

Wait, no, what?

It's my veins; my veins are actually glowing black, just like when I was five—but that wasn't real. It's as if they've been poisoned by this despair I'm feeling. And oh God, it hurts so badly.

The desire to be anywhere but here is screaming inside me, now more than ever.

I lose my legs, they give in to the pain. It urges me to make a last-minute attempt to dash towards the toilet, ready to throw my insides up, but instead my face smashes into the heavy door. For a second after impact, as I fall, everything is silent.

And then, instead of falling into the bathroom stall, I fall into my far away.

Chapter Two

Ella

Are you real?

I gently exhale to disrupt the dust around you, and yet not a speck of it touches you. My eyes interrogate every petal, but nowhere do they find a rip to the silk of your skin. The ground beneath you failed to fall, and the scorching sky did nothing to melt you down. You must have a special touch, a special design, that keeps you going day and night. I stand humble in the presence of you, surviving against any and all odds.

"How are you real?" I find myself whispering to the roses in the vase, inches from my face, cupped by my hands. My elbows knock the settled dust as they rest on the wooden table.

We stand in what was once a kitchen, perhaps a busy one. Now it's half alive, while the other half has fallen to rubble behind us. All the cabinets are open—either the doors have swung open or fallen completely off. Scattered across the floor lies uneaten meals of various packaging. I watch as Aiden scavenges a packet; he licks his full lips.

"That's disgusting." Benjamin creases his brow.

Aiden mumbles an attempt at mocking him; his deep black hair refuses to move as he drags a hand across his head. With glowing red eyes, a colour that works well with the dark complexion of his skin and matches the occasional glowing of his veins, he offers the packet to Ben with a trying smile.

Ben holds his hands up. "Oh, I'm good."

After the interaction fades, Ben turns to study the shattered window frame. Straightening his rounded lenses, he peers out the gap at the rubble below. He might be taller than Aiden; however, the hunching of his shoulders and the sulking of his head disguises his height. And while Aiden refuses to wear any more than the standard-issue trousers and a black vest, Ben is fully suited in the uniform we've been assigned, right up to the zipped and stuck jacket. His hexagon is poking out his back pocket, and I can almost make out the buttons on its screen. He pulls it out to take pictures of the scene around us.

"Over here!" Shui Jia shouts from behind us. "I think I've found someone!"

Aiden, Ben and I exchange stunned glances. No one thought there'd be survivors. I can't imagine what strength it must take to survive an earthquake like this.

Aiden leaps from the remains of the kitchen onto the rubble below, about a person-height drop. Ben sits before dropping, and as I attempt to recreate his methods, worn hands reach out to help me.

"I've got you," Will says, and I believe him.

Will's a mystery that even us, his closest and maybe only

friends, have barely begun to solve. With vast oceans for eyes and an apparent lack of a hair comb, his appearance leaves you with more questions than answers—is that a natural brown? His clothes are normally plain but occasionally distressed. His body is decorated with subtle scars; years haven't seemed to fade them. And he never does too much talking, at least with words. I've known him since we were twelve, and yet I barely know him.

We're rushing over to Jia, but it's overwhelming trying to take in what's happened around us. What was once a building, several floors high and home to many, now lies in ruin on unstable ground. We clamber over the stone; I grip a wooden chair stuck into the rubble and stumble as it slips into the unknown beneath. Through the gap it leaves, I see nothing. Pure darkness.

"Over here!" Jia waves her arms through the still air as multiple teams of protectors struggle towards her.

Aiden makes it first. He falls onto his knees and starts to shove stones from around him while yelling out, asking for any survivors to yell back. But there's no yelling. There's nothing. It's too quiet in the cold, where the only reaching sounds are us making our way to them.

Will reaches them next, then Ben. When I finally make it, I'm almost the last, so I waste no time getting to work. The pink fingerless covers to my hands gather dirt as they push aside the ash of crumbled stone. I dig and dig, and although I struggle to lift a single stone, I refuse to give in.

Where my physical strength has failed me, I use my gift. My veins glow white as the stones start to lift themselves under my silent instruction. They move slow, and although it's still better than before, I'm tiring quicker.

We clear a small gap that's wide enough for me to fit my arm through; I pull off my dirtied hand covers and feel around in the unknown.

"Anything?" Will asks.

I'm shaking my head when I change my mind; there's something soft—it's not rubble. But it's so cold as I squeeze it and search for its beginning. Then it squeezes me right back. I gasp.

It takes what feels like hours to pull them out. In reality it was probably mere minutes, but every second felt like it would never end. When they finally emerge, we witness the young boy.

Angelic blond hair escapes from the ash, a once-white turtleneck, and even his soft features feel so innocent. When he takes his first sight of the world around him, I witness his blue eyes, a rarity. So rare I only know of two other people that possess them—Will and I.

I look around. Are there other survivors? This building must've housed hundreds, so where are they? Somewhere beneath us. I start to move rubble again, forgetting to breathe as I lift piece after piece without moving my hands.

"Stop. You should take him to the base." Sloane, the mission lead, a member of the G team of protectors, stands over me, holding out my hand cover.

"No." I remember to breathe, and the pieces of rubble I'm holding that are floating midair crash down. "We're staying right here. We're going to help," I continue.

He sighs and pulls me up. "I don't care who you are, princess. I call the shots here, and I don't need dead weight getting in the way."

I gasp. "Excuse you!"

"All of you—" he gestures to Will, Aiden, Ben and Jia. "Go back to base. I heard the predators have arrived." In the distance I can just about make out the flashes of the recorders as they report on their version of current events. "Now that we know there are survivors, I can't have you all getting in the way. We need to get the machines out."

"What?" Aiden shouts.

Sloane shoves my hand cover into my hand and forces my fingers to close around it. "You all heard me. Go see your predator friends, and let the real protectors get to work."

Aiden's veins glow their familiar red until Jia places her hands on his arm.

I rise above. "He's awful, but he's also right. My gift isn't strong enough to lift the rubble as fast as the machines can."

"Well, maybe we can use one of our gifts?" Aiden adds.

Ben scoffs. "Fire is never the solution."

I pull Aiden away, and the others follow behind us. When Sloane thinks we're out of earshot, I hear him laugh. "Freaks."

"He can't do that." Aiden seethes.

Ben replies, "Actually, he can. He's mission lead. And he's on the G team. We're the S team."

"S for special," I say. "S for super."

As we approach base camp, I can see the predators with their recorders impatiently waiting outside. Two protectors ahead of us are trying to escort the young survivor through the frenzy, but they're meeting too much resistance from the predators. How can they not realise what they're doing to him? He's been in the dark for hours, and everywhere he turns are flashing lights.

It appears I'm not the only one concerned; Aiden decides to fill two holes with one shovel, metaphorically.

While the speeding ball of flames purposely just misses Sloane, he reacts is as if Aiden set him alight. Over the shouting of rage, Aiden proudly blows the smoke from his fingertips as his veins fade from the red. We struggle to hold in our laughter. The predators find a new target, and the survivor escapes them.

"Okay," Ben concedes, "fire is sometimes the solution."

❉❉❉

"How are you all so brave at only seventeen?" A predator shoves their recorder inches from my face. The recorder's lens is taking up so much of my view that I can't see the person holding it.

I smile so my rigorous dental hygiene shows. "We were given these gifts so we could help people."

❉❉❉

Another predator: "Aiden, can you set your whole body on fire?"

His hand lights up in flames. "So, I'm currently working on

the rest of my arm, but I'm getting there."

❖❖❖

"Benjamin, give us your best roar!" The flashes are so blinding I can't see who asked him.

Ben answers, "I don't think that's appropriate right now."

❖❖❖

"Jia, can you make it rain?" It's the fourth time this week a predator has asked her this.

She responds, "Do you have any other questions for me?"

❖❖❖

"Are you planning on giving up this work when you take the throne?" The predators turn to me, waiting for my answer.

Our coordinator abruptly steps in front of us. "Unfortunately, we're going to have to end this here. Have a great day, all."

❖❖❖

"Do you really think we were given these gifts to help people?" Jia asks me. She's lying on her back on top of the central table, the soles of her feet resting flat on the surface while her knees point up to the illuminator dangling above us. I pace back and forth next to her. Ben's lab has plenty of pacing room.

Aiden and Will sit on a side table alongside the left wall; Aiden's focused, trying to light more of his arm on fire. So far he's managed just below his elbow. Will's reading another book. I think Jia gave him that one.

"I do. And things will change. My father's going to convince the council to let us help more, especially with the Red Suits, because I think this is that prophecy. I think it's finally happening, and we'll get to save the world. I mean, we all saw it today—the world is literally crumbling around us. It's exactly what the prophecy said would happen."

"Yeah, I'd just settle for them to listen to my theories, hear my work," Ben replies from a desk chair, hunched forward with his gaze fixed on the screen of his hexagon.

"Well, we need to make them listen."

Jia lifts her head up. "And how are we going to do that?"

I pause. "Um…"

"Come on." Aiden flings himself off the table and grabs me by the shoulders. "You always have a plan!"

"And I'll think of one!" I pull myself from his grasp. "Because this is our time." Will looks up from his book. They're all watching. "We all know we were given these gifts for more than publicity. We're going to use them to save the world from the greatest threats and around us the world is crumbling and evil is finding it's face and soon the real threat will reveal itself and—" I stop to breathe. "And this is our time. We're going to figure out what happened to that building. We're going to start our own investigation."

As they're all nodding in agreement, the base-wide speaker springs to life. "Ella Day to discussion room seven. Ella Day to discussion room seven."

We freeze.

Aiden walks over to the speaker, climbs onto the table below it and whispers into it, "I don't know what you think you heard, but you should know—" he grins at us, "—I'll absolutely sell them out to protect myself."

"Aiden!" Jia exclaims as she throws the first object she can find at him, and soon the rest of us join in as a war breaks out.

Will scrunches loose paper into ammunition. Ben uses Will's book as a shield from Aiden. Aiden tries to pick me up, and we all run around laughing. At one point, Jia pulls me under a table to hide. At another point, I throw a paper ball straight into Ben's eye. Eventually, Will holds Aiden still while we pelt him.

I completely forget I have to be anywhere but here.

❧❧❧

Deep breath. "I'm so sorry." I rush into the room full of people. "We were just messing about and having fun—you know, as young people do—and I'm sure Aiden didn't mean whatever it was you know he did and I know he does a lot of things, okay, but he's just frustrated because he has this incredible gift and he's desperate to use it for something meaningful and—"

"What on Biack are you on about?" My father, Liam Day,

interrupts me. "I called you here to talk about the New Year ball that's now happening tonight."

I suddenly realise the room full of people aren't here to tell me off. "Oh."

"I don't know what you've been up to, and I have a feeling I don't want to know."

I shake my head.

The room is full of senior protectors, their aging complexions and decorated uniforms give them away. I recognise most of them, but there are a few new faces—this is probably not the time to introduce myself. My father sits at the head of the table, calm, collected and relaxed—how is he always so relaxed? He's never in a hurry; no matter how late he is, he somehow always arrives on time. But I guess no one would ever call him out if he was late, him being the king and all.

He continues, "Council member Derwood has recovered, although I only received news of it yesterday, and the timing could not be better as we really cannot wait any longer to host this ball. The first month is almost over, and it's hardly time to celebrate the New Year when you're already a twelfth of the way through it."

"Wait, did you say tonight?"

"This is the first chance I've had to tell you. Planning begun this morning, but luckily my new assistant seems to work miracles. Do you remember Scott Browning?" Our fathers are long-time friends. I haven't seen Scott in many years, though. "He's incredible. He'll be there later so do say hi."

"New assistant? What happened to Theresa?" My father

loved her; he took great pride in picking out the perfect gift for their work anniversary every year.

"Retirement." He sighs. But she was younger than everyone in this room. Odd.

"Okay, well…" I pause; there's so much to do suddenly. "Oh, is this the planning meeting?"

They all laugh. "No, we're discussing the collapsed building on sixtieth street. I was only just informed you'd arrived back."

I pull out an empty chair. "Odd, right? Buildings don't just collapse and there wasn't an earthquake so——"

"Apologies, your Highness." One of the protectors places his hand on my arm. "This is a private meeting."

"But I was asked to come here?"

My father smiles. "Yes, you were. But I think it's best you head to the palace now. I could use your help setting up, as I'm going to be stuck here for a while longer. Can I count on you?"

"Of course!" I start preparing my mental checklist. "Have a good meeting. I'll see you later!"

As I rush out the room, Will and Aiden immediately pounce on me.

"Oh, we aren't in trouble. He just wanted to let me know the New Year Ball is finally happening and it's tonight and he needs me to get to the palace and help set up. He's counting on me, you know?"

"Counting on you? To set up a party that probably has twenty planners working on it?" Aiden questions.

"Yes." My checklist is now three pages long. "I have to find Jia; she'll want to get ready with me, and I need to start heading to the palace." She's probably still in Ben's lab helping clear up. "You guys should get ready too—Aiden, your top is burnt."

"I know!" He's way too happy about that. "See? I did get the whole arm." He speaks to Will as he gestures toward the burnt sleeve of his top.

"What? That's amazing!" My excitement escapes with my words. We've barely scratched the surface of what's possible with our abilities, but Aiden is definitely making the most progress.

"Oh, please, he barely got past his wrist," Will interrupts. "He just waved his hand around enough to catch his top."

"That's not true!" Aiden raises his voice, but from the look in Will's eyes, he's already moved past this.

Will says, "Wait, the New Year Ball. This is perfect. Almost everyone will be there. The BCD will be almost empty."

I realise where he's going. "We can break into the investigation room."

"Why would we do that?" Aiden asks. "I mean, I'm not against it—I love breaking into rooms as much as the next person—but why are we doing that?"

"To steal any information they gathered from the building collapse. Or at least make our own copies of it." His face is still blank. "For our own investigation? What I said earlier about it being our time?"

"Oh, yeah! Ben started some kind of puzzle board for that while you were gone. I thought it was really stupid because none of the colours matched and it wasn't pleasing to look at and it definitely didn't make any sense—"

"Wait," I stop. "I need to be at the party. People will notice if I don't show up. I can't be in two places at once."

Will replies, "So we go and then disappear early. No one will be suspicious. We always do that."

"Okay, that could work, but how do we sneak out without anyone noticing?"

"I know a way. But we'll have to walk through the tunnels to make sure we avoid everyone."

"That'll take ages! I wish there was a way we could get there and back almost instantly." I sigh.

Aiden jumps in, "We could teleport!"

Will rolls his eyes. "Yeah, science isn't there yet, buddy."

Aiden huffs. "Oh, yeah? Well, I saw Ben working on that big orb thing the other day and he said, I quote, it would '*help Ella learn to use her teleport.*'"

"I think he said her telekinesis."

Aiden frowns. "Right, get out your hexagon and give Ben a call. He'll tell you I'm right." He smirks. "Oh, wait, you can't, can you? Because you lost your hexagon. Not feeling so smart now, are we, *buddy*?"

"I know exactly where it is. I just don't want to carry it around with me because then people think they can call me whenever they want and I'll answer."

"But what if it's me calling and I'm dying? And I use my last bit of energy to call you to say goodbye? And you don't answer and then I'm dead and you never got to say goodbye."

"I'm pretty sure I'll be okay." Will grins. "Because when I miss you, I'll just listen to that message you accidentally left me when you got rejected by Kai Jung."

"You said you deleted that! We're going to find your hexagon right now, and you're going to delete that message." Aiden starts to drag Will down the hall.

"As long as you stop by your rooms to get ready for later?" I chime in as they walk away.

"Don't worry, that's what we're doing," Will responds.

"Like death it is. You're deleting that message," Aiden says.

"Okay," I interrupt. "I expect to see the both of you there later, fully dressed in clean suits and with a change of clothing." I cross my arms so they know I'm serious.

Neither of them turn around, but Aiden decides to be helpful. "Jia's in her room. Something about meditation." I go to reply, but he beats me to it: "I know—we'll tell Ben."

As I rush off to find Jia, I can hear them continuing to argue behind me.

❧❧❧

Jia has the sweetest eyes I've ever seen, flecks of white lost in her warm gaze of the deepest brown. Her lids are dusted pink; it almost looks natural against the pale of her skin, and that red tint to her lips blends in so well when she laughs you can't see where her lips end. She toys with her hair, holding it in a high hold and then releasing it into loose waves.

She isn't just looks; deadly as she is beautiful, she contains the ability to manipulate water, sending oceans charging at you or subtly drowning you in plain sight. Well, with a bit more practice, she'll be able to; right now, she's pretty adept at knocking over glasses of water.

"Hmm." She studies herself in one of the mirrors of my dressing room. "Hair up or down, then?"

"How about half up, half down?"

She smiles in agreement. While she finishes with her hair, she walks around, examining various dress options. She's currently wearing a white corset and black tracksuit bottoms. "Hey, did you see Debjani today?"

I run my fingers across my jewellery options. "No, why?"

"She looked amazing. She had her hair in this high hold basically on top of her head. It made her neck appear so elegant, and it totally worked for her." She grabs a green cut-away dress with a deep V chest line and presses it against her. "I think this is the one. I can't wear anything underneath it though. See how low it goes—it's basically down to my waist."

"That'd look really good. Did you want to wear the corset underneath, though?"

"Kind of, but only because I love it so much I never want to take it off. Also, I could've just worn that and shorts later so it would've been easy to get changed." She admires herself in the mirror before walking over to another dress. "I like this one for you. The flower decoration should cover the marks on your shoulder—they haven't healed yet, have they?" She gestures toward a pink, laced creation. The actual dress is plain and simple but alongside it lies a garland of pink roses and leaves meant to be draped around your neck, with one side hung across your chest and the other side continuing to dangle towards your feet.

It's perfectly impractical.

I pull the top of my current dress to show the stitches on my shoulder.

She sighs. "I'm just glad this is a full-gown event; my legs are covered in bruises. It's not fair. Aiden caused all the damage, and yet he's completely fine. Why does he always think fire is the solution? And how does it always work out for him? Where are his bruises?" She tilts her head as if to pour the anger out. "Anyway, I'm doubting the green dress now. It might be a nightmare to get changed out of later."

"I had another nightmare last night," I blurt out. I didn't even realise it was on my mind.

Jia sits down immediately. "What happened this time?"

"Her brother moved out, and she caught her boyfriend cheating on her."

"Bad day," Jia begins to analyse. "Are you worried about any upcoming events?"

No more than usual. "The dream gets worse—her boyfriend cheated on her with her best friend."

"What? Scarlett? Yeah, that doesn't surprise me. She was always so mean. I really don't understand why they're friends."

"And it'd been going on for a while."

"Yeah, again, I'm not that surprised, sadly."

"But what was strange wasn't how truly awful her day was, at least no more than usual."

"What was the strange part then?"

"I think she was on Central Street."

"The Capital's Central Street?"

"Yes, she fell here somehow. I don't know; it was really odd. She lit up like we do, there was this darkness and then she was here. She didn't belong, though; she burnt in the sunlight." I start to pace out the racing of my heart. "I don't know, it's just the first time that's ever happened. She's never been on Biack before. You know I don't like to think about these nightmares or even talk about them, but do you think this one means something?"

Jia stares at the floor while she thinks for a few moments. Eventually she mumbles my own words: "And this is our time."

I end my pacing in front of a mirror. I can see Jess's face staring back at me in place of my own. She looks so sad. She's always looked so sad. But she has her whole life ahead of her with no expectations. She can be anything she wants. So why is she so sad?

But she's not real. Because Earth isn't real. So I know she's not real. So I won't think about her.

"Let's pick out jewellery."

Chapter Three

Jess

Biack 20/01/2014

The first thing I notice, before I open my eyes, is the smell of bleach. It's faint, but it's enough to make my nose scrunch. The air is warm, unusual for winter; it almost burns as it brushes by my face, and the taste of spices sit on my tongue, like walking past an exotic restaurant. Something's wrong.

The first thing I see, while my ears are incapacitated, is feet. In the distance, people are walking past in casual strolls. Where on Earth am I for people to not be in a rush? Every other direction is filled with the faultless grey walls of an alley—why do they look so futuristic? And where's the trash, the litter, the overflowing bins? Where are the forgotten humans who seek refuge in torn-up blankets? Where's the damage?

The first thing I hear, as I pull myself off the ground, is the clatter of voices, the mess of disjointed conversations not so distantly away. Why is the wind whooshing past me, blocking out the voices? I sound crazy. Have *they* made me crazy?

My hair gets blown across my face, my mouth, my eyes as

the cause of the wind comes into sight. It appears in the distance, behind the back wall of the alley, blocking out the burning bright of the sky. I move my hand to shield my eyes. A sleek, white, modern train slides across a single rail at a speed that races my heart. I've never seen a monorail before. But I have, in my dreams.

The train disappears into the horizon, revealing the sky behind as my eyes adjust to the brightness. Behind a shield of glass hexagons, the sky's on fire.

It's as if someone put a torch to the atmosphere and ignited all the gases, every single one; even the non-flammable chemicals fell victim. Because how else could it be so never-ending? My eyes burn as they turn to the middle. Is that their sun? It's hard to tell as it hides against the familiar colours of the sky. Its just a big space that's slightly more intense.

Providing some protection from the intensity of the sun, white panes surround each hexagon of glass that continues off beyond the skyline. They're so high up that each tile looks no bigger than the nail on my smallest finger. I know where I am.

This isn't real.

"Ouch," a stranger speaks.

With my arm shielding the sun, I look around to find I've stumbled backwards into the main street. "I-I'm sorry." I spin around.

The woman keeps on walking, soon disappearing off into the crowd, a crowd that doesn't push past me but instead moves around me. I reach out and grab a man's arm, and he just brushes me off. Can they see me? Am I really here?

Am I dreaming?

There must be a rational explanation. "Can you tell me where I am?" I try to speak to another woman. She walks straight past me. "Hi, I'm lost—"

Maybe this is a dream.

"Are you okay, honey?" A younger woman stops beside me; I'm not invisible.

"Yes, yes, I'm just, um…" Why did she stop and not the others? "Where am I? I think I've taken a wrong turn."

"Oh, you're at the end of Central Street."

"Yes…and where is Central Street again?"

She raises an eyebrow. "In the centre of The Capital, of course."

No. This isn't real.

"Where were you trying to go?" She rifles through her bag and pulls out a transparent glass device. It comes to life to reveal itself as a phone. I've never seen a make like this before. No, I have, but that's not real, so this must be a prototype from some new phone company. Yes, that makes sense.

I can feel my legs shuddering. "I actually don't remember." I need Everett. I need to be wherever he is. "Do you know where the nearest train station is? I just need to get to Newcastle."

"Newcastle? I'm sorry, I've never heard of that before. Whereabout in Biack is it?" *Biack*. Actually hearing the word out loud raises the hairs across my arm. "Wait, I think I've heard of it. Is it near Terra?" *Terra*? Okay, good, I don't recognise that word.

Is that good?

"Um, Terra?" I have to still be on Earth. I try to search a crude map of the British Isles in my mind, but I'm coming up empty. Why did they only teach us about rocks in Geography?

She clarifies. "Northern Biack?" I look blank. "Are you sure you're okay?" She reaches out to touch me, but my instincts jump me back.

"I'm fine." I need to escape this conversation; she's asking too many questions.

"Oh my life!" Another voice squeals behind us. Someone else has stopped. "Her head is bleeding!"

My hand rushes to my head to find a wet red has become entangled in my brunette strands. My fingers are trembling as I bring them back into sight.

"I'm calling the healers, don't worry!" Another voice shouts as the crowd begins to form around me.

This isn't safe. I shove past the original woman and break into a sprint down the street.

Oh, God. What the hell happened to me? How did I get here? I must've blacked out somehow. Did I get on a train? I must've tried to run away; it's not unimaginable. I probably got on the first train I saw, or maybe I picked a destination I'd never heard of before. Although none of this explains the sky and its weird shield. That can't be real. Wait, my head; maybe I'm hallucinating?

Yes, that makes sense. I'm hallucinating my dreams.

But she definitely said Biack.

"Your hand!" Ghost-skinned fingers clasps around my arm.

"It's burning!"

How ridiculous. I'm not an idiot. I'd know if I was burning. Wait. How can she be right? But it's true, my right hand isn't mine anymore; it's become an aggressive shade of dark red. "I'm fine!" But I am. Where's the pain that accompanies physical transformations?

"No, it looks like it's burning right now. Maybe the Dome is malfunctioning!" She cries out, eliciting the swarm around us to become frantic.

The *Dome*.

"Someone call the protectors. We could all be dying!" A man yells.

The *protectors*.

Ella.

Maybe the mayhem that's erupted can work to my advantage. Under the cover of raised voices and fast movements, I slip away from the spotlight and continue my descent down the street with a faster pace. Although I soon realise it's no use—the panic continues to follow me and I see no obvious escape. Why does this street never end?

What would Ella do? She'd stay calm; I take deep, shuddering breaths. She'd find out where she was. Okay, let's find a map. She wouldn't be alone. Ah, the key difference between my fantasy and reality.

Where are my friends? Sleeping with my boyfriend.

Behind an approaching building lies the gateway to the raised railway; the monorail map sits patiently outside. It makes no sense. There are three maps: one shows the continents of

Europe and Asia, another shows the UK, and a final one shows what can I only guess is this city. But it makes no sense. Simply no sense. That's where London's supposed to be. Why does it say The Capital?

All the place names are wrong, and where are the countries? *Salient, Moonglade, Ferox.* What the hell? I know those names, but this isn't their map.

Then again, I never saw a map in my dreams.

I stumble backwards in reaction to the tremors in my bones. A burning sky, a shield of hexagons, a raised railway. Unusual names and unusual words. The familiarity of the unknown raises every hair across my skin.

Ouch!

The wind stings as it knocks against my hand; there's the pain. Yes, I'm not crazy, I hit my head, this is all rational, yes.

My stomach is upside down, and it doesn't take long for my muscles to try follow suit. I'm so distracted in inner argument that it's taken me too long to notice the world around me spinning around and around and around. Is this me losing it? Is this what Scarlett did to me? How could I let someone hurt me so badly?

I lose my balance as I run, tripping on a rock or something. I don't care. I don't care as I fall backwards to the concrete. I'm too preoccupied with my inner conflict to care about anything other than my sanity right now.

The contact with the concrete ignites the fire across my skin as I realise the burns have spread. I watch my hand blistering. I have to keep moving. But I can't. I can't get up. I can't move. I have no strength. I have no energy. I have nothing.

I'm going to die here.

Chapter Four

Ella

Biack 20/01/2014

Jia leads me down the grand staircase; I try to not trip on her emerald trail. At the bottom, Aiden's impatiently pacing around while Will leans against the wood banisters. Even in a clean suit, Will looks out of place like a merman in a field, it's not quite right. Aiden, on the other hand, can fit into any scene; his charisma's so inviting and his appearance so adaptable. You'd almost think he was royalty, until he opens his mouth.

"Do you know what time it is? Do you know how much food they've already brought out?" Aiden pounces before we reach the final step.

Jia gasps. "What about those little sandwich things? Are there any left?"

"Well, I was saving you some, but you took so long I got bored and ate them." He invokes a frown and huff from Jia. "Okay, calm down, let me make it up to you." With a bow he holds out a hand. "Let's go dance with all those boring politicians."

"I guess you'll do until I find someone better." Jia grins before conceding, and together they race off to the great hall.

"Come on, I'll dance with you." Will reluctantly holds out his hand. "Only the one, though. We just need to show our faces before we disappear off."

"I thought you'd never ask." I smile as we follow after Jia and Aiden, at a much more appropriate pace, though.

Tiny diamonds adorn what could be thousands of illuminators above us; each one feels brighter than the next, but in reality, they're all glowing. They almost shield the artwork spread out across the ceiling, which would be a great crime, as I'm sure someone very famous painted it.

Footprints of glitter cover the patterned wood floors; somehow the glitter has managed to fill almost every space, even around the many tables and chairs in the outskirts of the room. And despite the hundred people spinning around in the centre, it maintains its hold on the entirety of the floorboards, vibrating slightly to the melodic hum of the hundred-piece orchestra.

This isn't even a particularly special ball; every few weeks, this picture is recreated in different dresses, suits and colour schemes. Although it's usually the same people in attendance, and the small talk is rarely new, and I'm sure they've reused a few themes by now, every time is still magic.

Will drags me through the rush of people into the centre; he doesn't give me any chance to respond to the people who call out to acknowledge me. Once we reach the middle, he spins me around too fast and I quickly slam back into him. We giggle like our twelve-year-old selves that used to sneak out of our rooms and play hide-and-seek under these tables.

"You look pretty," Will states as we start to sway like the crowd around us.

"Thanks. Do you like the flower decoration?"

"Um, yeah sure." He's hesitant. "Doesn't it get in the way, though?"

He's not wrong. "Aiden would appreciate it."

"Yeah, well, Aiden appreciates pretty things."

In the near distance we catch a glimpse of Aiden flirting with two of the most perfectly decorated girls, not a strand of hair out of place, and I think their dresses were made on them. Jia found someone better very quickly.

I change the topic. "We've been friends for five years now. And I still don't know what flavour juice you like."

"I don't like juice." He shrugs.

"Okay, what about your favour colour?"

Another no-hesitation response. "I don't have one."

"Favourite sport?" I continue.

"Nope." He shakes his head.

I raise my eyebrows. "Do you like anything?"

He shrugs. "I like you and the others, but that's probably about it."

"That's a start; it has been five years."

"I've only just started liking you all." He smirks, so I step on his foot.

We continue to dance in silence for a few more minutes. As the music turns slow, I rest my head on his chest, and my breath falls into a gentle rhythm with his.

His voice hums in my ear. "You know, when I used to live here, I'd sometimes sneak out of my room—"

"We snuck out almost every night," I interrupt.

Will moved into the BCD three years ago. His room used to be next to mine, and now it's next to Aidens.

"I know, but I'm talking about when I snuck out alone. Sometimes I'd come here to the great hall and lie in the middle of the room and look up at the artwork on the ceiling for hours and hours until morning came."

"I caught you doing that once."

"Yes, and you fell asleep in the doorway. I carried you back to your bed."

"I always wondered how I ended up back in bed." The song ends. "So, what was it about the art?"

"I'll tell you some other time." He gestures across the room. "Jia and Aiden have regrouped. Let's go."

I stop. "Wait, have you seen Ben yet?"

"No. He's probably late on purpose. He hates these things."

As we push through the crowd, I gaze around the room to find people I know. Most of the guests are businessmen, council members, county mayors and other such politicians or the richest of the wealthy. There are a few scientists from the BCD. I spot my father in the corner talking to a group of people in black attire, which is noticeably strange, considering the rest of the room is a sea of colour; they look like royal guards. Beyond the crowd I can just about make out the worry on his face.

"Something's wrong?" Will notices.

"Maybe." I lose sight of my father in the crowd.

The sound of Aiden's voice rings in my ears. "Good, you're both here. Tell them it was my *entire* arm. My *entire* arm was on fire." He's removed his overcoat and rolled up his sleeve to his shoulder. The two guys he's stood with appear far too invested.

I decide to help as I say, "It was up to his neck! I was worried he'd burn his face off, but look at him—somehow, not a mark." I brush glitter off his shirt. "It's amazing how it never leaves a burn, and what a relief. He's far too beautiful, don't you agree?"

Aiden smiles in thanks at me.

Will rolls his eyes. He turns to the guys to say, "We have to go. He'll find you later."

After the boys leave, Aiden slaps Will across the chest.

"Ow!"

"Two more minutes." Aiden holds two fingers in our faces. "Two more minutes, and I would've had both of their numbers. Then with the girls from earlier, I'd be at four."

Jia laughs. "Only four? And you had a head start?"

"You got more than four?"

She holds up six fingers before running off to the grand staircase. Aiden mumbles something incoherent as he chases after her.

"How?" I ask. "We had, what, two or three dances?" I glance back at the great hall. "And there's hardly anyone our age?"

Will shrugs. "You're asking the wrong person." I've never seen him with anyone, girl or boy. I don't think he likes people that way.

Jia and Aiden have completely disappeared, which is impressive, as the grand staircase is no easy feat to run up. As Will and I climb the marble steps, the people below us start to look like little dolls we could pick up and move. My gaze is fixed on one boy wearing a dress of every colour. He must be very indecisive, but it's worth it, as that's the best dress I've seen tonight. As I'm watching him throw his head back in laughter, I step into what feels like the edge of a wall and lose my footing. An arm reaches out to catch me, but it isn't Will's.

"Are you okay?" An old friend grasps my waist. His face is so youthful, it's hard to believe he's twenty-two.

"I'm so sorry. I wasn't watching where I was going." I find my feet. Will is steps ahead of me, I nod to let him know to go on.

Scott Browning gazes down at me with his brown eyes. "Oh, don't apologise." He releases his grasp on me to jokingly bow. "Your Highness, it's been a while."

Scott's father, Cathal Browning, is a successful business owner. I think he owns the company that makes those watches everyone wears; they're really uncomfortable. Our fathers have always been close, so much so that the Brownings accompanied us during a tour of The Plains almost six years ago. I had a huge crush on him at the time, but he was sixteen and I was only eleven; I was just some annoying child. I haven't seen him much since. He outgrew me.

"It didn't need to be. I haven't gone anywhere, and your father still visits every few weeks." All those old childish feelings come rushing back.

"If it makes it any better, I've barely seen my father these past few years. In fact, I think that tour of The Plains we went on together was the last significant amount of time I spent with him." He runs a hand through his auburn hair. Aiden would like him. He loves people with red hair.

"Was it that bad?" I think I'm fluttering my eyelashes too much.

"You, no. My dad, definitely." He rests his arm on the banister next to me, moving closer. "I just started working for your dad, actually. I'm now the king's personal assistant, which sounds just as glamorous as it actually is."

I smile. "So we'll be seeing more of each other? Good. We have a lot of catching up to do."

"Can—" Before he can finish his reply, the palace shakes like the full force of an earthquake has unloaded on this very spot all at once. In the near distance I can hear windows shattering and illuminators falling, glasses smashing and plates crashing, and within seconds the people start to scream.

Then the gunshots start.

"Was that a—"

"Explosion? Yes. You should go somewhere safe," I instruct while peering through the gaps in the wood banisters; people appear to be running from the great hall.

"Where? I haven't been in the palace for a while, and it's huge." His words barely register as I tuck a loose strand of hair behind my ear. I spot Jia, Will and Aiden speeding down the stairs in their pre-planned, all-black change of clothing—that was quick.

Jia grabs my arm. "There's something in your room you need to see."

Before I can respond, she's run off down the steps. I turn to Scott. "Just find a room and hide somewhere."

"What are you going to do?"

"Help." I need to find a weapon. Secret stashes are around the palace, but my favourites are hidden in my room.

As I run, screaming echoes in the background. I must be quick. What happened? And what does Jia want me to see? I try to distract my mind by planning my next hundred steps. Every possible outcome, I'm planning for; it's all going to be okay.

When I enter my room, the Screen across from my bed is blasting the news.

"We're reporting from the scene of an earlier panic that occurred on Central Street in The Capital. Current reports are suggesting a Dome malfunction occurred. There's currently one known injury. If you witnessed this scene—" I stop listening to the reporter when a slightly blurry, still image appears next to her. It's her.

It's Jess.

What if it wasn't just nightmares?

"Ella! Okay, you're safe. Come on, they need our help." Ben grabs me from behind.

"It's the girl." I point at the screen. "She's real."

"Are you hurt?" Ben starts checking me for injuries.

There's no time. I throw the image to back of my mind as I focus on the now. "I'm fine." I snap back and begin to focus. "I was looking for a weapon."

"Me too. You have multiple stored in here, right?"

On the side of my left bedside table hides a small button; it fits in so perfectly you wouldn't give it a second glance. It soon reveals a hidden compartment containing several guns. There are the more modern lasers, and then the old bullet versions. I controversially prefer the bullet versions; they're uniquely useful to me.

Ben grabs a popular laser pistol. "People broke into the ballroom; they blew a hole in the roof. The others said you were up here. They're fighting them off now." He fills in the blanks as we race down the grand staircase towards the conflict; we push through crowds running away.

The gunshots are getting louder and the people fewer. One man walks past in a daze; his right hand is clutching a dark red stain on his shirt. As he stumbles past, he bumps into me, smearing the stain onto the pink of my dress.

Outside the ballroom, several protectors stand hiding behind the double door's frame, occasionally poking out to fire aimlessly into the room.

"Your Highness!" A female protector notices us approaching. "You can't go in there, my lady. It's not safe."

We completely ignore her as we rush through the doorway, immediately finding cover behind an overturned table. I check the ammunition in my weapon, and Ben switches his on; a quick nod, and in unison we peer round opposite edges.

There's seven of them. Dressed in bright red suits sure to conceal any injury, which is smart but not odd. What's odd is their faces, or lack thereof. It's less odd and more terrifying. Red material is wrapped around their heads, removing any distinguishable features—hair, eyes, ethnicity, gender, they're all hidden beneath the mask. They're too far away to tell if they're wearing masks or several wrapped bandages; historically they've been known to use both, although we've yet to capture one, as they either escape or die trying, and those who escape take the bodies with them. They do everything they can to hide who they are. They could be anyone.

There are two groups. Across the room, four of them are poking out from behind another overturned table. One shouts something to a group of three farther behind them as they attach a frightened woman at the waist to one of several lengths of wire hanging down from the roof. They're kidnapping people?

Ben and I meet back in the middle of the table. "Cover me. I'm going to try shooting the wires," I say.

"Got it." He says.

Deep breath. I stick my head round the side of the table; the woman has disappeared, and Red Suits are now attaching a new person to one of the wires, a middle-aged man in a badly fitted blue suit. I raise my gun and attempt to aim; however, it doesn't matters, for as soon as the bullet leaves, I find the ability to direct it across the room, dodging other bullets and energy beams, even a fireball, until it reaches the wire attached to the blue-suited man. The wire snaps in half, and he attempts to run.

One of the Red Suits gestures to another before raising their weapon at the escaping man. However, they're soon knocked back by a warning blast from Ben's gun, allowing the man to escape out a broken window. Eerily slow, the Red Suit turns to meet my gaze; at least I think they are.

They've noticed us.

"Ella!" Ben jumps at me, pulling me back behind the table as I narrowly miss a foreign bullet.

I'm quick as I move to shoot more wires but before I can peer out, our table is bombarded by energy blasts. The metal shakes against our backs as Ben and I exchange worried looks; the fear trembles in his fern eyes behind thick black frames. Ready to return fire, we count down from five, but before we reach one, the shooting stops. All the shooting stops. There's a second of hesitation before we peer out from our safe place.

"You both owe me *so* big." Aiden stands above a completely still Red Suit collapsed on the floor a meter from our table. As we emerge from our shelter, I spot another Red Suit lying on the floor behind him, reaching for something.

"*No!*" I shout.

Aiden doesn't see them.

I throw my arms forward and scream, directing all the energy I have left to move him, but I move so much more. Everyone goes flying back, along with the tables, chairs and glass. I fall to the ground, gasping for breath. Aiden lies at the opposite end of the room.

As my veins start to fade from their white glow, I try to find my feet but fail. However, Ben's soon at my side, lifting me up. I glance around to see the Red Suits have all disappeared; Aiden looks annoyed.

"Your Highness!" Protectors start to swarm around me,

concern upon their faces.

My father's hand falls onto my shoulder; his gaze meets mine and with a smile he says, "That was new." A room full of people is a big step up from bullets.

I go to speak, but Ben beats me to it. "Where did they go?"

Aiden hobbles towards us. "Maybe Ella threw them out of the room." Yes, he's definitely annoyed.

"We'll find them." A senior protector approaches my father, who consequently breaks away from us to form a small group of important discussion with him.

Around the room, people are emerging from their hiding spots; more protectors have rushed in to help the injured, and the protectors who swarmed me, realising I'm fine, have now moved on to others. Our team reunites as Jia and Will approach. Will takes over from Ben in holding me up.

"T-they came me out of nowhere. S-suddenly the sky is falling and p-people are being shot." A nearby woman stumbles onto her feet with the help of a protector.

Jia squeezes my hand and whispers, "They were after scientists. That's who they took."

"How many," I'm still finding my natural breath, "did they take?" I whisper back.

"Three?" Aiden looks at Jia, who responds with a nod.

The once extravagantly decorated room is now swept in mayhem. Not a single chair has been left unharmed while tiny, lonely diamonds sparkle from all corners. The velvet curtains now adorn rips, and the air's become musky from the dust that's fallen alongside the ceiling. The only consistency is the glitter; it's still everywhere.

"Do we know if the scientists have anything in common? Any particular project?" Ben whispers while he shakes the settled dust from his blond hair.

"The Last King Project," My father unexpectedly answers. He's a few meters across from us, appropriately surrounded by his royal guard. He has this look as our eyes meet—faith. I thought we were whispering.

"That's a history project. Why would that interest them?" Ben continues to whisper as if we're alone.

"We have another problem," my father announces to the senior protectors gathering around him. Does he want us to hear him?

"What could be more of a problem than this?" Aiden whispers aggressively.

"The injured girl from the earlier chaos on Central street, she isn't in the database."

"What?" Ben half shouts. Jia jabs him in the ribs, and he returns to a whisper. "That's impossible."

"She's also missing the radiation treatment." My father turns to us as he drops all pretence of his closed-group conversation.

"Again, impossible." Ben walks over to the powerful people, completely unfazed by their seniority. "Someone's made a mistake. Everyone received that treatment, and it's hereditary."

I glance at Jia, who's already looking at me; she's thinking it too.

"How can someone not be in the database and not have the

radiation treatment?" Aiden asks.

"They can't. It's a mistake." Ben laughs unsteadily.

"What if…" I stop to breathe as everyone's attention turns to me. "What if she's not from Biack?"

My father, Ben, Will and Aiden—they all realise.

Chapter Five

Jess

Well, this is disappointing. I thought I died.

I awake to a woman in all white staring at me, and for several moments we remain in an awkward purgatory of silence. Despite the trembling of her body, she can't look away. I wait for her to perform some action, and finally she speeds out of the room.

Okay, where the hell am I now?

I tug at foreign tubes sticking out my left arm; my heart starts to race. Where was I last? At school. No, I was dreaming.

Did someone undress me? The basic white top and trousers itches at my skin. It's too clean; everything is too clean. Across the room, Everett's hoodie and the rest of my clothes wait in a neatly folded pile. Everything's too neat.

The room is decorated with strange machines. Is this a hospital? But it's too clean to be a hospital. Everywhere I look I see white—the walls, the floors, the machines, the furniture. It's unsettling. It's other-worldly.

"Good, you're awake." A man wearing all white—who'd have thought—enters the room. "How are you feeling? Has the treatment worked?" Treatment? "Your burns have healed, and you show no signs of distress." No sign of distress, my arse. "I just need your name."

Silence.

"Do you understand me?" I give him my blankest stare. "Perhaps you can simply tell me where you're from?"

How would that be any simpler than my name? In what world would someone know where they came from before what they're called?

Either way, I don't answer.

"Okay." He glances around for any task left undone. "I'll check on you again later."

No, he won't. I need to get out of here.

But where is *here*? I glance out the window; behind inches of frame and skyscrapers of steel, a shield of glass hexagons tries to block out the sky, the burning sky, under the burning red sun. I pinch myself. Ouch. No, I must still be dreaming. I must be asleep—or perhaps this is an oxygen-deprived hallucination. I feel for the burn on my hand, only to find it missing. I'm not crazy.

I need to get out of here. First thing, gently remove the tubes from my arm and hope they aren't keeping me alive. A little pressure to stop the bleeding. I don't know how much time I have, so I fling Everett's jacket on over the white top in a panicked rush; there are no shoes. From the door, I can see huddles of doctors and nurses, of which the differences are nonexistent.

They could all be doctors, or all be nurses. Either way, they're all dressed head to toe in that unsettling white.

There are no guards. Of course not. The people of Biack would never expect me to escape. They're not prepared for this. I mean, if this was real.

After waiting for the doctors or nurses to move on, I pull up my hood and sneak out of the room, head low. My previous guests are nowhere to be seen as I follow signs for the exit. When I finally encounter more people, everyone appears to be too swept up in their own lives and completely oblivious to mine. I don't stick around for them to notice me. I hurry down the hall towards the reception, and the exit, if the signs are right.

I blend in much better near the reception; the ocean of white garments is no more, and I fall under the cover of the crowd.

I'm about to make my exit, slowly to not arouse suspicion, when a girl standing at the desk steals my focus.

Her hair's carefully controlled in the perfect plait down her back, the blond brightening her lace top. She moves gracefully, almost regally, as her hand skims across the reception counter. The receptionist can't stop smiling. Meanwhile, the girl's companion, a lanky but well-kept blond-haired boy, engages in what appears to be a heated discussion with a nurse/doctor.

I'm definitely dreaming.

I'm almost through the door when she turns around and our eyes lock. For a moment, we share a stillness.

Crystal-blue, her warm eyes twinkle under the ceiling lights. I wonder what chill she feels in mine. Meanwhile, the soft of her skin gently moves as her lips skip between a smile and a tremor. Have I come face to face with my wildest dream? And if so, why is this pit within me still cold?

This is impossible.

But somehow…

Impossible.

The moment finally ends. "Wait!" Her shout alerts her companion.

I run. They chase.

Beyond the exit doors are more corridors. It's a scam, a maze. But maybe a maze will work to my advantage. They chase me down hallway after hallway; I seem to be slightly faster, socks sliding across the spotless floor. Although that's probably due to the four-inch heels on her feet.

Rushing past a doctor, I knock folders out of his hands, hoping the obstacle will secure my escape. The girl swings around him, and her companion jumps over him—the obstacle doesn't hinder them. Another attempt at creating the same obstacle only secures the same outcome; eventually they start gaining on me. Then I fall upon a dead end.

They stop behind me.

"Jess?" The word slides off her tongue like a melody. How does she know my name? I must've misheard.

I glance at an open window; it seems like a choice between this conversation and a three-floor fall.

"We don't want you to get hurt." She notices my glances. "We just want to talk."

That's what they always say in the movies. Right before you

get hurt.

Am I really that opposed to acknowledging her existence that I'd jump out a third-storey window? But she can't be real, she can't. This is impossible. Just like the sun and the sky's shield and the place names and everything. I'm truly losing it. And I'm not ready to deal with reality if I'm not. What if she can move things—no, that's not real. That's definitely not real.

It all happens in seconds. I lurch towards the window, she yells out, and her companion fires some weapon. I fall to the floor in a seizure of jerks as electricity shoots through me. He shot me!

In the final second, she's standing above me. How can she be real? How?

❧❧❧

I'm getting sick of waking up in different places. This time I've downgraded.

"You don't have to watch her; she's not going anywhere this time." The only physical thing separating us is a glass wall, and yet Ella feels a world away. Outside my metal room, her attention's focused on a scruffy-looking boy, whose attention is focused on staring at me. He's mostly obscured by shadows, but his sad blue eyes are piercing. I know him.

After receiving no response, she taps buttons that holographically appear next to a door in the glass wall, and then she enters my room. My cell. My hexagonal cell; half the walls are solid metal, while the other half clear glass. Across a hallway lies another identical cell, and next to it lies another. They seem to go on forever, or as far as I can see.

It's been a matter of seconds, but I'm already working on my escape plan. If this is real—which it can't be—the Biack I know isn't prepared for someone like me. They aren't prepared for someone trying to escape.

My attention is back to Ella. I've spent my life dreaming of this girl, and now that she's standing in front of me, it's…underwhelming. She's just a girl. There's nothing special about her.

For too long she paces back and forth across the cell. Finally her lips part, but words escape her. Odd, as she always knew what to say in the dreams. Maybe this isn't Ella.

"I'm Ella." She finds words. "But I think you may already know that."

She doesn't know me.

"And you're Jess." She pauses. "But I already knew that."

How?

She keeps looking at me, waiting, but I give nothing. She continues pacing. "It's okay. I already know the answer. I saw the way you looked at me before. It was the same way I looked at you." Nothing. She stops. "I wasn't the only one dreaming, was I?"

This is ridiculous, insane, preposterous, nuts, a load of bollocks.

She doesn't know me. She's can't.

"Where am I?" I finally speak.

"Biack."

There's this pit in my stomach. I don't know how much

longer I can deny all the facts around me, but I'm not ready to accept them yet. "You're lying."

"I'm not, Jess. I'm not." She's staring at the floor; strange, as she's never seemed to struggle looking someone in the eyes before. "I'm just as confused as you."

No, she isn't. She's a stranger, and how can a stranger even begin to understand how I'm feeling?

"I just... I just need to know." She pleads, "Where are you from?"

Nothing.

"Where are you from?" she begs.

If this is real— How could this be real? How could I come to be here, and how could this come to exist? Has it always existed?

"Please. I need answers." So do I. "Where are you from?"

She wants answers, but I only have one. The words fall easily. "Far away."

We sit in silence for several minutes before she gets up and leaves.

I didn't even get to ask for a cup of tea.

✿✿✿✿

His face may be still, but his eyes follow me as I move. I don't know what he hopes to achieve; it's unlikely I'm going to burst through the glass wall, being 5'2 with hardly any muscle on me. Although it is fun to pace around and watch his eyes try to keep up.

"Who are you?" I bang on the glass wall. I already know. He remains unchanged. "What do you want?" I bang again. "What do you want with me?"

His stillness only agitates me further, resulting in a swift kick to the wall, which I immediately regret as I fall to the floor clutching my foot.

He stifles a laugh.

It dawns on me: if this isn't real, my actions have no consequences. I can finally do and say as I please. Well, within the confines of this room. Hey, this might be fun.

Not long later, the companion from the maybe-hospital-thing appears; I'm finally able to size him up properly. Compared to my guard, he's quite skinny, but not in a feeble way. Instead, he appears healthy—his skin is practically glowing, enough that my prison feels less cold. Still cold, but just less. He stands with his head hung, although eventually he brings it up to talk, revealing dark green eyes protected by black frames.

"What's she like?" He straightens his sweater vest.

My guard shrugs. "Since Ella left, she's become quite vocal."

"In a threatening way? Should you come in with me?"

"I can hear you, you know," I interrupt. "And I bite."

"You'll be okay." My guard comforts the skinny boy. "And if she does bite, just bite her back."

They have a laugh; I try to join in, but it feels like I don't get the joke.

The skinny boy cautiously enters the cell, carrying a white briefcase of some sort; he walks over to the bed and opens it up next to me to reveal medical tools. Oh God, he's about to torture me. I really thought my guard was going to be the one to do that.

He notices the look on my face. "I'm not going to hurt you. I just need samples for tests. Besides, if anyone was going to hurt you, it wouldn't be me."

"Samples?"

"Blood, saliva, the usual." He shrugs.

Saliva? I decide to assert myself by spitting at his feet. He doesn't look impressed. My guard, on the other hand, finds it funny, much to the skinny boy's annoyance.

"Actually, I only need a swab." He hands me a tool. It's some kind of coated plastic, not a cotton swab.

"What if I refuse?"

He turns to my guard. "We'll take it by force."

I stick the swab in my mouth, assuming that's what he wants me to do with it. "What's your name?" I ask. I already know the answer.

He hesitates, looking puzzlingly back at my guard before answering. "Ben." The Invisible Boy.

"Why do you need samples from me, Ben?"

"For the same reason you're in here." That was vague.

"Which is?"

He takes the swab from me and pulls out a needle. "You're not in the database, and everyone's in the database."

"What's the database?" I know the answer. I flinch as he sticks the needle in my arm.

"It stores the identity of everyone on Biack." I always

thought that was a dangerous idea. But they've never met any resistance to it, at least as far as I saw. "I may not have come up with the idea, but it's basically my project. We've never discovered anyone to be missing…until you."

"Why do you think I'm not in it?"

"Well…" He pauses to change the vial attached to the needle. I can feel the blood draining from my arm. "The most popular theory is you were removed. Maybe an inside job."

"So you have someone corrupt on the inside?"

He shrugs. "That's what some believe. But it's a crazy idea that feels really unlikely." He massages the back of his neck. "Although I guess it's the less-crazy idea."

"What do you believe?"

Finally, he removes the needle. "A friend of mine has another theory."

"Ella," I whisper.

He unexpectedly yanks a few strands of my hair out. "She believes in people, so I think it's only fair to believe in her."

"What's her theory?"

He glances at my guard. "I think I've already told you too much." He starts to pack away his briefcase.

I grab his shoulder. "Please." My words come out rushed. "No one else has told me anything."

He hesitates before replying, "You're not from around here; Earth, to be more exact. Which is a place that only exists in old stories told to children. So you can see why Ella's having a hard time getting people to believe her."

"Will the samples help to prove her theory?"

"Or disprove it." He walks over to the door.

I ask, "So what do you believe?"

He stops to turn back to me. "Ella told us about her night-mares."

"You got everything you need?" my guard queries.

"Anything else was collected or implanted at the treatment centre." Implanted?

I rush to the glass to watch as The Invisible Boy shuffles out of sight down the hall. My attention returns to my guard, and suddenly it's cold again.

❖❖❖

Maybe an hour passes before more visitors arrive. This time there's two of them.

One's skin is as dark as ash, although the expression on his face reveals contrasting white teeth. "I've come to see what all the fuss is about," Fire Boy announces.

"Weird." The Girl of Oceans examines me, her brown eyes twinkling and her black hair windswept; how can it be windswept when we're deep underground, if we're where I think we are? She's wearing a sloughy cropped top underneath a uniform jacket matched with shorts, a stark contrast to sweat-er-vest-wearing Ben. "She's the same, right down to the scar on her nose." Did Ella tell them all about me? She changes her tone. "Why is she being kept in there? She's not a prisoner."

"That's what I've been saying," I say.

Fire Boy turns to face me with glowing red eyes. "You know,

for some reason people are talking about you more than me at the moment, and I spent last night with Rae Jones."

"Rae Jones?" My guard's surprised.

"Yeah, she wanted some company after the events of the ball." He turns to his companions. "Events which everyone seems to have moved past *really* quickly." He turns back to me. "Anyway, I've been trying to brag, but people only want to talk about *her*." He glares, but I can't take him seriously. I know him too well.

"It must be hard being overshadowed," the Girl of Oceans teases.

"Yeah, I finally get how you guys feel." He grins. "I'm Aiden, by the way." I already know. "I heard you're The Girl from Far Away?"

The Girl from Far Away. I like that. "That I am." I wave. "Congrats, by the way."

"Thank you!" He laughs. "I don't understand why no one else seems to care."

I shrug. "I don't know. I can't see how a mystery girl of unknown origin, falling from the sky, can even come close to overshadowing that."

"Oh, she's smug!" He grins. "You owe me now, though; you've taken away an opportunity to brag."

"I'll make it up to you when I get back to Earth. I'll tell everyone you spent the night with Rae Jones."

"Earth," he whispers.

Several seconds pass before Fire Boy turns to my guard and with a grin says, "I like her." Patting the guard on the back,

Aiden walks off, waving goodbye to me. I always liked Aiden in the dreams.

"I can't stay, either," The Girl of Oceans announces, "but you," she instructs my guard, "don't let anyone take her from here. Keep an eye on her. And you," she instructs me, "try not to go anywhere." Unlikely. She smiles. "I'm Shui Jia, by the way." I know. She disappears off down the hall, hair blowing in the nonexistent wind.

I examine my guard. I know who he is. His physique is just as impressive in reality as it is in my dreams; his muscles are carefully outlined by his rugged dark top. Like the rest of his clothes, it's frayed and torn. Does he take care of anything? His ocean eyes are still on me, relentlessly watching.

"Do I get to know your name? You've been watching me all day," I ask.

"Don't you already know it?" It's so cold in this room.

"I don't know what you're talking about. You're a stranger."

"So are you," he responds.

"If I'm just a stranger, why are you watching me or guarding or whatever? Why are you obsessed with me?"

"I'm not obsessed with you," he states.

"And yet you haven't moved all day," I tease. "Is it because you're afraid I'll leave? Do you really think I'm going anywhere? Will you miss me?" I move closer to the wall between us.

"I don't know what you're capable of." He doesn't know me.

I press my hands against the glass. "Do you really think I'm going to break through this wall? Are you afraid that all five-foot-two of me will attack you? Are you afraid of me?" I slam the glass; he doesn't jump.

"I don't think anyone's ever been afraid of you." He smirks.

I slide down onto the floor, back against the glass wall. How can he possibly think I might escape? I don't even know how I got here. After a while, I hear him join me on the floor; I can feel the pressure of his back on the opposite side of the glass. We sit together in silence for a while.

I whisper, "Will, did she tell you too?"

It takes him a while to reply, but eventually The Unbreakable Boy speaks. "Yes. Which is why I don't trust you."

Ironic. "I don't trust you, either."

❀❀❀

I'm lying in bed many hours later, pretending to sleep, when a hidden figure starts to knock on the glass. It's been a short while since Will abandoned his post for the night, believing I was asleep. I can't believe they've left me unattended, but I guess there are probably cameras somewhere.

I decide to maintain the rouse that I'm sleeping until I learn more information. The person keeps knocking.

"Wake up!" a male voice speaks. "I haven't got long; they've called an emergency meeting, and my absence will draw attention. And you don't want that."

I turn and look at him. "Why wouldn't I want that?"

"Because I'm your only chance at escaping."

I sit upright immediately. "What?"

"You won't be around long if you remain here. The emergency meeting is to decide your fate, and you must realise by now there's no happy ending. But I can guarantee your safety."

"How can I trust you any more than them?"

He pauses. "You can't, but you know you can't trust them—they locked you in a cell. You can't stay here, and I'm your only option if you want to escape."

"Where will you take me?"

"My boss wants to meet you; she can help you get back home."

This all sounds too good to be true, so the rational part of my mind's screaming at me not to trust him. Then again, I can't escape on my own. And Ella and her friends aren't planning on helping me. "Okay."

It's dark, but I think I can see him smile. "Excellent. When the time is right, just follow the signs."

"What signs? And who are you?" It's too late. He's gone.

Oh, Jess, what the hell are you doing?

Chapter Six

Ella

We finally have a seat at the table.

"Okay, let's begin." My father enters the overcrowded conference room. He continues, "Right, well, I'm sure you're all aware of the reasons behind this abrupt meeting."

"At this early hour!" Council member Donald Adams exclaims.

A protector from the back of the room responds. "So it's clearly of the utmost importance." His accent sets him apart from the rest; he must be from The Plains.

Another council member shouts, "Especially since the predators have already found out! Has 'classified' lost all meaning?"

"Not yet," my father answers. "To summarise for those who have no knowledge of recent events—despite the extensive press coverage—several floors below us sleeps a stranger, a girl with no trace within the database. A girl who's now been confined to a holding cell due to her previous attempts to escape questioning."

Scott abruptly dashes into the room. "So sorry to be late." He pulls up a seat next to me and passes a small toy bird under the table.

"Where did you get this?" It's my Alaria, named after a baby bird I nursed back to health when I was seven. My father had the toy specially made after we let her go. We were on a tour of the cities at the time, and Scott and his father had visited us; I always thought I'd lost it.

"I found it when I went through my old things recently," he says. "I guess I never had a chance to return it."

I stroke the wings; they're a soft as I remember.

"Ben, would you like to take over?" My father gestures to the already-standing Ben. They're finally listening to him. I'm so proud.

"As previously established, she isn't in the database. I ran her blood sample several times myself, but there were no matches. I then decided to actually examine the blood itself and—" He stops when he notices the yawns. "Basically, she hasn't had the radiation exposure everyone else has."

"Has she been kept underground?" Someone jumps in with a theory. "Hidden from the sun?"

"Unlikely. She isn't lacking in vitamin D, which would be characteristic of someone having never seen the sun." Everyone's silent. Ben looks down for a few seconds before continuing. I bet he's rolling his eyes. "No, she hasn't been kept underground."

"Maybe she has extra-strong skin or something," a protector exclaims.

Ben's answer is quick. "No, she doesn't."

"This is ridiculous! Impossible! There must be another explanation!" Adams interrupts. He's quite vocal, as usual.

"Hear the boy out, Donald. There's no one more qualified," my father responds.

"Hear yourself speak, Liam. He's just a *boy*," Adams fights back. "Growing up in a lab is hardly a qualification."

Ben's hands scrunch into fists. "If you'd like to have someone you believe to be more qualified look at the samples, that can be arranged. But I warn you, they'll just come to the same conclusion as I did."

Adams mutters something.

"I'm confused. What does all this mean?" Another council member asks, a younger one. I think her name is Adisa.

The room falls eerily silent; maybe everyone's afraid to sound ridiculous.

I hold Alaria tight. "I *think*—" I find myself having to answer the same question again, "—Ben's trying to say that the only conclusion, the only possible option—" everyone's staring, "—is that maybe she's not from Biack."

The room erupts into argument.

❖❖❖

Several hours later, we're finally able to leave after all other theories have been exhausted and the discussion draws to a close. Not that any sort of conclusion was reached.

"Nothing to say?" I manage to catch Will before he disappears off.

"I don't know anything about all that science stuff," he says.

"Neither does Adams, and yet he's never short of opinions."

He grins then turns, starting to walk away.

"What are you doing?" Will stops in response to my question. "The only time you've left her alone was for this meeting. You don't need to guard the cell. Because you know there's no way she can get out, right?"

He turns around. "No, I don't."

Before I can reply, a figure moves between us. "Good, Ella, I managed to catch you before you leave." My father waves to a passerby. "We have a council meeting later—"

"We?" I interrupt.

"Yes. After the events of the past twenty-four hours, there's a lot to discuss. And we're hoping to have an update from the A team about the Red Suits' attack." He stops. I can see the realisation across his face as he remembers what confused me. "But yes, we've been discussing lately the possibility of you sitting in on a few of our meetings. After all, one day you'll be leading them."

I hesitate. "Father, it's not that I don't appreciate this opportunity. It's just…"

"You wanted to spend today with the girl?" I nod. "Ella, I know she has this meaning to you, but the throne…" He stops himself. "Okay."

"Okay?"

"Yes, okay." He smiles. After a moment of thought, he continues. "As you can imagine, I'm under a lot of pressure from several commanders to allow their protectors to interrogate the girl. However, she's just a scared child. I keep thinking, what if that was you? And so I believe putting her through an interrogation will only further alienate her. We need to win her trust, and that starts with giving her ours."

"I do trust her," I state.

"I know you do." He smiles. "Which is why I think you spending the day with her is a great idea. You should show her around the BCD, although nothing restricted." A commander behind us gestures for my father's attention. "Hopefully showing her around will help earn her trust and make her more cooperative. And if possible, try to get some information out of her—if possible, any proof of her origin and how she came to be here." He gestures back to the commander.

"Thank you, Father! I know I can't neglect my responsibility to the throne, but this girl, Jess, she's…"

He's already disappeared off, completing his next task. He never rests; I hope I can find some way to live up to that.

Will's already outside Jess's cell by the time I arrive. The fact she's asleep makes it slightly uncomfortable.

"You don't think this is odd?" I ask.

He replies, "She's not asleep."

"How do you know?"

He just looks at her. Is it supposed to be obvious?

Across the cell on a metal plank, she lies silently facing the wall; she's almost as still as the Red Suit the other night. The treatment centre attire is still hanging on her body, while her tattered jacket has been placed on top of her as a blanket, or shield.

As I enter the room, she stays completely still, almost too still.

"Why are you here?" she speaks. How did Will know?

Why are you here? Until two days ago, this girl was a figment of my imagination, an idea, a dream. And now the victim of my nightmares is suddenly standing before me.

I wait across the room. "Your brother's name is Everett."

"What?" She turns around, facing us.

"Your boyfriend forgot to write in your Valentine's Day card last year." Jess twitches as I add, "Ex-boyfriend?"

"That toy's called Alaria." She points at the bird I can't let go of. "Although I thought you lost it."

I continue, "Your best friend made you cancel your seventeenth birthday party because it was the day before New Year." She pulls herself off the bed.

"She's not my best friend." Her fingers clench just like Ben's earlier as she says, "You have one of every Ella doll ever made hidden in a box under your bed."

Will bursts out laughing. "Oh, really? You do?"

"They're mementos!"

Jess stands before me; she seems taller, although I'm sure we're the same height. Her ivy eyes are searching mine. She's not scared. In fact, I think she's fearless. I've barely met her, and yet I think I know her better than anyone else. She pushes her hair out of her face; it's a complete mess. "I was jealous of you."

She whispers, "Of everything you had."

"I was jealous of you," I whisper back. "Your life isn't planned out for you." Her face is filled with doubt. "I was also terrified of your life." I smooth Alaria's feathers. "For me, they were nightmares."

"For me, it's my life."

I think that's enough for now. "How would you like to get out of this cell?"

"I thought you'd never ask." She puts on her jacket. "Do you want me to lead the way to Ben's lab? Or do you want the honour?"

❧❧❧

Jess leans on the central table, pushing a floating ball with her index finger; with every push, it swings straight back into its central place above a circular disc. Around the room, Will, Ben and I wait for her amusement to fade; it's been over ten minutes now. "This is so cool. It's floating. How's it floating?"

In the corner of the thirty-second floor hides Ben's lab. Home to both the newest advancements in technology and historical treasures, it's kind of an overflowing storage room. Looking around, there are plenty of signs that we spend the majority of our lives in here: the extensive collection of empty food packaging; the out-of-shape pillows thrown around the seater; the doodles amongst the science across the walls and the cardboard boxes overflowing with clothes.

"The disc creates an artificial gravity field," Ben answers

before grabbing the ball. "And it's not a toy. It's a decoration."

She rolls her eyes. "And what's this?" We follow the direction of her finger to a show box containing a depleted energy core.

"An object that was once useful but now just like that contraption is proving to be more hassle than it's worth." Ben throws the box in a drawer.

"These are some pretty cool toys, man," she says as she studies the room with her eyes.

Ben's voice is tense. "They're not—"

"Okay, Jess, why did you want to visit Ben's lab?" I interrupt.

How much of my life has she seen? My view of hers is riddled with plot holes; sometimes it'd be weeks between the dreams. Does she know about our abilities?

"To see the decorations." She picks up a portable screen. "Oh, and to ask about the Dome."

"The Dome?" I exchange a glance with Ben. "What do you know about it?"

She tosses the screen down on the table. Ben flinches. "All I know is it gets mentioned occasionally. It's a word tossed around. I know what it is, but I want to know *what it is*."

"Okay, how about an answer for an answer?" I propose.

The corners of her mouth rise. "Sure, but you first."

Ben waits for a nod before starting. "Our sun is nearing the end of its main sequence life. It's starting to become something we call a red giant."

"Yep, red giants. Learnt about them in school. Just a bigger, hotter star, right?" She pulls herself up on the central desk.

"It's not actually hotter. Its surface temperature is actually cooler. It's—" He stops. "Yes, sure, it's a bigger, hotter star. It's been increasing in both *heat* and size since the beginning of our records, but about a century ago the radiation started to get dangerous; everyone fled underground. We build hundreds of underground cities in caverns and then focused our excavating efforts on building tunnels to connect them. It was only about fifteen years ago that people returned to the surface completely. And that's because construction of the Dome was completed."

"Underground people, okay…" Creases form across her forehead. "So back to my original question. What's the Dome?"

Ben picks up a piece of metal on display in the corner. "We call it magic glass. It was discovered by pure accident, and it turned out to be our salvation. I'd go into detail about the chemical structure and properties that make it special, but it's probably above your intellectual level."

She mumbles incoherently as she mockingly imitates him.

"This—" he ignores her and instead beams as he holds up a piece of metal, "—is the Dome. The planet is surrounded by it, seven miles up. Its unique properties allow it to protect us from the harmful radiation from the sun. Meanwhile, machines we call maintainers placed around the inner surface control the atmosphere and temperature."

"So your planet is quite literally surrounded by a Dome."

"Yes."

"How long did it take to build?"

"About thirty years."

"And when you guys were children, really young children, you lived underground?"

"No, most of the Dome was built by the time we were all born. We lived above ground." Ben gestures to me. "At least, I know Ella and I did."

Will just smiles; he finds comfort in the mystery he creates.

"What happened to all the underground places?" As she speaks, she knocks over another trinket, a glass box. Ben jumps to catch it but misses—it smashes against the metal floor. "Shit."

His veins start to glow yellow.

"Shit?" I ask while grabbing Ben's arm. Slowly the glow fades.

"It's just something you say when you mess up." Her attention is elsewhere as she tries to brush the glass into a pile. She soon gives up when the glass cuts her fingertips. "So back to the underground places—are we in one now?"

I release Ben's arm and his veins return to normal; he smiles a silent thank you. I don't think Jess noticed, although I know she must know.

Ben answers, "Yes, it's a standalone complex rather than a city, though. The Biackian Centre of Defence, BCD for short."

I interrupt, "You already knew that."

Judging by the creases on her forehead and the tremors on her lips, it appears she's trying to figure out what to say next. "Tell me more about the BCD." She turns to Ben.

"Right. Well—" Ben looks to me for a further nod, "—it's the centre of operations for the protectors and the government. The complex has one hundred one floors but as far as the public know it only has ten, the other ninety-one underground floors are a closely guarded secret, which is kind of hard to keep, considering thousands of people work here." He pauses and looks to me. I nod again and he continues. "Floors ninety-one to one hundred are above ground but known to the public as floors zero to nine. Whereas the actual floors zero to ninety are underground. There are separate pods between the above-ground and underground levels to avoid any reporters asking questions."

"Pods?" she asks.

He replies, "Yes, devices that move you up and down levels?"

"Ah, where I'm from, we call them lifts." Earth. "If the above-ground levels aren't secret, what goes on there?"

"Mainly press briefings, publicised meetings, basic admin, but no one really cares about the above. At least not the people who know about the underground."

"Okay, you've had six questions. It's my turn now," I interrupt before she can ask another.

Her face tenses. "That's not fair. I didn't get to ask about the underground levels."

Will jumps in, "How did you get here?"

"So we're starting off with an easy one." She laughs before pulling herself off the floor and starting to pace around the room. "I fell here. Next."

I tuck my hair behind my ears and ask, "How did you fall here?"

"Backwards, I think."

"Have you been here before?"

"Never."

"Have you tried to come here before?"

"Why would I try to go somewhere I didn't think was real?"

Ben jumps in. "So you came here by accident?"

"Does anything happen by accident?" Destiny. "Maybe I didn't plan this, but maybe a part of me wanted to get away."

"So why did you come here?"

"Because I'm The Girl from Far Away." She smiles before starting to tut. "You're out of questions, princess. So, what happens underground?"

Ben, Will and I engage in silent conversation before accepting defeat. With a quick look to Ben, he begins to answer her question. "Mostly research, meetings, training—"

Will moves closer to whisper in my ear, "Next time, try asking her if she knows how to get back."

There isn't a next time, though, as shortly after Ben begins to answer her question, the base alarm starts to sound.

❖❖❖

"What do you think happened?" Ben asks as we make our way to the response site; Will agreed to return Jess to her cell.

I'm about to respond when I notice the chaos down the hall. Fallen lights, blackened walls. Healers are frantically trying to help the injured while scientists stand around assessing the damage. "Explosion," I answer. I find my father amongst the rush. "How could this have happened? Was it the Red Suits again?"

"Unlikely. This building is impossible to break into. It's the most heavily protected structure on the planet."

It must've been an accident.

"What's the damage? Who's hurt?" Ben asks as he pulls out his hexagon to take evidence pictures.

"Two scientists and a protector," Scott replies from behind. Stepping over a burnt briefcase, he makes his way toward us, exchanges quick conversation with my father followed up with a smile directed at me, and then rushes off again, all too quickly. Our hands brush as he leaves.

"This can't be an accident." Ben brings me back to the hallway. "There's no source here great enough to cause this damage."

"But my father said—"

Ben pulls me to one side. "Ella, I think the Red Suits did this. I think this was intentional."

"But, no—" My mind races through a hundred thoughts. Until yesterday, the Red Suits have never made such bold moves to attack us. What's changed? "If someone did this, why an unimportant hallway? If they could actually get inside—which is the biggest task—why not a lab, the cafeteria, an office? Why here? What does this achieve?"

"Nothing. It achieves nothing." But it did cause a base-wide alert, an alert that brought us here.

Will slides past the crowd. "What happened?" He's here, not watching her.

Ben shares my thoughts; at the same time, we answer, "It's a distraction."

    Jess.

Chapter Seven

Jess

"Is this the part where you say 'don't go far' and I make some wise-ass comment about the irony of that?" I say.

The Unbreakable Boy fails to conceal a smile as he locks me away before heading back Ella and Ben.

Again, I'm alone.

How long will I be trapped in this cell? Better question—how long will I be trapped in this world? God, I wish I knew how I did it. What if it wasn't even me? Every purified breath here feels like a bad dream, which is strange, because I used to dread Earth's polluted air.

I don't think my bluffing game is working on Ella. What does she think I've seen of her? What opinion does she think I've formed? What opinion have her and her friends formed of me from what she's seen; does she pity me or think I'm pathetic? Has she seen all the bad or only the few good? How do I come off in the story of me?

Perhaps I can return home the way I left it. After pulling

myself up onto the metal bed, I slam my head down, only to receive a nasty surprise, and no, it's not Earth. Something more uncomfortable than the metal is hidden under the pillow. I reach under to recover it—a badly drawn map paired with oh, God, a gun. Is this the sign?

Shit, does he expect me to shoot my way out of here? No, this isn't what I signed up for. Then again, none of this is. And what the hell is this map? Is that supposed to be this cell block? Surely it'll be packed with guards—wait, no, they'll be wherever Ella went. That alarm, was that a distraction?

Maybe I should just stay here. Maybe that's safer. But what will they think when they find this gun? Will they believe me when I say I don't know where it came from? Of course not. This time there's evidence against me.

Well, no point arguing anymore. I might as well get on with this. I mean, after all, it's no more impossible than the rest of today.

Everything happens fast as I realise my time is limited; eventually, my guard will return. I shoot the glass. It takes a few attempts before it comes crashing down, causing a great noise, but no one's listening. My arm catches on the jagged remains. I pay no attention to it. With the gun shaking in my grasp in one hand and the hardly decipherable map held up in the other, I proceed down hallway after hallway—luckily, without company.

I'm almost surprised as I fail to encounter anyone, but then I remind myself that in this perfect world, they're all too distracted by one crack in their flawless vision that they fail to notice any others. Maybe growing up on Earth has given me an advantage. God knows I never thought I'd say that.

Finally, I make it to end of the map's path, another strange lift—no, pod—when I hear the footsteps behind me. I raise my gun.

"Please, don't move." Ella speaks calmly and politely, but somehow the threat is still real. "Put it down."

Turning around slowly, I find myself the target of Ella and Will's guns. I thought I heard multiple feet. "Are you going to shoot me?"

"I'd like to think not," she replies. What a strange way of answering. "Are you going to shoot us?"

I glance at my gun. "Would you believe it's just a toy?" They don't seem impressed. My voice shakes. "I can't stay here."

I know they're capable of shooting, but am I? I couldn't even hurt Scarlett.

Ella's porcelain face glows under my gaze. I can't harm her. The Girl was always kind, endlessly supporting everyone around her. The only reason she's ever hurt anyone is to protect someone else. Although, I've only seen snapshots of her life, random days; do I truly know what she can do? Then again, Ben shot me, or tasered me—I don't really know. I turn to Will; maybe he's right not to trust me.

I fire at The Unbreakable Boy.

Her veins glow white. She raises her hand.

The bullet stops midair.

The bullet stopped.

She stopped the bullet.

She didn't touch it. No. That part can't be real.

"Jess," she begins to speak but it's too late; I'm already in the lift. She doesn't stop me.

My hand falls against the top button. What the hell. Okay, so, sometimes in the dreams she did things like that, but I thought that was just my own mind making it more interesting. People can't do that. Not with their minds. No. Not people. But I'm not on Earth. These aren't the people I know.

The lift stops too soon. It's the right floor. I'm just not ready to move. I feel dizzy.

Somehow I exit and discover the lift hidden in a closet; they did say the public didn't know about the underground levels. *Okay, just act calm, walk out, and don't look them in the eyes.* But they don't look at me. Everyone is oblivious, busy with their everyday lives. I stroll right out the front door, blood trickling down my arm, gun dangling from my fingers.

The outside is as terrifyingly pure as the inside. No litter, no dirt. Everything's too clean, and everyone's too happy. My lack of shoes doesn't dirty the white socks.

The wide road goes on endlessly, filled with people and pavements—I've never seen cars in my sleep. The buildings are tall but European tall. In the distance I can see American skyscrapers. Everything is made of pale stone with large windows; there's so much light.

After only several meters of aimless stumbling, someone reaches out from the shadows and pulls me into an alley. Their arm is over my mouth; I bite it.

"Life!" What? "I'm not going to hurt you, for King's sake.

I'm the one who helped you escape."

"Why, what do you want from me?" I struggle to break free from the man from this morning.

He stabs me in the neck with something, and the world immediately starts to fade. "Nothing. It's what my boss wants that should concern you."

※❀※❀※

They say before you die, your life flashes before your eyes. Every time I find myself blacking out, I wait for that to happen, and surprisingly no reminiscent flashes, but maybe my life isn't worth rewatching.

I'm done with waking up in different places; for once, can they keep me awake during transportation? This time it's a bedroom, like something out of a royal castle. I've been thrown onto a four-poster bed, complete with its own curtains. The bedding is blood-red, and a part of me wonders if that's to hide stains. The room's decorated further with a chair, desk, wardrobe and a dirty old mirror.

Whatever the man used to knock me out has left me feeling woozy; I almost collapse as I try to stand. I grab the bed to stop myself falling and notice multiple cuts and scratches across my arms; did I do that when I broke the glass? At least if they're painful, I feel too sick to notice.

Maybe it's this world that's making me unwell—perhaps something in the air? Maybe Ella never stopped that bullet; it was all in my head. Other worlds and other humans, I can find a way to rationalise that. But what she did, no, that can't be real. So it wasn't. But if I really believed that, why would I shoot at Will? After all, he has a pretty face.

A set of black double doors lie across from the bed; I try the handles, but they're locked solid and feel impenetrable. My next attempt to escape is the large window dominating one of the walls, and yet again it's locked; the glass seems unbreakable. This suspicion is confirmed when I throw the wooden chair. The glass remains unchanged but one of the chair legs snap off.

Beating the glass with the leg, I consider screaming, but looking outside, all I see are fields of green. There's no one here to hear me. I'm still alone.

Maybe I can find more tools to aid me. The desk drawers are empty, and so is the wardrobe, but it seems like a good hiding place. I climb inside and shut the doors from within; maybe the dark will somehow help me do whatever I did before to get to this world.

I've never wanted to be on Earth so badly. Biack was always my escape, my private paradise, but somehow it's turned out to be my prison. The perfect illusion has started to shatter as I realise Biack isn't the utopia I dreamed of. I'm no freer than I was on Earth. Here, everyone wants to trap me in a room; there, I'm at least trapped in a town.

Either way, I'll never see the outside of my entrapment.

I'm not sure how long passes before someone finally comes for me. Hours, minutes, they all feel the same from within the voluntary confinement of the wardrobe.

The doors fling open. "There you are."

I scream.

It's a male voice but muffled behind a head of red bandages, wrapped around so many times his face is completely obscured. He's wearing a suit of red that I've never seen up close. I continue to scream as he pulls me out of the wardrobe; I scratch and kick, but he's completely covered. I always thought if I was to be murdered, I'd scratch them till their DNA was locked so deeply beneath my nails.

He throws me onto the floor with such force I think I graze my hands. He could be anyone, a monster, disfigured. The worst part is not seeing his eyes. I spot the broken chair leg within my grasp, and when it smacks into his head, I can't tell if he flinches.

He waits for me to tire of fighting before he orders, "Get up."

I hesitate before standing. We leave the room and I'm still trapped, but I'm looking for new opportunities. "Where are you taking me?"

He pushes me down hallway after hallway of old stone. "To the boss. She's been waiting for you."

No open windows. "You know I've been awake for ages, right? You're doing a solid job."

He refuses to speak to me for the rest of the journey.

We end up outside another set of black double doors. A further two beings in red bandages and clothing wait outside. I think they're called Red Suits. They exchange grunts and glances with my transporter while we wait outside. They're monsters.

I can just about make out voices on the other side of the doors.

The man from earlier speaks. "I removed her tracker before I brought her. And I checked for more implants. They have no idea where she is. They're obsessed with the idea of a traitor in their ranks; I've been interviewing people all day, which is ironic. And now that she's disappeared, they're starting to believe she's a traitor too, instead of from Earth, which could work in our favour."

A female voice: "And what of our attack on their *palace*?" She spits the final word as if it's left a foul taste in her mouth.

"They've assigned the A and C teams to investigate, but they're useless." He laughs. "This girl, she's completely eclipsed everything. They're all too busy arguing about where she's come from to dedicate any brain cells to finding the people we took. It's perfect."

"Where is this girl?"

The Red Suits take that as a cue to open the doors. I guess they were listening too.

I'm pushed onto my knees in a room void of furnishings as the Red Suits return to their post, letting the doors slam behind them. I glance around the room, searching for any defining features that might indicate where I am. But the only space not empty is the space occupied by me, and *them*.

What is he to me? A friend? A foe? He has this distant, familiar face I can't quite place. The perfectly combed red strands of hair and clean brown suit he wears differs from the Red Suits, but then again, I don't think he's one of them, at least not to the people at the BCD. Maybe his hair makes up for missing costume.

And then there's her. Flowing from her back is a trail of black lace; I didn't know black could be so black. Meanwhile, falling from her head to her back are strands of the deepest brown—they sit so gracefully, regally. And that ebony dress, so elegantly decorated with golden metal that's adorning her neck and arms, while within her hand's grasp lies the most perfect rose finished with black edges. It's a picture of dark beauty I'm sure would create a cult following. Wait, maybe it has.

She turns to face me with the palest face. "Jessica Durand." The words slip from her red lips. How does she know my name? "Welcome to Biack."

Know that when I tell you I'm afraid, I mean it. But I've spent so much of my life afraid that I think it's become my comfort zone. At least this makes sense; I can work with this. "Actually, I'm trying to get *The Girl from Far Away* to catch on, so if you could spread that around that'd be great." She stares at me until I find a follow up with, "So, who are you?"

"The everyman's salvation." She smiles with her eyes. "And I've waited a lifetime to meet you."

"I did tell the guy who brought me I've been awake for ages; you should probably fire him."

"Scott." Scott? Nope, I still can't quite place him in the dreams. I'm sure he's no one important. "Order their execution for incompetence," she instructs the man.

I panic. "Wait, wait! I was just kidding around. I'm sure he's great at his job, whatever that is."

She hesitates for a moment. "Kill them anyway." Scott leaves. "I have questions."

If I don't answer, will she order my execution too?

"Did you know what you were doing when you travelled here?"

I answer quickly to keep my head. "I was asleep; that Scott guy knocked me out."

"No, when you came to Biack."

Of course not, or why do you think I haven't left yet? "No."

She pauses. "Were you in pain when it happened?"

Not physical pain. "No."

"Distress? Emotional distress." I think she's realised she has to spell everything out for me.

I nod. "Yes." I'll never forgive Scarlett for everything that's happened to me since.

"Interesting. Were you thinking of Biack at the time?"

How does she know I knew about Biack before I came here? How does she know more about me than me? "Yes."

"Interesting still." She walks close to me, smiling, and it's so sinister. God, she's creepy. "Five!"

"Six?" I'm confused.

A Red Suit runs into the room.

"Take her to Twenty-Two. They know what to do with her." She leans closer, a single black nail drawing blood across my cheek. "If you disobey any order, know you'll be wishing your life wasn't of value to me."

Why does everyone want to hurt me? I didn't even do anything. I've never done anything. Oh God, I've never done anything. I've never left Fairwater.

Five, the Red Suit, pulls me up before dragging me out the room. As I turn back, I get one last glance at the woman. "Who are you?" I whisper.

She hears me. "Don't you already know? I'm the Rose."

I need to get out of here, and this time I won't accept help from anyone. There's no one on my side.

"Who's Twenty-Two?" I ask the Red Suit.

They ignore me.

"That's cool. I didn't want an answer anyway. I just like to ask rhetorical questions."

They don't seem to be that much of a threat. Okay, so they're probably over six foot and they seem more muscular than the Red Suit from before, but they could just be slightly overweight, and yes, they're carrying a gun and some sort of baton. But let's be real, I don't have any other option.

One last breath while I eye the baton; as fast as I can muster, I grab it from their side. They start to react and I swing it at their crotch. I hope underneath the covers they're a guy. They fall to their knees. Boys are so weak.

I whack at the red bandages across his head with a strength I never knew I had—is this adrenaline? He falls to the floor, flat on his face. Another hit to the head to knock him out; blood starts to spread across the stone. Another blow; got to make sure he's really out. Then another, and another, and another. I don't know what's driving me. Maybe it's fear, or maybe it's a decade of built-up anger.

His chest is no longer lifting. His body is silent.

Oh, God. Is he dead?

I feel the blood run from my face just as it's probably running from his. The continuous pool causes my stomach to stir up a sickness; I haven't felt so violent in a lifetime. Did my heart stop? The repetitive motion has been replaced with a mute stillness. Can you die from inflicting death?

Please, time, stop. Please, I need a minute, just a second. I'm not ready to deal with the next moment; I'm not ready to deal with what comes next. But at least I get a next. He doesn't. What was his name? I don't remember. I don't know who he was.

Grabbing the gun from his side, I'm forced to deal with the next moment. I run to the nearest door. I stop. I glance back at him. Is this who I am now? I'm a killer. I killed someone. I bloody killed someone.

There's a list of people I wish were dead: Sam, Scarlett, my mum, that guy who coughed in my ice cream and gave me the flu that time, maybe even Ella, because she's the reason I know about this world. But that guy on the floor, lying motionless in a red lake, he wasn't one of them.

I move through the doorway. Inside it seems like some sort of meeting room, but from the medieval era. Yes! The window isn't locked; I think I can push it open enough to fit through. I use the baton to hold it open. I stick my head out the window and realise this is a castle. I didn't know they had castles. The distance is lined with a forest but ends with the hexagon shield they call a Dome. I'll never get used to that. Maybe I won't have to.

Two-storey drop, luckily onto grass. Okay, so it probably

won't kill me. That's a start. I mean, what other choice do I have? I pull myself up onto the window ledge. God, I wish I wasn't here. I wish I was a hundred miles from the body on the other side of the door. Closing my eyes, I slide out and tumble onto the grass. Wow, that was a short drop.

Oh.

Chapter Eight

Ella

Biack 22/01/2014

"You let her go?!" Ben cries out.

"She had a tracker implant!" I raise my voice to compete.

His eyes fume. "And you didn't think she'd remove it?"

I try to grab his arm as he paces around the meeting room. "She wasn't awake when it was put in! I don't know how she knew about it."

Will interrupts. "Maybe it's time to assume she knows more than she's letting on."

"It's a bit late for that now because *someone* let her go." Ben's stare pierces like a knife.

My father straightens his tie. "Enough. This isn't worth bickering over; our greatest concern right now is working together to find her before the Red Suits do."

"They might've already found her. Someone set up that explosion; that same someone might've helped her escape," Jia adds.

"Someone could've forced her into it." As I speak, Will

laughs.

He follows up with, "No one forced her to shoot me!" He's still seething from betrayal, although he never appeared to trust her, so I'm lost on where the betrayal was. As he sits in his chair, drumming his fingertips on the table with aggressive rhythm, I can't tell whom his anger's directed at. He hasn't broken his stare with the table since we sat down.

"Well, she wasn't going to shoot Ella," Jia replies as she sits cross-legged next to him. "And maybe she knew about you."

Will mumbles, "She seemed pretty surprised about Ella."

"It makes sense to me." As Aiden speaks, we all turn to him except Will. Aiden's leaning against the back wall next to a potted plant that's surprisingly unburnt. "If I had to spend a whole day with you staring at me, I'd probably want to shoot you too."

Will jumps out of his chair as Aiden roars in laughter. Jia pulls him back down.

"I said *enough*." My father slams his hand on the table. "There will not be a word spoken about this interaction with her. The council cannot know. We already suspect there's a spy in our midst. We cannot have anyone point a finger at one of you." We all nod in silence. "Right, well, both the B and E teams are working to find her as we speak, and when I have an update—"

"Shouldn't we be the ones to find her?" Aiden breaks our silence. "I mean, she knows us."

My father hesitates. "We can't risk the predators finding out about her escape. We're trying to play this under the radar, because so far, we're not looking great. She technically managed to escape from us twice in under a day."

"How would the predators find out just because we're the ones assigned to this?" Aiden challenges. We all turn to stare at him until he realizes—it takes longer than it should. "I don't draw *that* much attention…do I?"

Aiden was Jia's favourite shopping companion, but she had to stop taking him with her. It was too draining having to put out all the fires.

My father buttons his suit. "Continue with your schedules until you're told otherwise. When there's progress, I'll inform you."

Ben huffs before storming out; I try to grab his arm, but he shrugs me off. That's a battle I need to make peace with. Slowly and dejectedly, Jia, Aiden and Will leave as well. Eventually it's just my father and I left in the room.

I know this is a terrible mistake. "If she sees a team of armed men following her, she won't respond well." As I speak, he smiles. "Let me go after her. She'll listen to me."

He continues to smile as he rises from his chair. "You're in no way authorised to go after her. Nor have I or the council asked you to investigate this." As he leaves, he squeezes my shoulder. "And you should *absolutely* not try to find her first." He winks.

We're going to find her first.

"Scott!" I race down the hall as fast as my shoes allow.

He spins around with a smile. "Ella Day!"

"Were you present for the protectors meeting about Jess's escape?" I'm tucking my hair behind my ears when he pulls me to the side with one hand, the other is grasping his screen and a worn book.

"Keep your voice down." He glances around for eaves-droppers. "But yes, I was there. Why?"

I grin. "I need to know if they've made any progress, like if they saw what happened to her after she left the building? I wonder if she went back to Earth—" My attention's caught by a large plaster across his arm; he notices my gaze and quickly pulls his shirt sleeves down. "What happened to your arm?"

"Burnt myself with a cup of coffee. They really fill those things up to the top, don't they?" He laughs; it's cute. "You know, there's still no real proof she's from Earth, and you have to admit the whole dreams-of-another-life thing is a bit—"

"Bit what?" I interrupt. "You don't believe me?"

The edges of his mouth rise. "Of course I believe you. But I'm not the one you have to convince."

"So." I pause. "Would you say you're with me?"

He replies, "Of course—"

I interrupt. "Great, because I need you to tell me everything they know about her." Before he can answer, I interrupt again. "And what rank are you?"

"I'm an A rank—"

"Perfect! I just need your code then."

He hesitates, looking around us, before replying, "Okay, fine."

"Yes!" I must've shouted, because some nearby scientists turn around; Scott laughs as he waves at them. After they return to their own conversation, he fumbles in his pockets for a pen, eventually scribbling something on the inside cover of his book.

"I want dinner in return, though. Tomorrow night?" he asks.

"O-okay." I stumble; our hands brush as he hands me the book. "I didn't know you—"

"We have a lot of catching up to do," he adds. My heart drops.

I force a laugh as I start to walk away. "Yeah, of course, lots. It's been years and okay, yes, I'll see you tomorrow then."

"We'll probably see each other again before that." I must look confused, because he follows up. "It's not even lunch yet."

I smile before heading to Ben's lab.

❖❖❖

"Why do I feel so sick?" I ask.

"Because he's a boy and you like him," Jia answers.

I fall back into the sofa, pressing a pillow onto my face. I groan. I don't want to think about this; it isn't part of the plan.

"This is a weird look on you," Aiden states. "You're always so confident. It's fun seeing you all awkward." I throw the pillow at him, and his bowl of cereal spills down him. "Really?" He jumps off the side table. "Great, now I have to change."

While Aiden searches around the boxes of clothing, I crumble into Jia, and she strokes my hair. Will and Ben are completely oblivious to us as they stare at a screen on the other side of the lab. Since I shared Scott's codes, they've barely said a word to anyone but each other. I think Ben's forgiven me.

"Oh my life, put on some underwear!" Jia throws another pillow at Aiden; he hides himself behind it.

"I didn't realise you were so upset by—"

"I am when it's yours!"

"Well, that sounds like a *you* problem." He finally pulls on some underwear.

She scrunches her face. "You're the only one with problems."

"Hey," Ben abruptly yells, "there's no fire allowed in here!" He slaps a homemade sign on the wall.

I didn't even notice Aiden light up his hand.

The world excluded Aiden at ten. His parents taught him that you hurt the ones you love. So, when he walked into school that day and saw Sinead Flawn, an innocent beauty who showed him no interest, he thought the only way to win her affection was to set her hair on fire. They sent him here.

"Aiden, I'm serious, I'll get the hose!" Ben fights. He's always had little patience for Aiden.

"So, what's our next move?" I change the topic.

"Well—" Ben keeps an eye on Aiden, "—do you want the good news or the better news?"

Jia and I turn to each other. "The good news?" she asks.

He turns a nearby screen to face us. "The B and E teams have no idea where she is. They have no leads and are completely stumbling. Apparently they found her tracker in a side street, and that's the last trace of her. They're going to tell the predators so they can blast her face everywhere and hope someone spots her." He mumbles, "Didn't stay under the radar for very long."

I say, "That sounds like bad news?" Glancing at Aiden and Jia, they share my confusion. Will and Ben grin at each other.

Ben replies, "So you know that energy we emit when we use our gifts? I figured she must have a gift too, teleportation or something—I mean, how else could she get here? Anyhow, I set up an alert in case she used hers, and well, she used hers. Okay, technically she used it twice. I'm guessing where she teleported to and where she teleported from. But there's a second difference between them."

"Ella," Will says. His eyes are lit up in a way that's completely new. "We found her."

"Okay." They're all looking at me, my team. "Like I said the other day, this is our time. No more sitting on the bench, no more being used for the predators, no more watching the action from the sidelines. Let's go find *The Girl from Far Away*."

❖❖❖

"It's locked." Ben kicks the wall in frustration.

I examine the double doors to the stealth bay. "Not from the inside."

"No way. Absolutely not." He looks between us before sighing. "Fine, I'll do it."

He mumbles incoherently as his veins light up fluorescent

yellow, and in the quickest flash of light the Ben we know has disappeared into a pile of clothing. A small buzz rings through our ears as the tiniest fly jumps out from underneath his jacket and rushes towards the door. I lose sight of it as it disappears between almost-invisible cracks.

Not long later, the doors swing open. Ben hides behind them.

"Thanks," I say as I pass him his clothing. He continues to mumble incoherently.

Great machines dominate the room, twenty or thirty of them, with wings the size of two Aidens. Their blades of silent flight lie dormant, their skin coated in sleek black. We hurry on board the nearest one.

"Can you fly one of these?" Jia asks Ben while putting on her black hat; as she tips the front piece down, the huge sleeves of her oversized jumper slide up and down her arm.

"Yeah, can you?" Aiden adds, pulling up the hood from his jacket.

"I've read a few manuals," he shrugs; Aiden doesn't seem convinced. "Well, can you fly one? No? So, I'm guessing you're just going to have to hope I don't kill us all."

Will slaps his hand on Aiden's back. "When we go down, try not to set us on fire. Then we're definitely dead."

"I'm not going to kill us!" Ben straights his glasses as he finds his space in the pilot's seat.

Will removes his jacket and hands it to me. I try to conceal my distain. "What?" he asks.

I shrug. "I just don't think it'll go with my dress." They turn to face me, all in black; I stroke my pink satin.

"At least if we crash, they'll be able to easily identify Ella's body." Aiden laughs.

"We're not going to crash!" Ben cries.

As the engines start to fire, the silently known machine roars to life, as well as the alarm.

The stealth lifts off the ground as protectors race into the room, but they're too late. The machine speeds towards the exit tunnel as Jia grabs Aiden's hand. After several minutes of nervous waiting, the sound of the alarm fades and we emerge from the side of a cliff.

Several uneasy hours pass before Ben brings us to the ground. He was right, we didn't crash. Although, every slight turbulence caused a panic which would bring us closer to everything being set on fire; why does Aiden always think that's a solution?

"Over there, that's the only structure around here for miles. That must be where she's hiding out." Ben points at an ancient farmhouse desperately in need of restoration, or destruction.

"Okay, Will and Aiden; scout the outside. Ben, stay with the stealth. Jia and I will go inside and hopefully if all exits are covered, we can prevent her from escaping," I instruct.

"What if she teleports, or whatever it is she does?" Aiden asks.

"I don't think she can control it," Ben says. "And if you remember when we all first discovered our gifts, we could only use them accidentally, when we were panicked."

"So don't panic her? Yeah, that seems easy," Aiden replies.

"Okay, how about this," I offer, "if you see her try to travel, go with her?"

They all nod in agreement as we pass out weapons we'd never use on her.

Aiden and Will run off, weapons out, towards the structure. First scouting the barn while Jia and I await the all-clear, next they move onto the exterior, peering carefully in the windows, followed by a head shake to us. Jia knocks her gun against mine as she starts to run to the entrance.

Rickety outdoor steps try to give us away but nothing appears to startle, so we continue. Inside, strings of silk decorate the reminiscent images; a short breath causes dust to dance through the air, throwing itself at anything in reach. Everything seems untouched, but maybe her touch is silent.

What is a ghost? Is it an unexpected presence that leaves as invisibly as it enters, with the only footprints left behind hidden in the mind of tenants, and the only sound hidden within the whistles of the wind? What about it's tainted touch that leaves you doubting your own eyes? Is Jess a ghost? After all this is over, will people believe she ever existed?

Jia points to a set of treatment centre clothes faded by dirt. She's been here.

Exhausting the downstairs, we approach the stairs with a shared uncertainty; considering the age of this house, it's going to be impossible to climb them without alerting a hidden guest. If my mind was strong enough, I'd lift Jia upstairs without creating a sound, but that's where limitations get in the way.

As slow as we can, we rise up the steps; we make it most of

the way before a creak sneaks outs. Frozen, we stand while we wait for a reply to our intrusion. Nothing happens, so we continue our ascent. A smell of stale existence spreads across the upper floor; how long has this place been alone?

The only room disturbed looks to be the main bedroom. The mattress has been dragged off the broken bed onto the wooden floorboards; a lack of dust highlights a recent host. Next to the makeshift bed, a crude drawing is sketched into the wood with what seems like chalk. There are two figures: a woman holding something in her hand, and another that appears like an attempt at drawing herself. The woman's eyebrows form a giant V. Is it me? Does she see me like that?

"Ella!" Aiden shouts from below. We race downstairs to find him aiming at Jess, who's aiming at Will as she stands behind him. Seems she found us first. "We have a situation. It was Will, I swear."

"You set your hand on fire!" Will argues while standing hostage.

"It's starting to get dark out. I couldn't see anything!" Aiden yells.

I ignore their bickering. "Jess, we don't want to hurt you."

"That's what everyone says." She's replaced the white treatment centre clothes with dark jeans that barely fit and an oversized black top. The tattered hoodie seems to be a constant.

"Whoever helped you escape, they're dangerous. I don't know what they want with you but they won't care what happens to you when they're done," I say.

She bites back, "What about your people? Wherever I go,

I'm a prisoner."

"But I'll keep you safe," I plead.

Her forehead scrunches. "What good is that if I'm still trapped?"

"Is it better than being on the run?" I reply. "Look, I get it. Your feel like your life has been turned upside down. Do you think it's easy for me to accept that you're real?"

"I don't know what's real anymore. You— No." She fights with her emotions as they escape into her voice.

"Well, let's figure it out together."

For a second, I think she considers it. But then she takes a step backwards. Her veins start to glow black. "I can't."

"You can," I whisper, but I think she still hears.

It appears behind her slowly, this stretched circle of darkness with undefined edges that blur into the evening around it. But it's more than just a pit of black—there's something glimmering in the darkness, revealing itself as an illusion. There's no sign of what lies beyond it. A person would just have to hope it'll take them where they need to go.

She starts to stumbles backwards as she says, "You're wrong. You don't know everything."

Maybe she's right. Because I don't see it coming when she steps into the darkness. I don't see it coming when Will turns and runs after her. And I don't see it coming as in the shortest second, together they disappear through the portal. I didn't see it coming.

For a moment, we're all frozen.

"Well," Ben says, "at least we know it's portals, not teleportation. Too bad we now have to explain why we let her go twice. What was that word Jess uses again?"

Shit.

Chapter Nine

Jess

I can go home. I know how. Kinda. It's a start.

The setting sun dominates the sky as it blasts its scorch above what I now know to be a safety net. So, it isn't Earth, but it's not where I was before. Turns out I jumped into this game playing my ace, and now I'm learning the other cards. At this point, I'll take any progress.

My mind returns to this world as I witness The Unbreakable Boy reaching for his gun. I lift mine to aim, and we find ourselves caught in a draw. Relentless, we stand for what could become hours. It's like putting seven and seven together, trying to achieve fifteen.

"I'll shoot. I did before," I say.

His face tightens.

"You're not going to shoot me, are you? Can you imagine how angry that would make Ella?" As I speak, he doesn't budge. "Although everyone's trying to hurt me, I know no one wants me dead. So, put the gun down." He still refuses to lower his arm. "But I could shoot you. No one's going to stop me, and I don't need you alive."

After considering my last point for several moments, he finally lowers his weapon. I quickly grab it from his hand and tuck it in the back of my jeans; I don't know how they do it so naturally on TV—it's uncomfortable as hell.

Surrounded by pale brick, I side-step towards the only exit to this alley while keeping my aim on Will. Skyscrapers, monorails and unaware people. Are we in The Capital again? That's where the BCD is. Okay, so I need to get out of here. And this time I won't let Will follow me. I try wishing, wanting, as hard as I can, but my veins won't glow and nothing seems to change. Shit, I thought I had this.

"You don't know how to do it," he states.

I look up in distain. "You don't know me."

"You like telling people that, don't you? Does it make you feel better to be different? Is it cool feeling misunderstood?" he spits.

"Stop talking."

"Just because everyone wants you right now doesn't make you special." He continues, "You're no fighter. You're going to get yourself killed before the attention wears off."

"Stop talking, or I swear I'll blow your tongue off," I growl.

Whether he's threatened or not, he does stop. For a few minutes, at least, while I fruitlessly try to recreate a portal.

"It's getting dark. Are we going to stand here all night while you pace around brooding?" he asks.

If I can't make another portal, how do I get away from him? Should I just run for it? No, this is his world. He has the advantage of knowing the playing field. I have to either accept I'm stuck with him, or shoot him, and actually hit him this time.

Wait, maybe this is a good thing. He knows this world. He could be useful to have around. I just need to keep running until I figure out how to work this portal thing and get back to Earth, and he can help me do that. This could work.

I state, "It's not safe here. We're too close to the BCD."

"I don't think three hundred miles is close." What? "We're in Terra." He points at posters plastered all over the alley walls, clearly advertising an event in Terra. It's oddly less clean here—still clean, just less. Amongst the ramble, a wanted poster stands, boldly showing my face.

"That's a bad photo," I state.

He turns to see. "That's how you look." He shrugs. What a dick.

Under the fast-setting sun and awakening nightlife, I decide it's probably best to wait until the early hours to leave this place, hopefully guaranteeing a lack of people. Placing my gun against Will's side and my hand on his arm, we head up the street to-wards what appears to be a residential building. Inside, we climb the stairs as I search for signs of empty homes.

"Break down this door," I instruct.

He laughs. "No."

"Do it!" I insist.

"Why?" He presses on the handle and reveals the door was never locked. "I could just open it?"

People don't lock their doors here? Why are they so weirdly trusting?

Inside, we quietly confirm there's no tenant. Magazines lay carelessly thrown around the sofa, while a half-eaten meal sits dead on the coffee table. The dishes wait patiently while showing days of gathered dirt; has this place ever been cleaned?

Will watches as I grab a pair of scissors off a kitchen shelf. "What are you doing?"

I cart him to the bathroom. "They're not for you. I'm cutting my hair."

He waits quietly on the edge of the bath while I start to chop strand after strand. "Have you done this before?"

"No," I say.

"Couldn't tell." I catch him rolling his eyes.

"Okay, so I don't know what I'm doing. I'm sorry if I'm not special enough to have spent my life running from people. You act like an expert, but what do you know about being on the run?" I argue.

"I meant with your hair," Will states. He looks at me for a moment before continuing, "I'm sorry I said you weren't special." I hope he isn't feeling pity.

"I don't want to be special. I don't want this attention. I don't want any of this," I say as I cut myself a block fringe.

"What do you want?" he asks. I don't think anyone has ever asked me that before.

What do I want? I want a house in the countryside, far away from the crowds. A view of the ocean beyond a cliff, where on the dark days I can stand and imagine what it'd be like to fall. I want a porch where I can sit in the rain and paint the sun. An empty mailbox that waits for a never-appearing guest, while I argue with thoughts that are mine to protest.

But instead I answer; "To be where I belong."

"Why do your answers give more questions?"

I answer, "Because you aren't asking the right questions."

My stomach rumbles, prompting him to get up from his perch on the bath edge. "I'll go find some food."

"No!" I speak quickly, reaching for my weapon.

"Relax. I'm just going to the cooler." He leaves before I can stop him. I listen to the sound of him searching through cupboards. He doesn't try to alert anyone. I guess he knows I'm serious about threatening to shoot him.

My long brunette locks are now cut to my neck while my eyebrows hide behind my fringe. Hopefully it's enough of a change to prevent recognition from the posters. People are pretty oblivious here, anyway. I kinda like it. In the living room, Will lays on the couch, eating a foreign packet of what I hope is crisps.

He holds the packet towards me. "It won't kill you." It tastes dry and bland. He reads the disgust on my face. "Yeah, they're disgusting." Did he enjoy my displeasure?

I sit opposite him; I think he hates me.

"What next then?" he asks.

"I don't know." I don't. Where do I go next? "I need to go home."

"And you don't know how."

Yes, thanks for reminding me. "No. So until I figure out how, I think I'll just continue running."

"You know, eventually you'll have to stop."

"Can you just not? Can you please be quiet for five minutes, just five minutes, so I can think? You're supposed to be the boy of few words."

He laughs. "Do you believe everything you see in dreams?"

I didn't. And then I saw her stop that bullet. Is it all true? The fire and water and shapeshifting and, no, it can't be. If it was, I was never a threat to him, and then why hasn't he tried to alert someone or take me back to Ella? "I don't know what to believe anymore."

"You know, I've never met someone so untrusting," he says, the corner of his mouth twitching. "What happened to make you like this?"

"I could ask you the same."

Ah, an impasse.

❖❖❖

We barely sleep, even though we both bear clear signs of exhaustion. But it appears this is another trait we share. Most of the night consists of voluntary silence sometimes met with vague conversation. He definitely hates me, and I think I hate him.

Soon enough the sky begins to light, and without bothering to clean our mess—the owner won't be able to tell—we head out of the city. The streets are morbidly quiet as the city sleeps. Occasionally we pass fellow pedestrians but they never acknowledge us; maybe I didn't need to try so hard to change my appearance. After a while we come across a café struggling to wake up.

"In here," I instruct, shoving him through the door. I hide the gun in my jacket pocket.

Inside, a few victims of the morning wait. Why are they here right now and not at home? What has dragged them from their slumber? Or were they, like me, never asleep? Behind the counter, a skinny man dreads his future; he has this weird expression on his face as he eyes up Will.

I look up at the menu. "Two corn sandwiches." Does that mean actual corn? It seems more appealing than a grape sub. Will shoots me an odd look—did I order something weird? Or is he shocked I got two?

I wait while the skinny man prepares in the kitchen; darting glances at the other diners show they share a disinterest in my presence. Why is everyone here so ignorant to events around them? What made them so isolated? When the skinny man returns, I try to figure out a distraction. "And two teas."

He seems unimpressed that I didn't tell him earlier. "What kind of tea?" he mumbles.

I don't understand their menu at all. "Surprise me."

Okay, now I kind of want to stay. I could really do with a cup of tea.

Nope, got to get out before I'm in too deep, so as he turns his back, I grab the sandwich bags from the counter and yank Will with me as we dart out the door. No one bothers to look up. The skinny man half-heartedly shouts after me, but I don't think he bothers to leave his safe confinement behind the counter.

"Run!" I grab Will's sleeve and continue to drag him down the street. Even though no one's chasing us, I feel so alive; I can't help but laugh. Stealing is fun.

Eventually we slow to a walk, and I hand him one of the stolen goods.

"How kind of you. It's almost like you didn't try to kill me yesterday," Will says.

I ignore him and dissect the sandwiches. Inside they're filled with some kind of meat; it's weirdly chewy. "I didn't understand anything on the menu. What is corn? It's not what I thought it would be."

He answers, "Unicorn meat. It's expensive too, so I guess you chose the best thing to steal."

I laugh. "Ha, unicorn meat. Good one." He doesn't understand the joke. "So, who were you before you met Ella?"

"I was Will." Sarcastic too. Am I starting to like this boy? Or at least dislike him less?

"Okay, but who is Will? Is it short for something? What's your last name?" I enquire further.

"It's just Will."

I accept that's all I'm getting from him. "Does Ella know who you were before?"

"No," he answers in between mouthfuls.

I remember dreaming of their first meeting. Ella was twelve but her heart was fully grown. She snuck out of her bed that night to practice climbing the palace walls, but as she approached, she noticed someone else trying to climb in. He was so thin she feared he'd fall and snap, so, with disregard for her own life, she ran to catch him as his grip slipped. Guards overheard the commotion but were unable to arrest him when Ella claimed he was her long-lost brother. So that's what he became.

"It must be a lonely life, not having anyone really know you," I state.

He laughs at me. "And that's coming from you?"

"I have my brother. Who do you have?"

He says, "But do you? Where is he now?"

Earth. "Okay," I concede, "so what does that make us, then? Two lonely souls?"

"Human."

Not much later, we stop as we come across an old— no, very old—pickup truck waiting at the edge of the city. Will seems confused by my excitement. But how could I not fall in love with that familiar red that was discontinued long ago?

"You know what this is?" he asks.

I yank the driver's door open. "I've never seen one in the dreams; I didn't think you had cars."

"We don't. This must be at least a hundred years old." He wipes decades of dust off the wing mirror. "Ella did say your world seemed less advanced."

I'd take offence but I'm too preoccupied with the discovery. Reaching under the steering wheel, I attempt to start it the way Everett taught me; luckily the design is familiar and so with a bit of chance, I manage to get the engine running. I'm taken aback by the luck I must have for this to actually work. Maybe cars on Biack are more durable?

"How did you do that? I didn't know these still worked."

"My brother taught me. It's basically the same as his friend's car." I jump in and adjust the driver's seat for my little legs. I catch him staring at me. "What?"

Smiling, Will shakes his head before walking round and yanking the passenger door open. "You know, hundreds of these are just lying around Biack gathering dust. They were used before everyone went underground and when people returned to the surface, they'd outgrown them."

"I hope that means there's more out there with fuel in." I look disappointedly at the fuel metre—half full. How far will that get us? "So, where do you want to go?"

His face says it all. Unfortunately, we can't go there.

"Okay, so I guess the hunt for a good cup of tea begins."

Chapter Ten

Ella

Biack 23/01/2014

"I stand by my actions," I recite. "I take full responsibility for the events of the twenty-second of the first."

To stand in this room is either an honour or a burden. Around me, the council sit on raised thrones of the oldest stone that represents the centuries of unity amongst the people. I can feel their stares piercing my bones and yet I can't bring myself to return the eye contact; my gaze is instead planted at my hands, as if the script I'm reciting is held within them.

"The other participants were coerced into their involvement, and so full punishment should fall solely on myself, and myself alone." I stop and take a moment to remember the next line. "I'm grateful to be granted this audience to confess my actions. Long reign the king, and may he continue to bring prosperity to the people."

I wait to be dismissed but instead of the pre-planned end, one of the council members decides to go rogue.

"Was it your actions that lead to Will—" Donald Adams stops to look up Will's full name, "—of no last name, disappearing with her?"

I didn't prepare for questions; I glance towards my father. "Yes?" Was that right?

"And it was your actions that led to him aiding her on the run?" he asks, leaning closer.

I don't know what they're doing. "I instructed everyone to stay with the girl if given the opportunity. He must've come to a decision, influenced by myself, to follow after her. I believe he's being held hostage and if he was able to, he would've made an attempt to contact us."

He pauses, appearing deep in thought. "If he's being held hostage there's the possibility he may die at her hand, and if so, it'll be your fault, as the whole idea was conceived by you?" The edges of his mouth twitch.

I turn to my father, who sits on the central throne; his eyes try to convey the answer, but I'm unable to decipher it. "Yes?"

"Ah, so you, Ella Day, first princess of Biack, confess to the greatest crime known to our laws—murder." He slides back in his throne as a smug smile emerges.

My father abruptly pulls himself out of his throne before declaring, "This confessional is over." He hurriedly ushers me out of the room. I'm sure he already has a plan.

I speak first. "What was that? I thought all I had to do was repeat the confession Scott wrote? Why were there questions?"

He checks the buttons on his suit. "Donald was being difficult before we started; I should've expected this." Behind another set of closed doors, I can hear shouts of questions—the predators. My father looks to Aiden, Jia and Ben waiting further down the hallway. "Go to your friends. I need you all to keep away from everyone for a while; they can stay with you in the palace until this dies down. You need to keep the lowest profile."

"But—" It's too late; he's gone. The council has appeared, and so my father has moved to damage control. I wonder how much extra work I've given him.

Jia sits with her head resting on Aiden's shoulder while the boys flick through a tattered journal; they have that look of guilt I tried so hard to master.

"If I ask what you're doing, will knowing the answer get me in more trouble?" I ask.

Aiden doesn't even look up. "Yes, but not with the council. With someone even worse."

"Do you think he's alright?" Jia stares gloomily into the distance, which is the other side of the hall about ten metres away.

"Who, Will?" I reply to Jia.

"I mean, I know he'll be alright but I still worry. He's not immortal." She talks at us. "I just wish he kept his hexagon on him."

"He knows what he's doing, and maybe he'll find a way to get through to her and convince her to return." I slide down next to her. "And if anyone's in danger, it's Jess. Do you remember how mad he was that she tried to shoot him?"

"Yeah, we might have to accept the possibility of not finding her alive," Ben adds, his gaze also fixed on the tattered journal.

"I don't know, that girl has a fire within her," Aiden says.

"And I'm guessing you mean that as a positive?" I glance

over at the words their eyes are following; I recognise the handwriting. "Hey! That's Will's journal."

Neither stops reading. "Yeah, I know. It's hilarious." Aiden laughs.

"When he comes back, he's going to kill you," Jia states with a blank expression. "If he comes back."

I snatch the journal from their grasp. "Not if I kill you first." They look at me like I just stole their lunch. "Where did you find this, anyway?"

"Well, I'll tell you, it wasn't easy," Aiden starts. "I've been trying to find it for ages. I even tried sneakily taking it out of his pocket once, but he never lets his guard down or leaves me alone in his room long enough to properly search."

"As soon as we got back, he ran to search for it," Ben chimes in.

"And guess where it was?" He doesn't give anyone a chance to answer. "In his treatment cabinet. There were, like, nine of them in there! Luckily, he numbered them."

"I'm going to put this back, and you're going to promise me you won't 'find' it again," I instruct.

"Don't you want to know what it says?" Aiden teases, "It'll make you change your mind."

"No! Will is our friend. We should respect his privacy," I say as I smooth the pleats of my skirt.

Aiden, defeated, resorts to comforting the worried Jia. He kisses her head softly as she leans further into him.

"You know, it's funny." Ben looks to me. "I really thought today you'd wear black."

✿✿✿

There's something about her face; I stroke the pixels on paper. Spread out around my bed is every documentation of Jess in existence, from pictures to witness interviews to DNA results. If I stare hard enough, maybe I can get inside her mind, something everyone seems to think I'm capable of doing. Do they not re- alise I was a mere observer during all those dreams? I was no more able to hear her thoughts than I am now.

"So, this is what happened to dinner." Scott stands in the doorway, arms crossed.

"Oh, that was today, wasn't it?"

"Yes, yes it was." He picks up one of the pictures. "Is this really better than an evening with me?"

"It's not an alternative." I grab the picture back and return it to its perfectly organised place. "I'm trying to get inside her head, and I guess I left my own for a little too long."

He finds a spot beside me. "I thought you've been doing that for years?"

"I actually think I'm getting somewhere—"

"You can finish getting there later," he interrupts. "I heard about today. More specifically, I heard about the *lay-low-in-the-palace* thing. So I brought our dinner here."

I look up. "You did?"

His hand finds a place on my knee. "I did. This other-world-girl stuff can wait."

"Actually, I think she prefers The Girl from Far Away." Why

did I say that? "But sure," I correct. "It can wait."

He squeezes my knee. "Do you like surprises?" No. "Put this on." He shrugs his tie off and places it around my head, engulfing me in darkness.

I try to remain graceful, but in reality I must appear a fool as he escorts me through the palace. Soon the smell of ancient stone changes into the warmth of an ending winter as we step outside. I almost trip down every step leading to the gardens, but thankfully he keeps me upright.

"Are you ready?" he asks; I nod, and he removes the tie. "What do you think? It's like that scene in your book, *Finding Penelope*."

It's just like that scene. Everything is as perfect as the words that wrote it, from the pink blanket stretched out across the grass to the vase of freshly picked daises amongst the picnic. Around us, illuminators twinkle across the shrubbery. He even managed to organise a selection of my favourite cakes, and are those Ashley Savont plates? Is that champagne? Is this real? All this to just catch up?

"I know you're not supposed to drink until eighteen, but I also know no one's watching us," he says as we find space to sit on the blanket.

"It won't be the first rule I've broken." I smile as he pours me an overflowing glass; it fizzes over onto my skirt, so I quickly hide the stains under a napkin. "Do you like your job?" I stutter. I stutter?

"I'd say it was the best thing that ever happened to me. It brought me back to my home city and everything I left here."

He has this look in his eyes I don't understand. "Everyone I left here."

"That's good," I reply. *That's good?* Have I lost the ability to make small talk?

"So, why all the pink?"

"My father taught me that how you present yourself is just as important as your actions. People form most of their opinion before you open your mouth. And I just really like pink." He wanted to catch up. "Are you still close to your parents?"

"Not particularly. I grew up and found my own life," he states.

"That's a shame," I say.

His eyebrows rise. "Why?"

"Because you're the most important part of your parent's life."

He laughs. "I somehow doubt that."

"But they made you. They created life." I stop to take small bites; presentation matters. "I can't imagine how that must feel, to create a whole being from nothing and then watch as they grow and experience all the world can offer." He's staring. "To know that everything good or bad they do will only be possible because of you, and so everything they achieve is your achievement. I imagine it's the same as building a house and then watching all the life that gets to exist within it. Or climbing a mountain to look out at the world and seeing all the potential left to be had." I sip my champagne.

He may be looking at my face, but I can see in his eyes he sees something else. It's a different look from before, somehow less perfect but more real.

"I don't even know what to say to that." He laughs in an unsure manner that could be misidentified as nervousness.

"You don't always need to say something back." I shrug, filling up my plate with the tiniest delicacies. "You don't need to reply so someone knows you're listening. Your actions show that."

"Actions speak louder." He has this pensive smile I don't understand.

Before, all I could smell was the freshly trimmed grass, and now as he edges closer I detect the hints of Kapurwood and Burnskey. He tucks the loose strands behind my ears and uses the opportunity to pull my face towards his. I can hear the symphony the evening birds sing around us as if an audience has gathered. I always imagined in a moment like this, time would stop for me as the universe watches on, and maybe it does, because as his lips touch mine, everything stops.

Yet somehow my blood continues flowing.

Several hours later, he escorts me back to my room with a kiss goodbye. I fall onto the bed without a care for disrupting the papers laid out around me. When my attention finally returns to this world, it's stolen again by Will's journal on the pillow next to me. Although I'd never admit it to Aiden, he tempted me.

I can't help myself as I flick through the worn pages; it's mostly a collection of dull statements about each day.

Aiden did that thing again with the cake.

Too hot to go outside. Ben said maintainers malfunctioning. Glad to have cooling inside.

Lost another bet, think Aiden's cheating

Got new hexagon. Still can't find last one. Can't let Aiden know.

And then, as I brush through the pages, near the end it gets interesting.

Girl found in field. Seems to be same girl from Ella's dreams. Locked in cell, too sarcastic. Wish she'd bitten Ben. That would've been funny.

SHE SHOT ME.

She escaped. Knew she would. Need to find her before she leaves for good. Can't lose her, not now. She completes us. It's just like the prophecy. Also she's pretty funny—Aiden approves but she still shot me, so.

My eyes flick back to the words they just read.

It's just like the prophecy.

I slam the book shut.

How did I miss that?

Chapter Eleven

Jess

He's trying not to laugh as he adjusts my beanie.

"Do I look invisible?" I ask.

"Like a ghost." He sits back and admires his handiwork. "But ditch the jacket. It's too different."

"People didn't seem to notice me before when I was wearing it," I say.

He shakes his head. "But you weren't doing anything then. If you want to pull this off, you need to completely blend in."

"Okay." I open the car door. "So, just walk out with it in the basket? Really?"

"If you're not up for it, I can do it," he offers.

"No, I am," I quickly reply. I'm half out the car when a worry pops into my head. "This isn't some plan to get us caught so we get sent back to Ella, is it? And I'm not going to come back to find you've taken the car and driven off, am I?"

"Wow, I wish I'd thought of that." He was never this sarcastic in the dreams. "I don't even know how to work this piece of junk." He kicks the dashboard. I frown. "No. It's not a trick," he states.

I follow his instructions to the letter—don't walk too fast or too slow; find something to look at and don't look anywhere else; keep walking even when grabbing items; keep as much distance from other shoppers as possible without altering course; don't speak to anyone.

I've never stolen anything from a shop before, but I think if I did this on Earth I'd do something similar, although it'd be harder to blend in. There's an instant distrust for the young, because why would they be shopping when they're riddled with student debt, getting by on minimum wage?

When I return, having encountered no obstacles, he's writing something on an old yellow pad notepad. At least, I think it's a yellow pad; it may just be really old.

"Okay, what'd you get?" He puts the notepad down. Where did he get it from?

I empty out my accomplishments from the basket into the space between us. Various types of food—I have no idea what any of it is—a pair of clear glasses, some ugly grandad cap, a slouchy brown backpack, the strongest but thinnest rope I could find, cheap makeup, an ugly sweater, a cabin-sized black suitcase and a pale blue woolen shirt.

Will searches through the haul. "You forgot the hairbrush."

"That's fine, I'll just use my fingers," I demonstrate, tidying my hair by running my fingers through the knots.

He frowns. "Okay, we might be able to pull this off."

"So what next then?"

He passes me the shirt. "Put this on." He shoves the sweater over his unkempt hair.

As he arranges the cap on his head, I yank my top off. I'm halfway through doing up the buttons when I catch him staring; he immediately turns away and distracts himself by applying the glasses to his face. I smirk, but it was nice to have someone look at me and not feel like their doll.

We prepare in silence as he shoves everything, including my jacket and top, into the small suitcase. Meanwhile, I plaster the unfamiliar makeup onto my face, unsure if I'm using foundation or eye shadow. When we finish, we look like different people.

"Pick a name, I'll be Ewon," he says.

I say, "Meghan Armland."

"That was quick. Have you done this before?"

Only in my daydreams. "So where's this hotel you saw?"

Hiding the car in the same manner we found it, alone with no effort on the edge of a town, we embark with suitcase in tow. An unlikely alliance has formed between The Unbreakable Boy and The Girl from Far Away.

He holds the door open—an act, or is there a gentleman behind those cold eyes?

"We have a room booked under Armland." He's so nonchalant as if he's done this a million times before.

The redhead girl, a bubbly beauty, taps away on some computer screen. "Hmm, it isn't coming up in the system."

I turn to Will. "I shouldn't have left you to sort this; of course you'd find a way to mess it up."

He scoffs. "You only *left* me to sort this because you've been too busy at work to even think of anything else lately."

"We can't both sit at home and do nothing all day!" I start to yell.

"This was supposed to be our weekend getaway, but I saw you pack that screen." He looks disgusted.

I have no idea what he means by "screen." I'm going to guess it's something you work on, maybe a tablet? "Maybe if you did something with your life I wouldn't have to work as hard to support us both, *on my own*," I shout.

The redhead interrupts, "Oh look, I found it! If you'll kindly wait one moment, I'll go collect your keys."

After she's left hearing range, I whisper to Will, "How did you know that'd work?"

He grins; God, he's so cocky. "Because everything has to be perfect."

She returns shortly and escorts us upstairs, three floors to be exact. The room she opens up to us is incredibly bland but would put any hotel on Earth to shame. A huge TV lights up as we enter; is it a tv, or is it just part of the wall? Everything appears built in: the desk, the light, the sofa. And that bed. I cannot wait to sleep.

"A bath," I gasp. "I've never been so excited about water!"

Removing his cap, he starts to fall back to the Will I recognise. "You sound like Ella. She's always getting excited about every little thing."

"Hm." I kick off my shoes. "I never thought I'd have anything in common with her."

He's smirking. "Me neither."

I throw one of my shoes at him.

Unpacking the rope from the suitcase, I pull the gun out and for a few seconds hesitate. The room turns cold as I direct the weapon towards Will and walk over with the rope. He remains still while I wrap the golden strands around a pole of the headboard and then tightly across his wrists.

"I'm not going anywhere," he states.

I collect a towel. "Not now." Hitting aimlessly around the tv-slash-wall, eventually it turns onto some sort of entertainment channel. "I'm having a bath. Watch TV."

As I close the door behind me, I can hear him mumble, "What's TV?"

It takes 'til the waves turn still for my memories to haunt me again.

There will never be words that can explain the bruises the water's strokes are drawing across my skin. Or the emptiness in the freezing air and how it reminds me of a home that's never been a home. For words are both unable to protect you and then unwilling to provide you the comfort you crave to go on. And after they fail to articulate your fears and allow your demons to push you, they will refuse to save you as you fall. They create the very definition of loneliness but tempt you with ideas of love that always prove to be false. And there's no combination that can explain the impossible things I've seen. So, what good are words? I wonder as I hide under the water's waves. It's not like they can save me from anything.

Life quickly pulls me out of that claw-foot tub.

I slip the shirt's woolen embrace over my arms. Outside, Will waits in apparent boredom, briefly glancing from the TV to my bare legs and then back again with a remorseful stare. Perhaps people aren't as liberal here.

Our relationship seems to have evolved to the stage where there's never a need to fill the silence. Or maybe it's always been this way. As I untie his wrists and toss the stolen food onto the bed, we never say a word.

My gaze is on his hair as he brushes his hand through the mess of thick brown, and then the scar across his lip; what misadventures led him to it? I didn't realise I was staring until his gaze catches mine for a moment that lasts too long.

The words come spilling out. "My dad got really mad once because I didn't know how to use gravy properly." I find myself beyond control. "He kept saying I needed to cut my potatoes and roll them around to soak it up." My eyes don't budge from his. "And then he was mad because I wasn't using my knife right." The words keep spilling out. "And I didn't understand why I kept getting everything wrong." He's silent, listening. "But later he gave me a hug and apologized. He said even grownups have bad days." I pause. "I told him I didn't even like gravy. And he said, 'that's alright, we can have ketchup.'" I look away and force an uncomfortable laugh. "I don't know why I just told you that."

It's silent while he figures out what to say. I can see his eyes searching for something. "Once when I was younger, long before I met Ella, I fell down some stairs and had this huge gash on my knee," he responds. "I tried to find someone to help, but people kept passing me by." Sounds familiar. "Eventually I tripped over this woman, and she thought she caused my injury and panicked. She let me stay with her for two weeks." He pauses. "People notice you when it inconveniences them." He smiles. "I don't know why I just told you that."

There we sit, The Unbreakable Boy and The Girl from Far Away, in the first moment of truth either of us has experienced in far too long. It's short-lived, but at least it existed.

"What were you writing on the notepad earlier?" I offer a new topic.

He shrugs. "Just making notes."

"On what?"

He finds the notepad in the suitcase and tosses it at my hands. "The day."

Travelled from Terra to outskirts of Sagitam. Jess talked about the car the entire journey. Taught her how to steal supplies from an Everystore. She'll probably mess it up.

"Nice to see you have faith in me," I say as I playfully slap his leg. "Why did you write this, though?"

"Aren't you afraid of forgetting?"

"Despite my many, many fears, no, that isn't one of them," I shrug.

He looks puzzled. "You don't seem like someone with lots of fears," he states.

"I don't?" I laugh.

"Yeah, you're kinda fearless." Fearless? That's his take-away, hmm. He changes the subject. "I have journals full of notes like this back home."

"Where is home? Ella's home? The BCD?"

"The BCD for now." He offers me bread. Yep, that's definitely bread.

"What do you mean, *for now*?"

"Well, I just don't think we'll live there forever. Ella talks about us moving into the palace once she's queen," he says.

I think for a moment before replying. "So, home is wherever your friends are?"

"You know I don't have all the answers, right? Just checking before you ask me the meaning of life."

I kind of love it when he's sarcastic. I feel like I taught him that. "Where do you think you'll you end up? Can you answer that, or are you going to remind me you're not an encyclopaedia again?"

"What's an encyclopaedia?" he replies.

A stroke of creativity splashes over me as I grab a pencil from the desk and rip a page out of the notebook. Will curiously looks over, but I think he ultimately decides it's best to leave me alone. A while later I drop the drawing on the pile of food wrappers; despite having only one colour, I think I managed to capture the blue of the ocean and the yellow of the house walls. "This is where I want to end up. The house on the cliff," I state. "I like the romance of knowing it's mine alone to experience, as one day the cliff will erode enough for it to fall into the sea. Hopefully I can be with it."

"Depressing." He strokes the porch swing. "Maybe I'll fall

with you. If you don't shoot me first."

Maybe in the future we're sitting on that swing laughing about the time I pointed the gun and tried to convince him it was a toy. Or maybe not; maybe I'll kill him before then. Maybe he'll kill me.

Soon enough the light falls and the food is eaten. Maybe we should've saved some. I tie his wrists again, this time to his side with a separate strand joining it to the headboard. I try to be kind as I give him room to move. The TV turns off, leaving us lying in silence, although it carries a comfortable sound.

For a while we stare at each other. I was right before when I first met him; I said his eyes carried sadness, but I didn't mention how it matches my bones.

"I'm sorry I shot you," I whisper.

He whispers back, "It's okay. You missed."

We don't try to fill the rest of the quiet as we lie still besides each other. In the end, he falls asleep before I even produce a yawn. Hours may pass as I listen to the hush of his breathing; rhythmically, it soothes me until mine slows to match.

I never knew the comfort I would find in this bed.

Chapter Twelve

Ella

Biack 25/01/2014

I had another dream last night.

The chill of the air dives me further into the claw-foot tub; my fingers tiptoe along the porcelain slides. It feels as if the universe built it for me. I watch on as the water gently dances around my skin and protects me under its warmth. I feel safe here.

Yet images of my dream proceed to haunt me: the gunfire, the blood, and the silent people. The horrors she committed and then calmly walked away from. How could she do that? How could he let her? And how could my father allow those protectors to hunt her like that?

It must be the council; they have no care for finding her alive. They simply want an end to the burden she's created. She was defending herself. How could I expect her to act any differently when I've seen the world she's from? She just wanted to escape. But she can't escape. I need her—we need her. And Will, what if she takes him with her? I saw the way he looked at her in the dream, the way she looked at him. What if I lose them both?

But did I ever have them in the beginning?

We've been summoned to the blue dining room, the smaller one. My hair is still dripping as I pull up a seat. Beside me, Jia sits decorating hers with freshly picked flowers. Aiden's attention has been stolen by the fireplace, his face so serious as he tries to shape the flames. And across from us, Ben's tapping furiously at a screen. It's strange—he normally takes good care of his devices. Despite the size of the palace, we're still trapped. And after the first day of searching for any means to amuse ourselves, the second feels impossible.

"I have an update." My father strolls in, documents in hand; everyone gets up to bow. I remain seated.

"How could they authorise that?" I ask; my fingers tremble.

His forehead creases as he stops in his tracks. "Authorise what?"

Everyone's attention is focused on me now. "I dreamt it. I saw what happened. She killed them, she killed them all. But they attacked her; they were going to kill her."

"What?" Ben drops his screen on the old table. The thud vibrates through the wood.

Aiden is by my side, grasping my hand.

"The council sent protectors after her," I state. My lip tremors as I can't escape the images. I knew them.

"No." My father shakes his head as he finds his seat. "Well, yes. We are going to send the E team after her, although they haven't left yet."

"They haven't left yet?" How could that be? I saw them. I

saw it all.

Jia places her hand on mine. "What did you see?"

"They were in a hotel," I begin.

My father places photos before us. "The Ivy Eagle." That's them, in the reception, then the stairwell. "They arrived yesterday, and our most up-to-date intelligence suggests they're still there."

"No, no they left when the E team came after them." I flick through the photos and shake my head. "They're gone."

"Like I previously stated; the E team hasn't arrived yet." He shakes his head. "They're still there."

"They are?" I continue to flick through the photos. What if… "It hasn't happened yet," I whisper, my mind racing. "My dreams of Jess. What if I didn't just dream of her life? What if I dreamt of her future?"

No response.

Ben finally breaks the silence as he turns to my father. "You can't send that team after her. Ella saw Jess kill them."

My father's hexagon beeps. "It's too late." He looks up. "They've just left."

"They're going to die," I half shout. "Everything I've seen previously, it's real; it came true. Before she first came to Biack, before she stepped foot on Central Street. I saw it, I dreamt it. I was right then, and I'm right now. Those people—" I choke on my words. "You need to call them back."

"She told me about that dream," Jia says. "She dreamt it before it happened."

"You need to call that team back," Ben repeats me.

"I can't. The mission's already been set in motion," my father says, worry across his face. "I can tell them to proceed with caution. That's all I can do."

"How can that be all?" Aiden finally speaks up. "You're the king. Call them back!"

"It's not my decision alone. The council—"

"The council are wrong!" Ben interrupts. He interrupted the king. "Call the E team back and send us in their place."

"I can't throw out the political system, the political rule book, over this. I can't go against the council. The people would never understand." My father shakes his head.

"What if they did?" I whisper.

He turns to me. "I can't throw away thousands of years of peace over this. I can't be *the Last King*." He could never be him. "This discussion is over. I'll keep you updated."

My father gets up and leaves. The discussion's over: the council have won again.

❖❖❖

It's half nine when Scott wanders into my bedroom. "I come bringing goods!" The packaged baked treats fall from his hands to the bed as he stops and notices the expression on my face. "What knocked your crown, princess?"

"She's going to hurt people, people I know. And it's too late to stop her," I answer.

"Ah, so another Jess problem." He falls beside me. "I'm not sure I can help you there. But I can try distracting you."

Despite the warmth of his lips, the anxiety doesn't budge.

"I actually had another idea that doesn't involve tainting your innocence," he says in between kisses. "I'm interviewing suspects today for the explosion investigation."

I break away. "Can I join? I'm really good at reading people and I've known most of the senior protectors and scientists my entire life. I know I'm not meant to leave the palace, but if we just avoid the main corridors, no one will know and I could really use a distraction from—"

"Hey, Ella," he interrupts, "just going on a hunch here, but do you want to help me interview the suspects?"

I smile. "Yes, I do."

❖❖❖

In all honesty, when he asked me to help, I thought I'd take on a more proactive role. Instead, here I sit, in the surveillance room next door.

"I don't think it's him." Tola, a protector from the K-team, leans back in his swivel chair. "He doesn't have the technical skills to disable the security cameras."

"It can't be him. We had lunch a month ago, and this just doesn't fit his character," I reply while our gaze is fixed on a large screen. Next door, Scott sits across from Antony McArthur, ex A-team protector and now the head of recruitment.

"That's exactly what you said about the last guy." Tola kicks up his feet. "But it has to be someone."

Next door, Scott's face softly moves with his voice. Meanwhile, McArthur trembles in his chair; his innocence is stark, and still the interview proceeds. Although, none of the people who have yet to sit within that chair have carried a shed of guilt, and I'm hard-pressed to think of anyone who would.

"I've already told you; I was in my office working," McArthur states.

Scott raises an eyebrow. "So why is there no record of you signing into your account that morning?" He tosses documents across the table.

"I don't know." He sighs.

"You don't know much, do you? I thought you were the head of recruitment; shouldn't you know everything that goes on around here?" Scott continues.

"I'm the head of recruitment, not internal security. I can tell you all about the new recruits, like you, but I can't speak for all their constant whereabouts." He tilts his head. "Scott, I've known you since you were a small boy. Do you really suspect me of this crime?"

"I'm just following the facts, Tony." Scott leans back in his chair. I admire how dedicated he is to his work, overlooking personal connections and all.

Tola whistles. "I'd like to be interviewed by him." I almost forgot he was next to me. "He's gorgeous, isn't he?"

I brush my hair out of my face. "I'm dating him."

He slams the desk. "No way!" He huffs. "I'm so jealous of you, it's not fair. I never considered you guys together."

"Why not?" I ask, reaching for a glass of water.

Scott's family are high up the political hierarchy; the council would approve. My father would approve. And he's the king's personal assistant. It just makes sense.

He shrugs. "I guess everyone always thought you and Will would get together."

I spit out my drink. "What?" I laugh. "No way. Will's my brother."

"Adopted brother, and not even officially." Tola grins. "I'm just saying, though, if he was my adopted brother—"

Playfully slapping him, I say, "Don't be foul. I'm dating Scott, and it makes complete sense. He's a gentleman and he ticks all the boxes and—"

"He's stunning." Tola's attention has been stolen by the screen again.

Next door, the interview finishes up as Scott prepares to hush McArthur out of the room. While we watch, I rearrange the water jug and glasses on the desk before us; all this waiting and watching is failing to distract me from my dream. I can't escape those images.

I continue to search for the glasses' perfect positions. "Tola, do you believe in the prophecy?"

He doesn't seem fazed by my change in topic. "Well, you exist, so yes."

"And what would you think of a dream, about events that have yet to happen?" I continue.

"I'd think that anything is possible," he replies.

I'm quick to follow up with, "You wouldn't think it's impossible?"

"Well, two decades ago if you asked someone about moving objects without touching them, wounds healing in a matter of minutes, controlling water and fire and changing your physical form, yeah, people would've said that was impossible." He leans back. "And yet, here we are."

"I hope this is the one thing that proves impossible," I state.

He shakes his head. "Nothing's impossible."

Scott smiles at the recorder. He's smiling at me; my insides flutter.

"Up next is Damien Griffin," Tola read off his file. "Oh, he's new! Also rather cute."

"People are more than their appearance," I say.

"Yeah but that part is never very cute."

Next door, a second person enters the space. He must be new, as his face is almost completely foreign—oh, wait! I find his place in my memory as the protector who spoke up against council member Adams. The protector from The Plains; his skin reflects the long days in the sun, and his hands wear the pain of the world slowly being regrown. It can't be him, either; his eyes are too warm.

"How was the most recent harvest back home?" Scott begins.

Damien studies his tactics. "Like the rest."

Scott smiles; this feels like a game. "I'm sure your father's still keeping busy."

Damien hesitates. "There's always plenty to do."

"So when was the last time you spoke to him?"

Another pause. "Recently."

"How recent? Would you say the last few months?"

Damien slowly nods. "It's plausible."

Scott grins as he slides a folder across the table. Damien's quick to flick it open. "Do you still think it's plausible?" No response. "Your father passed when you were ten." The blood leaves Damien's face. "So my question is, who's been maintaining the family plot? It's against the law for a child to tender the fields, and your father left no money to hire outside help."

"My mother," Damien states, trying to remain composed.

Scott leans forward. "That's odd, because I heard a rumour that she struggles to walk."

"She can walk just fine." His expression has gotten tense. "Why are you doing this?"

"Well, I thought we were being honest with each other." Scott shrugs.

"Just ask whatever you brought me here to ask."

Scott smiles. "Where were you on the twenty-second?"

"My family home. I wanted to spend a few days with my brothers and sisters."

"That wasn't authorised," Scott states.

"No." Damien leans in. "It wasn't."

Both next door and within this room, we all sit in silence. Eventually Scott leaves his seat to come visit us. Meanwhile, Damien waits patiently.

Scott shuts the door to our room slowly before turning to say to Tola. "It's him. Make your arrest."

"What?" I try to grab Tola's arm as he leaves his position beside me. "No, no. It's not him."

Tola turns. "Come on, Ella. You said it wasn't the last person either, or the person before them, or before them, and I'm pretty sure it won't be the next person too. But it has to be someone."

"Then we haven't found the right person yet," I say, "because it's not Damien."

"Why?" Scott asks. "He's already confessed to lying about multiple things, his family needs money and he's from The Plains—he has motive."

"Because—" I stop. They're right, but they're wrong. It's not him. "I just know it isn't."

They exchange glances before Tola proceeds to leave. I chase after him.

I make it to the hall before Scott restrains me. I can't save the E team, but maybe I can save Damien, because I can't allow someone to be wrongfully convicted. So, I focus all my energy on the door to the interview room; I can feel the white spread through my veins. I think they tell me stop, but it doesn't register properly as my mind is no longer grounded within me.

Tola struggles with the door, pulling with all his might; his muscles tense like the creases across his forehead. The world goes almost silent as only a faint hum twinges through my ears. I can see their mouths move, but their shouts are deaf. I'm not sure how long I can keep the door shut as my gaze starts to blur, overcome by its own inexperience.

Eventually I slip up.

"What did that achieve?" Scott yells as he releases me from his hold. After a few moments to calm, his tone changes. "If you can't see the good in people, you make it up. But Ella, sometimes people are just bad."

"No, you're wrong." I stop to catch the breath still escaping me. "There's always good."

Moments later, Ben appears at the end of the hall. You can tell from the look on his face he knows something's happened, but he also doesn't care to know what. "The E team are about to arrive," he states. "I thought you'd want to watch."

Not particularly.

Chapter Thirteen

Jess

Biack 25/01/2014

The average human gets seven hours and fifty minutes sleep a night. Let's round that up to eight hours. That's almost three thousand hours a year. If they were to live for sixty years, twenty would be spent in a state of unconsciousness. A third of their life. I wonder how much could be achieved if we didn't need to spend all that time resting? And why were we created this way? Surely it's in nature's favour for us to be more productive, unless it's not? Maybe the human being is too dangerous when awake.

I wake before the sun but I'm still until after its scorch rises. There's a strange kind of comfortable feeling within me that I'm struggling to understand; it's not found in the weapon to my side or the rope around his hands. Its origin lies inches before me with hushed breaths of cold air, another bittersweet melody. What answers hide behind his closed blue eyes? What can he tell me that I could never see? Eight hours a day over seventeen years, and somehow I managed to learn more about him in one night. It seems there's more we share than a hotel bed.

Eventually my legs ache for movement. Giving in to their

wishes, I move towards the window, peering out at the foreign world below. In the distance, a monorail speeds past at velocities yet to be achieved on Earth. Do they sleep less here? Is that how they managed to overtake us in advancements?

Flowers drift from the trees' hold as the wind whistles an inviting tune; meanwhile, the people of the world embark on the first journey of the day. In the distance, buildings of glass reach above the clouds in an attempt to touch the stars; shame they're trapped in a Dome.

This isn't the perfect world I came to know in my dreams, but maybe it's not as far off as I previously thought.

"What happened to your dad?" Will asks; I'm not sure how long he's been awake.

"He killed himself when I was eight. Post-traumatic stress disorder." I let the curtain slip from my fingers. "He was a pilot in some war. There's been so many I forget which one."

He doesn't say anything. He just lies there, and somehow that's the best response.

"How'd you get the scar on your lip?" My turn.

He states, "You're not safe when you sleep."

I wait for him to take his turn, but before he speaks, a figure in the distance steals my attention. A group of protectors, dressed head to toe in black, spread out across the street, guns held high. I've never seen protectors carry guns before, but I guess you don't need guns to rescue people after a hurricane.

"You did something. You told them where we are." I chuck everything I can reach in the backpack while pulling my jeans on.

His brows raise. "No!"

My hand shakes as I lift my weapon to him. I detach the rope from the headboard, but his wrists remain stuck together. I throw the backpack over my shoulder and push him forward. "We're leaving."

We get as far as the door before I realise we'll never make it out that way. Shit, what other exit is there? I rush over to the window. Three stories—am I crazy? It doesn't take much force to shove it open, and the window ledge feels quite strong as I press down my hand with my full weight.

"This way." I move back inside to push Will towards the window.

"Okay, but are you going to untie me, or is this how you plan to kill me?" He holds out his wrists.

Hesitantly, I tuck my gun into my jeans and grab scissors from the desk. More hesitation follows before I cut him free. I guess I don't want to kill him, at least not today.

It's probably not the gentleman in him that lets me go first. Did I mention I'm terrified of heights? My stomach fizzes as I peer over the edge, and the world starts to spin. Will must notice the colour fade from my face as he grabs my arm and holds me back against the brick.

Deep breaths.

"I didn't tell them," Will says as we shuffle towards a drain pipe.

I reply, "You're right; I forgot your world was full of psychics."

"What's a psychic?"

His hands are ready to catch me while I mount the pipe; I'm hoping this thing is stronger than it looks. Maybe it's just chance, but it feels like things may be going my way as I manage to shuffle down the pipe to the ground with no issues. Will follows shortly behind me; it even managed to support his weight. Why is the universe not against me for once?

We glance around the alley, searching for the safest exit. How can everything be so clean here? Even the dumpsters are spotless. It's crazy, and yet I've never seen a cleaner.

"Any ideas?" I ask.

"I thought you were in charge?" He's useless.

"Stop." We freeze. The backdoor slams. Her deep voice is unfamiliar. "Turn around, slowly."

"Just do it," Will whispers. Although I have so many reasons not to listen to him right now, curiosity takes over. I have a right to face my attacker, after all.

She's way too young. Early twenties at the oldest, fifteen at the youngest. There's a ruined innocence in the rigidity of her black hair; why won't the wind move it? It matches the heavy weight of her clothes and the firmness of her grip. What made the stiff child into a solider in a world with no war? The BCD logo is displayed on her upper arm, shaped like a hexagon in a nod to the dome.

I remove the gun from behind me. "You need to leave."

She remains set. "Not without you."

"Please," I beg. *Please don't make me do this.*

"Drop the weapon and release him," she orders.

I shake my head. "I can't do that." I can't.

What makes a murderer?

Do they need to have a cold, unloving heart that's impenetrable to remorse? Or perhaps it's speed, to be able to perform the worst crimes so fast the brain doesn't realise what's happened and so is unable to experience all the guilt that follows. All I know is when I aim my weapon and take her life, I know what I'm doing. And in that moment, I define ice.

Will just stares.

"We need to get back to the car," I state and point the gun at him; he's not on my side.

"There's almost no fuel left. We can't get far. Where do you plan on going?" His eyes flicker back to the body in the alley.

I have an idea. "What if we didn't have to go far to end up far away?"

"You're crazy, and if it's not enough to get yourself killed, you've selfishly dragged me into this." He refuses to move.

I yank him forward. "You got yourself involved the moment you decided to guard my cell."

"I did that because I didn't trust you!" He throws his arms around; the gun doesn't bother him. "And guess what, I still don't trust you."

"Will." I laugh. "I really don't give a crap whether you trust me or not. Either we're in this together or you're with them." I lift my loaded arm. "So, what's it going to be?"

He pulls a face of disgust then shoves past me.

We're almost at the car when a further gunshot rings through the air. They've found us. It's a mad dash, just a few feet farther towards the car's safety, and we soon find ourselves trapped behind it, unable to enter without risk of serious injury. They're much too close much too quickly.

"Give me the other gun in your backpack," Will orders; where did he get this authority?

"Now you're the crazy one." I laugh.

"Look, there's many of them and one of you. Even Aiden could do that math. Now give me the other gun."

"You're the reason we're in this mess!" I can't believe his nerve.

He starts to yell. "Why won't you listen to me? I didn't tell them where we were. I have no idea how they found us, but it was nothing I did!"

"Listen to yourself!" I peer over the car boot, only to have a near miss with some sort of energy beam; was that to stun or kill me? "After everything that's happened since I quite literally fell into this world, do you really think I'm going to be like, *oh yeah, man, great idea.*"

He doesn't fight me anymore.

How do I take on a number of protectors, which can only be described as many, when I can't leave the safety of the car's side? And while I try to figure out a plan, they're getting closer.

"Get down!" I yell as I pull Will back behind the car. The idiot tried to sneak a glance, only to have gunfire unleashed upon him. They're trying to shoot him too—maybe they can't tell us apart? Surely they must care.

That's when a spark of genius strikes. I lie flat and take aim from underneath the pickup truck. Although all I can see are feet, I know with certainty they're all going to belong to protectors; anyone else would be utterly stupid to be out here right now.

I count five people in the open. Okay I can do that. With no remorse—maybe my actions are too quick—one bullet completely misses, but I manage to shoot a second into a soldiers's leg. He falls to the floor in pain, only to receive a further bullet to the head. I can't believe that worked. And I only missed once.

They're just pawns, I tell myself as I continue to shoot until I run out of ammo. Although half of my bullets flew past their targets, I manage to take down another two soldiers with the rest. It's not everyone, but hopefully I've somehow evened the playing field. Although, there are still many protectors and only one me, and now that one me has only one weapon left.

"I take it by the silence you've run out of bullets," a voice yells out. I think it belongs to an older man, although at seventeen, almost everyone is considered older.

"Maybe I ran out of—" I stop; no one's going to understand my absurdities.

"What?" he shouts back.

I try to act more serious. Maybe they'll listen. "I don't want to fight. Let me leave, and no one else has to die."

His laughter echoes in his words. "We didn't come here to let you leave."

If only he could hear me roll my eyes. "Wow, you sure know how to make a girl feel special."

"If it's special treatment you want, let us know your demands?"

I give up on taking this seriously. Maybe I've lost it, or

maybe I somehow hit my head again. It's just like before when I met that woman with the rose. I do feel afraid but also, even more so, I think I feel alive. "I'm British, so obviously top of the list is a cup of tea. And by God if you put too much milk in, I'll start a massacre."

Will quietly laughs at my jokes even though I'm sure he doesn't get them. Is he having as much fun as me? And why is this so much fun? This shouldn't be fun.

"Some cake won't hurt, although I'm allergic to anything remotely healthy, so carrot cake is probably pushing it."

Will mouths, *What are you doing?* and I shrug.

"Actually, all I want is a lifetime supply of tea; I want all the tea in this world. I'm sorry, but the real reason I'm here is to steal all your tea. This is teagate."

"I get what you're doing," he shouts in response.

Searching through the backpack, I pull out the other gun. "Okay, what am I doing?"

"Using humour to cover up your fear. But you have no reason to be scared; we don't want to hurt you. We just need you to come with us and answer some questions."

I'm not letting fear stop me, I can survive it. "No, seriously, I'm here for your tea. There's your answer. Now you no longer need me to go with you for your questions. So I guess I'll be on my way then."

He gives up on me as his tone changes. "You have five seconds to surrender yourself up before I order my men to advance on your position."

I swing my backpack on.

"Five."

I check the gun's safety is off.

"Four."

I look under the car for his position.

"Three."

I gesture to Will to stay where he is.

"Two."

I prepare for another cold-hearted act.

"One."

I stand up and kill him where he stands. His gun wasn't even raised.

Taking advantage of the chaos as their leader falls to the ground, I push Will into the car and reach under the seat to quickly start the engine; it soars to life and so do our hopes, for a second, until we see the fuel meter. We're screwed.

"Where are you going?" Will asks. I drive head-on through the soldiers. We hide in our seats while bullets and energy beams aggressively assault the vehicle; luckily, they all either miss or do little damage.

"The beach," I say. Behind us some high-tech aircraft silently emerges from behind the skyscrapers. "What the hell is that?"

"A stealth. Yeah, whatever it is you're planning, you might want to do it right now." His head shifts from the aircraft to before us and back again as the city starts to disappear behind us.

Okay, here goes nothing. I think of the waves crashing against my feet to the childish laughter of innocents. And that no matter how hard the sun tries, it can't compete with the cold air the wind blows. And why does everything taste of salt when there's nothing to be bitter about? It's just us; it's just us in the quiet, calm, peaceful embrace of the endless sand. Everett and I running towards parents who wait with open arms; crouching over rock pools with our fishing nets; pretending to be asleep as my dad carries me to the car. My arms start to glow black and my head begins to throb, but I can't let it distract from the image of the ocean beyond the sand. My hands release the steering wheel to clutch my aching head.

"Jess! Are you insane?" Will yells as we speed out of control towards a cliff that's appeared as if from nowhere. The final ingredient—an urgent need.

"Do you trust me?" I ask although I have no reason to suspect his answer has changed from earlier.

He's hesitant; who'd blame him? But he does finally answer. "Yes."

There's that moment again. That gaze that lasts too long.

If my head wasn't already in pain, the screaming would do it. I press hard on the breaks. My eyes close in doubt; he distracted me. I wait for the cliff, the terrific fall and the maybe not-so-tragic death. But all that comes is warmth, and the brightest of lights I can see despite closed eyes. I think it worked. I'm too scared to look.

I don't need to open my eyes to see the ocean. I can hear it; taste it, smell it, feel it. That familiar feeling of deja-vu rushes through my blood, although there's something different; opening my eyes, I see the burning sun—we're still on Biack. He did distract me.

The Unbreakable Boy looks at me, and we erupt in a roar of laughter.

"That was—" He pauses to find the right word. "Something else."

"Why was that so much fun?" I ask rhetorically.

"I thought you were going to kill me."

For some time we sit there, The Unbreakable Boy and The Girl from Far Away, in a pickup truck on a beach in the middle of nowhere. After a while we get out and give chase into the ocean. I think hours pass while we splash and play. The January air has brought the water to near freezing, but we don't care. We dance to the sound of the waves. The sun is finally setting when we climb into the back of the pickup truck and sit back to watch the world fall asleep.

There's something about the way he looks at me as I say, "Why does it feel like this is what my life has been leading to?"

He replies, "Because maybe it is."

Chapter Fourteen

Ella

I sit in bed pretending I don't already know everything being told. "How many casualties?" I ask, knowing the answer is five.

My father looks relieved. "None."

"W-what?"

Jia squeezes my hand from beside me.

He nods with joy from across the room. "There were five injuries, but no one died. Her aim wasn't very good."

"But in the dreams…"

He laughs. "Maybe they're just that, dreams."

"No, there's some truth to them." Ben speaks up from his spot on the floor, surrounded by my obsessive collection of Jess memorabilia. "Ella was right about what happened, just not the injuries." He pinches the bridge of his nose while we wait for him to continue. "Maybe they're distorted by Jess's perception of events?"

"But I don't see things through her eyes. It" more like I'm an observer on the sidelines?"

"They could still be distorted. There's obviously some link

between the two of you—you're not tied to the events, you're tied to her."

I run a hand through my hair, searching for something to cling to. "So I see events, future events, the way she thinks she experiences them? And she must see the same for me?"

Ben shrugs. "We'd have to ask her." And we would.

"Okay, so." Aiden lays on his back across the floor next to Ben, but with his legs up on the end of the bed. Is he comfortable? "How do we use that tie to find them?" He pauses to pick up one of the documents from the floor. I can't see which one. "Like, you have a lot of things in your lab. Which one will do it?"

"I have no idea." Ben snatches the document from Aiden before turning back to my father. "So they lost her?"

"Yes, she disappeared." We all turn to each other, sharing a common thought. And wherever she went, she's surely moved on by now. My father brings us back to reality. "This happened yesterday," he reminds us.

"So no leads." I slump back into bed. I miss Will.

I still remember the first time I knocked on his door. Sometimes the nightmares were too real and my father was too busy, so I'd get into Will's bed and tell him the horror stories; he was never scared. It's like he'd already faced every demon and tamed them into his pets. He was this kind of fearless that was shrouded in mystery.

A while later, once everyone disappeared off around the palace, I find myself stumbling around searching for him. I see his touch on the oil stains across classic paintings, I hear his step in creaks of this one floorboard and I feel his presence all across the great library—all two stories of paper.

Eventually I arrive at the one place I can find him, but instead discover Aiden on Will's old bed, unsurprised as I enter. He moves his feet so I can sit opposite. It takes a few minutes before either of decide to speak; maybe we're waiting for our missing friend to hear us first.

Aiden speaks first. "We've never been apart this long before."

I reply, "None of us have. Before now, the longest was that time Ben locked himself in his lab during first exams." I smile. "And that only lasted thirty hours before you broke down the door."

"He was so mad." Aiden laughs. "But I left my hexagon in there! And thirty hours is a long time!"

We laugh but eventually return to Will. "Do you ever wonder what happened to him before I found him?" I ask.

"He didn't tell you? I always thought you knew but he'd sworn you to secrecy."

I shake my head. "No, he's never said a word about anything that happened before that day."

"What could've happened that's so *hard to say*?" He nudges me with his foot. "Hey, can you imagine what a conversation between him and Jess is like?"

"I bet they just sit in silence staring at each other, waiting for the other to crack," I say.

"I've never met two more untrusting people. He'll say something like *can you pass the water?* and she'll be like *why what are you going to do with it?* and then he'll be like *why do you want to know?*"

I reply, "Do you think they even sleep? It's been several days now. They must be exhausted."

"Has Will ever slept? No matter the hour, when I look for him, he's always awake," Aiden says.

For a while, we sit laughing and sharing ideas of Will and Jess's exchanges. Eventually it stops being all jokes.

"The Girl from Far Away," I whisper. "Maybe she can bring him what life never has."

"There's an opportunity to make fun of his virginity there." He doesn't take the opportunity. "I think you're right. I'm not worried about him," he confesses. "But I'm worried he might not come back."

"He'll be back." I don't hesitate. "Because he's our brother, and the family you create without common blood, well, you can't just walk away from them." I pause. "Besides, he believes in the prophecy, so he'll be back."

"Wait." Aiden leans forward, grinning. "You read his journal?"

I nod, and he bursts out in laughter.

After a while, he calms down and decides to change the subject. "So, you and Scott?"

"Tola told you?"

"Actually, a lot of people told me. It's getting really annoying now."

I squeeze my hands together, "I'm trying not to make a big deal out of it like everyone else."

"Really? You? The girl who hired an orchestra to help tell a boy you loved him when you were eight years old?" Aiden raises his eyebrows.

"Oh, I forgot you knew about that. Well, I really thought I loved Pladum," I defend.

"I think you fall in love with ideas and plans but not so much people," Aiden states.

"What? When did you become this expert on love?" He's never this serious.

"Oh, I'm not. Sex maybe, but not love. However, I am an expert on you." He finds my hand. "Promise me you'll let yourself be happy when it doesn't turn out how you planned."

"Why?" I don't know why I'm so defensive.

He laughs. "Because sometimes it's okay to not be in control." No, not for me. "And sometimes people aren't as perfect as you believe." But they are. "And sometimes the people are so much better than the ideas and the plans."

I exhale as I smooth out the creases in my dress. "So." I hesitate. "Sex."

His eyebrows shoot upwards. "Really?"

"Yeah, I wonder—"

"No," he interrupts me. "I'm not going to answer any of your questions, okay, because like I said, I know you. You'll ask too many questions and overthink and get trapped inside your head and create this picture of how it needs to be, and nothing will ever live up to that."

"I wouldn't—"

"Yes, you would," he interrupts, lightly laughing. "Look, this is one of those things you shouldn't plan. It'll just happen. Or it won't. But live in the uncertainty, okay?"

Live in the uncertainty? Who does he think I am?

❖❖❖

"Oh! Sorry."

"No need to apologise, Ella." My father sits upright in the Throne of All, eyes softly closed and hands gently placed on the armrests.

I consider leaving him be, but something forces me to stay within the confinement of the high walls. Tiptoeing across the marble tiles, I almost trip across the tree roots dancing in and out of the ground. Like all rooms in Day Palace, the throne room is a real chameleon, filled with people, rows of benches or predator-led recorders. Currently it's bare. Stretching to the Dome above us, the First Tree patiently waits for the next court; at its perch, a throne formed from its skin holds the king. It's said the palace itself was built around the Throne of All, which the First King forged from a dying tree.

"Do you believe in the legend behind the origin of the throne?" I ask.

He smiles, eyes still shut. "Where do you think you inherited your faith from?" Awakening from his conscious slumber, he moves from his seat to offers it to me. "Would you like to sit? After all, one day you will."

Hesitant, I oblige. My fingers stroke the fraying wood, traces of leaves from the previous season crinkle across the floor.

Around the thick of the trunk, engraved in the bark, lie six grooves meant to hold six gems. But that's another story.

I sit down; it's uncomfortable. "I thought it'd feel…" I can't find the word.

"Natural?" he suggests. I nod. "The first time I sat there was my crowning. It felt wrong in every way, and yet it was too late to change it." He gestures me. "That's why it's important you sit here now and understand it's always going to feel too big; you'll never feel ready. It'll always feel as if you're living in the shadow of those who came before you."

I do feel tiny on this ancient monument. "When do you stop feeling like that?"

"Never." He laughs. "But like me, you were born for this."

"But…" I hesitate. "What if I was born for something else?"

He smiles. "The prophecy." I nod. For a little while he's still, deep in thought. And then with a sigh he finds a seat on the edge of the platform the throne sits upon. His back is to me. "My father had a hard life. Born in the dark, a son himself of a king who never saw the stars. His life was decided at his birth— he was to be another Dark King, and his destiny was to keep the people alive in the underneath. Then one night he dreamt of a Dome that towered above the land and sea. And thus his destiny became to lead the people out of the dark. He was to be the last Dark King.

"But as you know, when I was nineteen, my father passed. However, what you may not know is it was due to a construction accident during the building of the Dome. Hundreds of miles of the structure was destroyed, and hundreds of people perished, which is sadly fortunate as it could've been far more. And the construction of the Dome was prolonged for another decade.

"I was another king born in the dark, but my destiny was to be the First King of the New World. So I always felt lucky; those who came before me had to carry all this weight so I could experience the worth. I would rule a utopia. But like my father, and most likely every father who came before him, I've ended up with a different legacy. Because it was me who led our people out of the dark. And so I became the last Dark King.

"When you were born, well, you'll be the First Queen after a history of only sons. That was and is the life expected of you, a legacy far superior to any that came before you. And yet at age nine you discovered your gift and instead of being one extraordinary being, you became two." He finds his feet as he turns to face me.

Our eyes meet as I say, "But what if I'm average? What if I'm an average queen and an average protector? What if I have this great destiny ahead of me and the person I am falls short?"

Crouching before me, he takes my hands within his. "Ella, my daughter." He looks up at me. "I don't know what your life will be. I don't know what title you'll find or what story you'll leave behind. But I do know that whatever it is, it'll be extraordinary."

"Ella." Aiden runs into the room. "Oh, sorry to interrupt."

"It's okay, what's wrong?" I ask.

He pants, "It's what's right. That thing Ben did to find Jess the first time, it was something to do with energy and knitting and our gifts. Well, he did it again."

I turn to my father. He says, "Go find her. Go live your story."

Bring her home; complete the team; continue the prophecy.

Be extraordinary.

Chapter Fifteen

Jess

Biack 26/01/2014

I didn't know The Unbreakable Boy had that much laughter within him.

I didn't know I did, either.

We've been walking aimlessly for hours. Hunger is starting to win as we come to accept we shouldn't have eaten all the food the other night. A while ago we left the beach to enter fields of nothing but grass, which soon merged into skyscrapers of endless trees.

I may be a galaxy, or a solar system, away from Earth, but without looking up I can almost convince myself I'm back. The melodic tweet of the birds is in chorus with the wind as it blows the river on. And have I seen that tree before? It looks like the one Everett and I spent a summer climbing. What about that river stream? Didn't I ruin a pair of shoes in it? Or how about that smell of freshly grown earth? Or do they refer to the dirt of the ground as biack here?

"This is what Earth looks like," I state. "It reminds me of this place in Brecon where I spent a summer." As we walk, I let the low-hanging leaves slide through my fingertips. "It felt like my own private paradise, my own adventure waiting to be lived." Just like how I thought of Biack. "So much of Earth is ruined, and so finding something as untouched as that is…" I can't think of a word. "Worth remembering."

After a long pause—perhaps he's deciding what to share—Will speaks. "Most of Biack looks like this. Although amongst it, you'll find ruins." He stops to stroke an undecipherable tree carving. "People used to live here, and then they all died out." He continues moving. "The new people are different."

"Do you mean since everyone came back above ground?" I have to ask; he's speaking in riddles. Did he learn that from me? Did I learn that from him?

"I was barely born when that happened, but I do know that crimes we didn't have laws against when I was young now exist." He shrugs. "Either people never used to do bad things or they were really good at covering them up. Because the protectors were always just that, *protectors*. They helped people during natural disasters instead of investigating crimes and fighting the Red Suits. *The Red Suits*. I guess that's really where it all started to go wrong. Crime appeared when they did, maybe twelve years ago at most."

Really? Crime only started twelve years ago? I laugh. "Somehow I find that hard to believe. On Earth, people are inherently bad. Where there are humans, there is war."

"There's never been a war," he states.

"Impossible. How many people have lived on Biack?"

He thinks before responding. "Millions?"

"And you're saying that not once in your world's history has any of those millions of people ever felt like rebelling. People don't like being told what to do and how things are; it's in their blood to spite it." People like to create conflict. They need to have something to argue over.

"Maybe on your world. But here everyone believes the king and the council will do what's best for the people."

What happened to the queens? "Can women not lead here? Why is it always the king?"

"Our current king, Liam Day, Ella's dad, calls it a history of sons. Every king has only had one child, and it's always been a boy."

Wait a minute. "Ella's a girl."

"Ella's the First Queen. Or she will be one day."

"So, she really is special. It's probably just the male swimmers are strong in that family line." There will be some science to explain it. "I bet that drives the fanatics crazy, though."

"She's special." He doesn't care much for my logic. "When I met her, I was…" He pauses. "Like you, I guess. Running from everything and everyone." What was he running from? "But she has this way of seeing the best in people. Seeing the best they could become. And no matter how many times you disappoint her or make a mistake, she always defends you and believes in you. Her faith is never shaken." He smiles. "And she believes in people so intensely and unconditionally that after a while, you start to believe in yourself too."

We walk for another hour while the hunger grows and the sun finishes its rise; eventually the forest falls back and we find ourselves standing on one side of an open field. The woods en-circle it, but why is it here? Far off in the distance we spy a cab-in; it's almost invisible.

"This doesn't feel right," Will states.

I nod. "You took the words right out my mouth." We stand at the start as we try to figure out a plan. Eventually I give up. "To hell with it. I'm starving."

A device below me starts to emit a loud and repetitive beep.

"What is that?" Will's referring to the device I just stepped on. He seems to have no knowledge of this tech, but luckily, danger is very common on Earth. Although maybe not in this form; we don't have a lot of mine fields in southern England.

I'm frozen on the spot. If I bend down to try disarm it, I might activate it. And I have no idea how to disarm bombs anyway. Whenever they show it on TV, they cut a random wire. What if the bombs on Biack don't have any wires? And my companion will be no use; he probably doesn't even realise the threat. "That's something we call a mine on Earth. And not the underground-rock-gathering kind of mine. The bomb kind of mine," I reply. In his eyes I can see the rapid thoughts. "We have to run," I follow up.

He frowns. "That's your answer to everything. Maybe if I look at it, I can turn it off somehow."

He moves close enough for me to grab his arm. "No, Will, we have to run. It's a risk, but I've done the math. We have to run!"

All hell breaks loose.

Our hands intertwine as we take the plunge. Behind us,

explosions of earth, or should I say black, shake at our feet, but we don't stop, we don't look back, we just keep on running with our grasp tight. Luckily there's about a second delay behind each explosion. Is the purpose of these devices to warn rather than to injure?

How come I could never find this stamina or speed during PE? Maybe schools should implement mine fields onto their grounds, but then I guess they'd have to buy warning signs— health and safety and all.

As we run, our glances meet and laughter break out. Why is this so much fun? Why is all of this so much fun? I'm absolutely terrified but by God, I've never felt so alive.

The sprint ends in a terrific fall resulting from the explosions catching us up and throwing us from their ground. We land hard, uncomfortable but fortunately with minor damage. Maybe we hit our heads, because when we turn to each other instead of expressing concern or checking on our safety, we burst out in further laughter.

"The risk we took was calculated. But man, am I bad a math." I'm hoping he doesn't realise I stole that joke from the internet. Wait, of course he won't.

For a few minutes, we lie there in breathless laughter.

After a while, I speak. "These new people, they seem a lot like the people on Earth."

Pulling himself up off the ground, he offers me a hand up. The cabin isn't far now; I can see the broken windows dressed in cobwebs and the overgrown garden climbing the walls. As we move closer, the stench of abandonment is overwhelming, but why would someone hide mines to protect something they no longer want?

Inside it's no different. Everything looks frail; if I sit on that chair, will it crumble beneath me? I clasp my hands around a teacup. It doesn't break, but a crack in the bottom shows it's already useless. The kitchen shows no signs of life; maybe no one's ever lived here. From the empty fridge—damn—to the dusty but desolate cupboards, I search but find nothing. I'm not even sure if there ever was anything; the fridge has no plug.

I'm trying to find where Will went when I walk past the bedroom. Scars decorate his bare back like a tapestry of tragic art. What happened to him? As he turns, I catch sight of his chest, the pain embellished in white marks. I'm working my eyes up his body as they meet his. Nothing is said.

Minute later when I'm searching through the bathroom, no surprise there's no running water, Will yells out from the living room. "I found food!"

"What about a cup of tea?" As I walk in, he chucks what seems like a chocolate bar at me. It tastes more like an energy bar. "Where was this?"

"Here." He reveals a not-so-dusty box hidden under a blanket.

Is this a safe house? Inside the box is further food, bottled water and a rose. Don't ask me how it's still alive. Instead of questioning it, we shove as much food as we can into our mouths while drowning in somehow-fresh water.

Soon enough I feel sick and I think Will shares my discomfort, because he too stops eating. I stash the rest of the supplies in my rucksack.

"Why is that in there?" The Unbreakable Boy gestures at the rose while placing a dusty old book in the back pocket of his jeans.

It's familiar. "I've seen one before."

"Yeah, they're quite common on Biack." I can't tell if he's being sarcastic or stupid.

"No. I meant the people who helped me escape." I've caught his attention. "Their leader, she had one in her hand." I stroke the black edges. "It had tips like this."

"What was her name? What did she want with you? Where did they take you?" He asks too many questions.

"This isn't my problem," I reply. "I don't want to get involved in Biack's issues."

His head shakes in disbelief. "You already are." Those blue eyes haven't looked at me like this since I tried to shoot him. "You can keep on running and avoid responsibility, but that doesn't mean you didn't do those things. You killed someone. You killed people. Good people." I had to. "Your existence proves legends, and your abilities…" He pauses. "You could save lives."

"I'm not from here. I don't owe your world anything."

He's stood up, half shouting now. "You came, you caused chaos, you hurt people and now you're going to run off back home, leaving a trail of destruction behind you." His words spit like acid. "You were right about the people of Earth. You've just proven nothing good can grow there."

I storm out of the cabin. How dare he insult my world, my

world that he knows nothing about. As I stomp around outside, I start to wonder why I'm so mad. The only good thing I've ever found on Earth is Everett. Will is somewhat right; almost nothing good can grow there. And anything good that does grow is beaten till it wilts.

While still stomping around in a confused anger, I notice the trees starting to part as the wind increases; it's like a helicopter's coming in to land. But they don't have helicopters here; they have stealths.

"We're going." I run inside and grab my rucksack. Will doesn't move. "Now!" I point the gun.

Maybe we can lose them amongst the overgrowth. Maybe we can hide within the untouched trees. Maybe we can avoid their stalking eyes. But what if this never ends? They'll follow me to the ends of Earth—no, the ends of Biack. They won't follow me to Earth.

"Jess, please listen to me." Ella's voice echoes through the forest.

Will and I stand still as we exchange a look.

"You're not in trouble; I understand why you tried to hurt those people." I pull Will on as we continue running. "I know you want to go home. And we'll do everything we can to help you if that's what you really want, but you have information we need. Please understand that. You know things that could save someone." The sun catches my eye as an end to the forest becomes visible. "And you have our friend." I glance over at Will. "We need him back."

We run out of trees as we exit the woods and find ourselves

trapped on the edge of a cliff. Peering over the side, I examine the adjacent waterfall. I think I could survive that. But it's a risk; can I really force that on Will?

"Will!" The Girl of Oceans breaks out of the forest and runs towards us. She stops still when she notices my gun.

"Jia, wait." The First Queen emerges from the trees. Closely behind her follows Fireboy and The Invisible Boy.

For a moment, we wait in silence as we all acknowledge each other without words.

"Ben went through your journals." Aiden breaks the silence. "I tried to stop him, but he overpowered me, buddy."

Will's face tenses. "I'm going to kill you."

"Jess, please." Ella ignores them. "I'm not going to force you. I want you to make the choice. Come with us. Help us."

"I don't belong here. I can't stay," I reply.

"You're wrong, you do." She starts, "Don't you feel it? Don't you feel like this was meant to happen? You were meant to come here. I think you're meant to stay."

Will looks to me; he must be remembering our conversation last night in the back of the pickup truck.

"I have a life on Earth." But do I? My best friend's sleeping with my boyfriend. My mother's emotionally absent, and my stepfather's abusive. My only friend is Everett, who, I have no idea how to contact. And truth be told, I feel closer to the people standing around me than I ever have to any friends on Earth.

"Maybe so, but if you ever wanted a life on Biack, you have one."

I think it's the first time I've seen her in anything other than pink. And even so, a white sundress isn't a big change.

"You're one of us," Ben adds.

What?

"You're meant to be here," Jia joins in. "It's written in the prophecy."

Prophecy? I'm no hero. But maybe this is where I belong.

Before anyone can say another word, a further humming noise appears behind them. The leaves fall as the trees shake and the wind rushes through them. Soon some kind of drone bursts through the woodlands and rushes towards us, I almost slip retreating further back.

"Is it true you're from Earth?" A blinding light, emitted by the drone, attacks me. It's accompanied by a booming voice. *"Tell us how you got here."*

"W-what?" I stutter. What's going on?

"Leave her alone!" Jia shouts at the drone. It emits a second light upon her.

"Tell us about Earth," The machine booms. I stumble further backwards; Will grabs my arm to stop me falling into the river below.

"Ignore it, Jess!" Ella shouts above the noise of the drone's blades.

But I can't ignore it. I can barely see past it. This is what a life here would involve; this is the downside to what I saw in the dreams. The people they call predators and the photo ops disguised as missions. I don't know how to live like that. I like feeling hidden. They locked me up; they'd experiment on me; they'd use me for the cameras. I turn to the drop behind me. I could survive that.

Will yanks my arm, forcing me to look at him. "Jess," he whispers. "Stay."

"Why are you running? Why do you have a gun? Who is Jess?" the machine shouts.

Who am I? I try to look around at the only real friends I've ever known, but I don't know them. Ella knows them. They were never my friends. I look at Will; none of them are my friends.

My grip of the gun starts to slip.

"Come with us." Ella continues to fight. For a moment there, I thought I was done. But that's not who I am.

I turn to the machine and shout, "I'm The Girl from Far Away!" I yank my arm back from Will; he was never mine to take. "Go home." I let go. And finally, I turn to Ella to say, "The Red Suits are led by a woman who calls herself the Rose. She has someone working for her in the BCD." As the final word slips out of my mouth, I let myself slip off the cliff. They shout after me, but it's too late, I'm falling.

Before I hit the water, I witness Will diving in after me.

The water pushes us downstream until it finally releases us on the river's edge. "I'm not going with you!" I splutter while I try to drag myself out of the river's hold. Behind us I hear a gunshot; we ignore it.

He helps me onto the land before pulling himself up too. "I know you're not." His hand pushes the dripping strands of hair back across his head. "Which is why I'm coming with you."

He picked me.

Someone picked me.
He stayed.

Chapter Sixteen

Ella

The gunshot rings through our ears as the predator's device falls to the ground. Aiden puts his gun back in its holder.

"No!" Jia yells after Will and Jess. Running to the edge, she looks in anguish. "We need to go after them."

I halfheartedly try to grab her arm as she searches for a safe way down. "No, leave them."

"You saw it, right? In her eyes? She was going to stay." Jia paces around. "We have to go after them. That stupid machine ruined everything!" She kicks the lifeless metal.

"No Jia." I hold her still, looking straight into her eyes. "Like you said, she was going to stay. But she just needs a little more time, and we're going to give it to her."

Jia pleads, "What about Will?"

"He's going to convince her."

"He chose her," Aiden whispers. "I didn't even know he liked girls."

I need to focus on something else; I change the subject. "Look, let's just think about the information she gave us and hope the machine wasn't able to transmit it in time." I glance at the smoking scraps. They don't live-stream what they see but there may have been enough time for it to back itself up. "The Rose. What do we know about that name?"

We all glance between us before turning to Ben for the answer. "Nothing? I mean, that name doesn't exist."

Less than an hour later, in Ben's lab, we discover he's right. That name doesn't exist. There's never been any mention of roses, let alone *the Rose*, in any mission or investigation reports.

"Maybe she lied," Aiden suggests.

"She's telling the truth," I state.

"You know what that means for Damien, right?" Aiden says. She didn't say it was him. "And if she's telling the truth, why haven't we found any mention of this Rose?" He taps the screen. "Maybe she made it up to get us off her back?"

"No!" They turn; I didn't mean to be so loud. "She's telling the truth. We need to keep searching."

He laughs. "You're blind. You're always blind."

"I am not!" I shake.

The vein on his forehead starts throbbing. "You are! You have this delusional rainbow-filtered view on life and—"

"Jess was telling the truth," Ben interrupts. "I found something." He passes the image to a screen behind us; it's a single rose. And then more images start popping up, all of lone roses. There must be hundreds. "I searched for images of roses in the database. They appeared in over half of the missions the BCD has completed," he tells us.

"Out of the missions this year?" I assume.

His face drops as he realises I don't understand. "No. Out of *all* the missions."

What?

"What?" Aiden speaks for me.

"But that's thousands over years. And for crimes and disasters." I try to piece it together. "When did it begin?"

"Since the start of the database, since we began collating all records. It was created seven years ago but it has documents from missions from maybe up to twelve years ago?"

Twelve years.

"That's when the Dome was finished," I state. "But why has no one noticed before? All these roses, you'd think they'd draw attention?"

Ben pulls up a program on the screen, although none of us speak that language. "I didn't search for the word 'rose.' I had to use this to compare a stock image. The roses have never been catalogued in crimes or mentioned in reports."

"They're hidden in plain sight," I whisper. "Who are you?"

"I wonder what will happen if I burn one?" Aiden says. "Maybe we should try it. Do you have any of them?"

"That's a terrible idea. And I just told you, no one has noticed their presence before, so why would you assume we have any in storage?" Ben questions.

Aiden's hand lights on fire. "It was a great idea."

Jia smirks as she tips a water bottle with her hands. The flames sizzle out. "Notice how I don't even need to use my gift to stop yours." Jia's always had a way of dealing with Aiden that the rest of us haven't managed yet; their powers counter each other.

"What about the place Jess travelled when we went after her the first time? A team was sent there, right?" My eyes are focused on the screen.

"Yeah, the H team. It was an old castle on the coast and by the time they arrived, it'd been completely cleared out," Ben replies.

"We have to go there," I say as I spin around, causing my white dress to twirl. "There's nothing we can do about Jess, and we know now that Will is working on that."

"Yeah, he is." Aiden snickers, resulting in a quick slap to his arm from Jia.

"So let's follow the intel she gave us. Let's find out what's really going on," I say.

I turn back to the image on screen. A rose. The Rose. *Who are you?*

❧❧❧

The rest of the day flies by as I struggle to tear my eyes away from the photos; how did everyone miss this until now? Roses are common flowers, but not that common. In one incident, the first reported murder on Biack, a rose was placed in her hand. How did we miss that? How did we not realise the significance?

"Whoa!" A protector narrowly avoids me as I trudge down the corridor with my face in a folder. "I'm sorry, but you should pay attention—" I look up. "Oh, sorry, ma'am. My mistake."

I manage to make it home to the Palace without any other

near-miss collisions. And as I'm settling into bed for a long evening of searching through report after report, an uninvited but much-welcomed guest appears. With food.

"I come bringing dragon noodles," Scott says as he strolls into my room.

I move over to make space for him. "Thank life, I'm starving." As I dig through the food, I notice he hasn't touched his. Instead, he's more occupied with the reports spewed across the bed. "Your noodles are going cold."

"Sorry, I just—" He hesitates.

"What?" I move the food to a bedside table as I inch closer to him. "You can tell me anything."

His arms fall around me as he smiles. "I know. That's why I'm so crazy about you." I flush. "So, why are you going through all these reports?"

"Have you ever noticed a rose at the scene of a crime, or on top of a crumbled building after an earthquake?"

His face goes pale. "No. Why what does it mean?"

"I don't know, but I'm going to find out. Tomorrow we're going to visit the castle Jess escaped from."

"What are you looking for?"

I'm honest. "A distraction. Scott, she rejected me. Again. And Will chose her. I need to do something right."

"What happened isn't on you, it's on her," he says.

"Then why do I feel so...cold?" I ask. "What if I'm a terrible queen? What if I ruin everything?"

"Do you want to know how I know you're going to be the best queen?" he asks, but I don't need to answer. "Because sometimes, sometimes you'll say something, and it changes the way I see everything." His stare feels so intense. "And you have no idea you do that."

My lips are on his. His lips are on mine. I fall into his embrace as the world around starts to slip away. This is what I needed, a distraction. We inch further back until I sink amongst the reports; I don't care about the clutter. Closer he moves until the space between us runs out; it's almost as if he can't stand the gap. That's okay, because I can't, either.

I never want this to end. I never want to leave this moment we now coexist within. I never want his lips to not return to mine. I never want his touch to leave my body. I never want his breath to not fall against my neck. I never want to return to a life in which we're not intertwined.

My fingers tug at his top until he breaks our embrace to remove it. Several kisses later, his hand starts to rise up my leg; my body shivers under his touch. That's when I take the leap and pull off my sundress. He just stares. There's that look in his eyes again; this is real.

But then he pulls away. "I can't do this."

What? I whisper, "Why?"

He replaces his top as he stutters, "I can't take that from you." He stumbles out of the room, seeming confused by his own actions. "This is a mistake. I'm sorry."

He leaves me alone with my worries.

What a terrible place to be.

❀❀❀

The castle's walls are crumbling, and the moat has long since dried up. Is that a flower bed? No, it's just weeds. It seems the people who were here had no interest in restoration or preservation. What is true evil? Is it the want to only destroy, to hurt? If so, this place has been touched by darkness.

Maybe I have too, why else would Scott not want me?

We cautiously enter through the front gates, guns, fireballs and claws drawn. Ben, the great master of deception, changed his form to that of an eagle but upon entry of the castle grounds decides a human's more fitting. With a glow of yellow veins, the Ben I know best appears besides us, awkwardly replacing his clothing.

"What did you see?" I ask about his scouting journey.

His head shakes. "Nothing. They've definitely abandoned this hideout."

"Should we split up?" Aiden asks.

"No, I think it's for the best if we stay together this time," I reply. Bad things happen when you're alone.

Inside, the building has been completely cleared out. All the rooms are void of furnishings, as expected, but why was it so necessary to remove them? What secrets hid in the dining room table or the mirror on the wall? What stories would the rug tell, and what tales would the picture frames share? What happened here?

Am I doomed to be this empty? Will everyone eventually leave me?

"What were they doing here?" Jia whispers.

"You don't need to whisper." Aiden leans against the stone

wall. "There's no one here." The wall crumbles further under his weight, causing him to slip onto the floor, making a great noise.

"Well, if anyone is, they definitely heard that. So now there's no need to whisper," she replies as we all move past him.

The corridors are so narrow I'm surprised they were built this way. Surely this was a poor idea. If an earthquake struck, I can only imagine the chaos as people tried to escape down these halls. Then again, they build a moat—an old ideology that a wall of water could protect you from the forces of nature. That must've been a nasty shock.

As is rejection.

"I have something," Ben says. We rush over.

"What is it?" I ask.

He points a light at the ground, and the floor lights up blue. "Blood. A lot of it. Enough to kill anyone."

"Hey, look at this," Jia shouts from a nearby room. "Someone propped this window open with a baton."

I piece together a theory. "Maybe this is how Jess escaped."

"After she killed someone," Ben states. "She's a cold-hearted killer."

I shake my head. "No, she's not."

"Face the facts, Ella. She tried to kill five people the other day. Five of our people. And from the video feed, it seemed like she didn't even hesitate," he argues.

"To her, they weren't the good guys," I argue back. "To Jess, they're all people trying to capture her. The Red Suits, the protectors, we're no different."

"That doesn't change the fact it's a cold thing to do, killing someone."

He's right.

"She wasn't born cold; life made her that way. And right now, our world isn't helping," I say. "But there's something coming, a change, and someone like her, from a world like Earth, would be really useful."

Ben doesn't have a response.

"Ella, Ben. You might want to come see this," Jia shouts from the distance. Somehow during my chat with Ben, Jia and Aiden disappeared.

We follow her voice down the hall and through a set of black double doors into a small tower room. They stand in wait around something on the floor, decorated by a stretch of light escaping from a small window. My stomach is upside down as we move closer to the spot.

There's that voice again, the thousand worries, the hundred fears. I'm not good enough. I'll never be good enough. If Scott doesn't want me, will anyone? Will the people of Biack accept me? Will the people of the BCD accept me? What if I can't solve this? What if I can't save the world? What's waiting for me in this room? Is it more doubt?

But it's not. It's another black-tipped rose. And under its petals lies a hand-written card.

Welcome to the rebellion.

Chapter Seventeen

Jess

He didn't leave me. He picked me. He stayed.

Awkward looks are the only sound during our journey out of the forest, besides the shaking of our damp bodies in the chill of the air. And the looks don't go away as we move through a desolate town. If anything, they only get more powerful, more painful and more frustrating. Many times I attempt to make conversation, but words fail me. How do I express my gratitude without showing my fractures?

As we walk, his hand brushes against mine; neither of us reacts. It seems like we're going to continue this pretence of ignorance. After all, we're self-preserving people.

He opens his mouth as if to speak but then a quick decision snaps it shut. Does he want to ask me why I didn't go with them? I can't answer that. Maybe that's why he hasn't asked.

I go to talk, but words can't form. The question is clear in my head: why are you here with me? But the only answers I can think of, I don't want to know. Either he's still gathering intel, or he doesn't trust me on my own, or he's going to try convince me to go back to the BCD. Or he wants to be with me. Maybe it's all four. I don't know what's worse.

I'm beginning to wonder if this silence will ever lift when we make another exciting discovery, an old station wagon.

"These are old even on Earth." I rush over to it, admiring the red paint work and the still-inflated tires. A sharp pull, and the door swings open. Without meaning to, I manage to blow dust everywhere. This car is *so* old.

"Does it work?" Will finally speaks.

A bit of fiddling, and it roars to life with a long-held cough. "Yeah, it works."

He climbs into the passenger seat after removing as much dust as possible, and that's when I have an idea. "Hey, do you wanna learn how to drive?" I ask.

"I'm good right here," he responds.

I'm going to pull him out of his comfort zone. "If you're coming with me, you might as well feel what it's like to be in the driver's seat."

Reluctantly he finds himself behind the wheel. "No one drives anymore."

"Where I come, from it's cool to learn useless skills." He doesn't seem impressed. "The peddles go clutch, break, acceleration. Like the alphabet backwards." I start the lesson. "First put your foot on the clutch." The engine roars. "Okay, now try the *other* clutch." No more roaring. "Now move into first gear, and then find the biting point while pressing the accelerator with the other foot."

"Biting point? First what?"

"Gear." Blank stare. "Okay, I'll do it." I move the gear stick. The car lets me, but he still looks confused.

"Now what?"

"Slowly lift your foot off the clutch," I say, "and I mean slowly. Like, think old-lady-at-the-checkout slow."

True to my order, slowly the car starts to move. But then it quickly stalls.

He hits the steering wheel. "I did what you said. This stupid thing is too old."

"Hey, it has feelings. Probably. Try again, but when you feel the car start to, like, judder, give it some gas."

"Judder? Gas?"

"Shake and acceleration," I answer.

He gives it another go, but again it stalls. The repeated failure increases his anger, which leads to him unleashing a vicious attack on the steering wheel after his third failure. I can't hide my laughter.

"You think this is funny?" He's so mad. "These stupid machines died out for a reason. They're trash." He spits out, "Why do you need three peddles? What's wrong with stop and go?" The more he talks, the angrier he gets. "What's the point of this gear thing, and why does the car stop every time it starts? I thought cars were meant to move." He's not wrong. "I don't need to learn to drive this stupid thing, and I also don't want to. They're old and they shake too much and they don't do what you want and…and…argh." He hits the steering wheel again.

I suck in my lips, trying not to laugh. When he looks up, I avoid eye contact.

He sighs. "Just say it."

I can't hold the laughter in anymore. "I guess you could say it's driven you up the wall."

It's clear he doesn't understand my joke, but after a while he starts to laugh anyway. We soon decide it's for the best we switch seats; after all, this is my journey. He does express a grunt of annoyance, though, as I'm able to start the car smoothly without stalling.

After we travel I don't know how many miles down the road, Will gets out the book from his back pocket. Normally I'd be more focused on the road but considering its long empty stretches and there's literally nothing to drive into, I think I'm allowed a nosy glance over at him.

"What are you reading?" I ask.

He replies, "*The Drought*. It's a love story set in The Plains."

"A love story? You know, where I'm from, if a guy's reading something, it normally has a lot of action, blood and guts."

"That's stupid," he states before adding, "I'll read anything I haven't read yet."

"So what happens? And what's The Plains?"

"The Plains is the continent where all the crops are grown and all the livestock is kept. And it only takes one disaster—one drought, one earthquake, one hurricane—to destroy people's livelihood. So it's a pretty depressing place."

"And I'm guessing the love story somehow involves a disaster destroying a farm?" I suggest.

"When I get more than a page into it, I'll let you know."

I leave him in silence to read, although I can't help but

wonder what I've missed about The Unbreakable Boy. In the dreams, he was always the quiet one in the background, and no amount of years would reveal any more about his character. Who knew he would read love stories, he could get so angry when he couldn't do something or that we share the same taste for adventure? Who knew?

"So what do you do for fun?" he asks after minutes of silence. "Besides driving off cliffs, running through minefields and getting into messy situations."

"That sounds like a typical day on Earth for me," I flash him a smile, "but when I'm not off risking my life, I drink tea." He wants more. "And I draw."

"What do you draw?" He turns to me. "Things like that house?"

"Normally what I see in the dreams." I shrug.

"You've seen me in your dreams," he teases. "Are there pictures of me all over your bedroom wall?"

I release my hand from the steering wheel to slap his arm. I lie, "Actually, I'm more of an Aiden girl."

He laughs. "Aiden? Wow."

"Well, not since I met him. Turns out you're all terrible."

"Well, Ella made you seem so... so—"

I interrupt, "So what?"

"So nice. But you're just as terrible as us."

After a small break, I say, "I was lying." I quickly clarify, "You're not all terrible. I mean, you are, but they're okay." He grins. "I guess it's just... Like, the more time I spend here, the more I think maybe this could be my world. Maybe you guys are my people? Because I could never find my people on Earth."

"What happened?"

It's strange; I haven't thought about any of it for a while. "I tried to fit in on Earth, but I could never find my group. I'm not smart enough to be a nerd, creative enough to be artsy or scary enough to be a rebel. Too privileged to be working class but not enough to be middle. Everywhere I looked I never ticked enough boxes." I shrug. "So I found a pretty best friend all the guys wanted and a popular boyfriend all the girls wanted. My grades were average; my life was average. I went to parties but I wasn't the life of them. I had a circle of friends but I couldn't talk to them about anything. And I thought that was what I was supposed to do. I thought that made me happy; I thought I just had to act like I belonged."

He takes some time to think before replying. "I think you've got it wrong. People are complicated. They're more than ticks in a box."

"But everyone belongs somewhere."

"Yes. But fitting in isn't belonging. You can't belong to a label or a place or a value." He opens up his book. "People are too complicated to be defined by something so vague."

I frown. "So what am I meant to do? How do I find my people, my place, my home?"

He flicks the page. "You build it."

We're starving by the time we arrive in the next town.

Rows of detached houses line the wide streets as the sun sets in the distance, creating a beautiful shadow over the world before us. The rising moon has a tint of pink, probably caused somehow by the sun, but oh God, is it not the most beautiful thing to witness.

As the shadows spread across what lays before us, the house lights start to spark to life, a useful tool when trying to decide which houses are vacant. And as luck has it, many seem to be so.

"Wait with the car," I instruct.

He jokes, "Why? Afraid someone's going to steal it?" As I head off, I can hear him mutter under his breath, "Piece of trash."

Much farther down the road sits a house with no sign of life. So much so that I can see the cobwebs forming across the windows; how marvellous they look under the pink moon. Upon the doormat lies an edge of snow. At least now I have confirmation it's winter here too.

I try the door, remembering Will's previous statement about locks, and just as he assumed, it opens with little sound. Inside, coats hang from the wall; there's a tenant. Maybe they're away. Either way, it encourages me to move slow as I head for the kitchen.

Slinging my rucksack around to the front, I start to shove the kitchen's contents inside. People must live here—there's way too much food. I'm halfway through the cupboards when I hear the car horn. Shit, is that a warning? Is the car even close enough to see? The front door starts to open to the sound of a happy couple. Shit.

After I dive into the pantry, I watch through the gap in the door as the couple falls against the countertops. Something about this is too familiar. Why are these strangers creating this pit in my stomach? I grab a shelf as I struggle to stand; I feel myself slipping away. What's happening to me?

I can't escape it.

It was a school day. My mother was out running errands with her friends after she'd dropped Everett and I off at school. I'd forgotten Scarlett's birthday present and she'd told me that without it we couldn't continue to be best friends. It wasn't hard to sneak home; I wouldn't even call it sneaking.

The spare key was hidden under a plant pot containing white roses. I thought the house was empty. When I entered my dad's study to find wrapping paper, I had no fear of discovery. Then I heard someone come in the front door. I was hiding in the cupboard and watching through a gap in the door when he walked into the room.

As the happy couple starts to spin around the room, dancing to silence, I remember how my father paced. Something was wrong; I was too young to understand what.

I watch as their lips fell against each other in a way my parents never got to experience again.

I was too young to realise what was happening. I kept waiting for him to leave but he didn't. He fell into that desk chair and never got up. When he picked up that pencil, I thought it was to sign documents, not write a letter. And when he started looking at his gun, I thought he was thinking about where to place it. So, when he put it to his head, I didn't understand.

The sound overwhelms me; it's so real, I can't distinguish between reality and memory. And what a terrible memory to be trapped within.

Just as I did when I was eight, I run.

Straight past the couple, past my dad. Straight out their house, out my house; I don't stop. Then someone grabs me—it's my mum. No, it's Will. They ask me what's wrong but I can't hear; I can't escape the sound. That sound, the start of what my life became.

He shakes me through my tears, but I can't escape. A lifetime of running won't get me away from that scene. A lifetime of suppressing memories, of pretending to be someone else. The Girl from Far Away will never be far enough.

"I don't know where I'm going." I finally form words through the waterfall. "I don't know where I'm going," I repeat.

"That's okay." His hands hold me still. "Come with me."

I shake my head. "I can't," I mumble. "I can't escape."

"You already have." His voice is so calm. "Come back with me to the BCD. Work with us. Stay with us."

"No." I shake him off.

He follows me away from the car. "Why not?"

"Because I'm bad," I turn and shout, but the anger isn't aimed at him. "And you're good. And I'll ruin everything you've built as I drag my disasters around with me." The tears stop as this great fury replaces them. "I belong on my own where I can't damage anyone else with my cracks." Where no one else can leave me. "I belong far away, far away from everyone."

He's mad. Worse than before. Worse than I've ever known him to be. "What's it like to pity yourself so much?" he shouts back.

"What?" I rage.

"You heard me," he continues to yell. "What's it like to see yourself as this tragic being?"

"I don't—"

He interrupts, "Because you're right. You're not good. You're a mess. You show no guilt for the people you hurt and you don't care about the chaos you've thrown our world into." It keeps going. "And maybe, maybe, we'd be better off if you never stepped foot on our soil. But you did." His voice is enraged. "Jessica Durand, you're cold, and lonely, and tragic." A pause. "But you belong with us."

I don't have a response; I don't have a plan. I just stand, right there in the middle of the street, as the rain starts to pour. And by God, it soaks everything as Will's words start to sink in. And that's when I move towards him.

The Unbreakable Boy and The Girl from Far Away.

Finally, in a long-awaited moment, we intertwine. A moment that pushes us against the car as my lips crush into his; a moment that rips at our clothes as if they're wet acid to our skin.

He breaks away. "Are you sure?"

"Yes." I push his hair out of his face. "Are you?"

He picks me up. "Yes."

And so it's here, in the middle of the street, that we have sex in the passenger seat.

Chapter Eighteen

Ella

Aiden paces back and forth across Ben's lab. With clenched fists, it's easy to see how much anger this confusion's stirring within him. Small amounts of soot start to decorate his arm as the flames burst out in sharp and quick attempts at existing. But their attempts are in vain as Jia, resting against the wall, puts out the fire.

"She was tipped off." Aiden starts to work through his confusion. "Someone who knew about our trip is her person on the inside." He stops. "Who knew about the trip?"

Ben looks to him. "After I booked it with the stealth leader, I came back here. I didn't speak to anyone else until we left."

"I went back to my room too. I called my parents, but the call cut out before I could tell them much," Jia says. She rarely gets to speak to her parents; they aren't exactly the easiest people to get hold of.

Jia's parents are travellers. Like her, they were born on a ship somewhere in the ocean; they were birthed in waves and grew in storms. They report to no higher authority, they follow no particular plan—they just travel where the winds take them and witness what they have to show.

I think for a while Jia knew of her gift, of the oceans she could control; her parents called her their good-luck charm, but they had no idea what she really was. It wasn't until she was eleven and found herself in the worst storm of her life that she fully unleashed the control within her.

They happened to have a special passenger on their ship that day, a protector from the BCD. And so it wasn't long before she was pulled from the only life she knew and brought here.

"I know I didn't tell anyone, so unless it was the stealth leader, it has to be someone you told, Ella," Aiden says. "Who did you tell?"

"Scott," I reply. "He must've told someone."

"Where did he go after he was with you? Do you have any idea who he would've told?" Jia enquires.

I shake my head. "I don't know where he went." Far away from me. "He could have told anyone; it wasn't a secret."

Aiden kicks the table. *"Argh."*

"Okay, so it could be anyone," Jia states.

"Why didn't Jess tell us who it was? *She has someone working for her in the BCD."* Aiden gets her voice all wrong. "That's great, but we already knew that."

I say, "Maybe she doesn't know who it is? If she doesn't know their name, then how is she supposed to tell us?"

"It's still no help telling us something we already know," Aiden mutters.

Ben bangs on the table to draw our attention. "Why are we

missing the important issue?" We all glance between us. "The note?"

"Welcome to the rebellion," I repeat.

"Yeah." Ben gestures in relief then continues to question us. "But what rebellion?"

Jia speaks. "The one written in the prophecies?"

Ben applauds. "That very one."

"This is our time," I whisper.

Ben hears me. "It's beginning to seem that way, yes."

"So what's the story again? I wasn't listening when you told me," Aiden asks.

Ben's mad. "I've told you so many times."

Aiden shrugs. "Yeah, but most of what you say is so boring."

"It dates back to the *Last King*," I interrupt before they erupt in argument. "With his dying breath, he swore vengeance on the six. He swore that one day their peaceful world would erupt in flames of rage. And that the only way to save their crumbling world would be in a great sacrifice, which would only be possible if the six were reunited." I smooth down my skirt. "Jess being here reunites the six."

"But," Aiden says, "she wants to return to Earth."

"If we help her go home, she'll never come back to help us," Ben says.

They all turn to me.

I reply, "We don't know that." They frown. "What if we ask her to help us first?"

"Hmm," Aiden starts slowly, "but what exactly do we need

her help with?"

"I don't know." I turn pleadingly to Ben.

He speaks. "Right." Grabbing markers, he draws an idea map across the wall. "What do we know so far?"

"The Red Suits are led by a woman called The Rose, who wants to start a rebellion," Aiden says. "And she's been involved in most crimes and disasters since the creation of the Dome."

"If not all crimes and disasters," Jia adds.

I say, "And the Red Suits wanted Jess for some reason. Either for her specific gift or because she's from Earth and that's somehow useful to them."

Ben continues to draw. "They kidnapped scientists working on the Last King project, and anyone they couldn't kidnap they tried to kill. They really didn't want us to work on it."

We all stand back and stare at the wall. It's a mess of scribbles, drawings of roses and Red Suits mixed amongst words. But what does it mean? Why did they kidnap scientists working on a history project? And why did they need Jess? And what, oh what, does any of this have to do with a rebellion?

"The Last King. The crown. Jess. Portals. The gems," I mutter until it hits me. "I have it."

❖❖❖

There's a weird duplicate feeling that accompanies my visit to the prison cells on floor forty-five. As the other side of the glass starts to come into vision, I look for her. I search for her tattered jacket that used to lie on the bed, and I scan the floor for the small drops of blood that escaped the vial. I hunt for the human who can't exist but somehow does. Instead I find Damien.

"Hey." I wave.

He's lying on the bed, staring above. I wonder for a second if he didn't hear me. Maybe my guilt swallowed my voice. But soon he turns to meet my eyes before jumping at the sight. Within a beat, he's standing before me, hands pressed against the glass.

"Your Highness, I'm... I... You—" He finds himself. "Do you have news?"

My words fumble. "No. Yes. Well. We saw Jess." His eyes light up; even if he isn't the spy, he still knows her name. I guess everyone in the BCD knows by now. "She confirmed there's someone here working against us."

"But..." He pauses. "She didn't exonerate me."

I shake my head. "She didn't give us a name."

"It's not me. I didn't do this," he pleads.

I place a hand on the glass opposite his. "I believe you. Someone leaked a recent trip we took. The Red Suits were there not long before us." I press against the glass, almost hoping I can touch his skin. "They left us a note."

"But surely that proves my innocence."

I don't know what to say.

"Why did you come here?" he asks.

"To let you know I'm going to get you out."

He backs away, and our hands forever part. "I believe you'll try, but you can't save everyone." He chokes on a laugh. "Have you heard my punishment? Death. They want to send a mes-

THE GIRL FROM FAR AWAY

sage; they're upset with the continued losses against the Red Suits."

I shake my head. "No. My father would never allow that."

"They don't listen to him anymore. He can't save me." He's panicking; he paces around, grabbing his head as his chest rushes up and down under his breath.

"So I will." I raise my voice to draw his attention back. "I won't let them do this to you."

Suddenly he stops pacing. After a brief moment he comes back to the glass, this time pressing a single hand on the barrier. "Just promise me you'll make sure they're okay."

"Who?"

"My brothers and sisters."

I nod. I decide it's best not to ask any more questions and risk upsetting him further. He retreats back to the bed, continuing as before to watch the ceiling. I wait a few moments then leave; I don't think he notices.

❖❖❖

Day Palace is undeniably beautiful. Sitting proud at the top of the city, I'm still not sure if the hill is man-made or natural, although I'm sure I should know. It watches guard over The Capital. On one side, it's protected by the river Tenebris, which separates it from the rest of the city. And on the other side it's enclosed by vast gardens stretching out beyond sight. Over the last ten or so years, protectors have started to patrol the walls and guard the historic structure.

There are over five hundred rooms, including multiple ballrooms of varying sizes, formal, informal. Spare dining rooms, a kitchen to serve for hundreds, offices for the staff, guests and anyone who might need one. A few modest museums, uncountable bedrooms and bathrooms. It's a vast building.

Every detail is pre-planned. From the ivy crawling up particular exterior walls to the sparkling of the jewels that hang from the illuminators as the light hits them from designated angles; the floating petals dragged in by the wind that proceed to drift across the indoor pool before returning to the outdoor pool. And the gentle movements of the sheer curtains as the breeze flows in through windows that have been opened just the right amount. Every place setting at every table is measured in accuracy, every bush is trimmed to the right concentration of neat and every book in the two-storey library is located in just the right place. Oh, the order of it all.

But something's different.

As I enter the hallway outside my room, I can already feel the warmth of the candles that I soon discover decorating every surface. Ordered across the bed are identical, freshly picked daisies that give the appearance of being tossed casually around. Carefully placed on the bedside table, between my trinket dish and my solid-gold lamp, lies my favourite pink champagne and two flutes, each resting on an appropriately sized glass coasters. And the windows have been sprung open, allowing the breeze to shoot the sheer white curtains around the room, dancing through the air but not dislodging the candles or daisies.

"Are you sure?" I ask him.

Behind the fluttering curtains, Scott nods. "Are you?"

"Yes." And I really think I am.

So I let go of myself.

And together we fall into pre-planned disorder.

Chapter Nineteen

Jess

If only this car had a radio.

It's not awkward as much as it's uncomfortable. As I drive us in no real direction, I wonder if he thinks he's won. And I wonder even more, has he?

There's that fight for words again. He'll go to speak then stop, and then I'll try in his place but we'll both fail. If I could have a superpower, it'd be to read minds; that would be useful right about now.

But I do have a superpower. I'm special. No—Ella has one too. So we're both special. Wait, in the dreams the others did too—no, that can't be real because then Will… No. So it's just me and Ella, and now I get to decide whether I want to be a superhero or supervillain. What if I want to be neither? What did Jia say? Something about a prophecy. Normally I'd immediately dismiss that idea, but since I've discovered this ability to travel great distances in an instant, I'm starting to open up to it.

The sun is almost in the middle of the sky when I break the silence. "What do you know about this prophecy?"

Caught off guard, he takes a moment to reply. "I've never thought much of old stories." Something from our time together is telling me he's lying.

"So you don't believe it's true?" I say. "But then, why all this talk of me belonging?"

My brother would stress at how much I look away from the road while I drive, but as Will takes longer to respond, the road loses more and more of my attention.

He finally speaks. "I want you to stay."

The car swerves as I only just miss a tree. Good thing Everett's not here.

"And—" he's grabbing the door handle, "—I'd like to stay alive." I laugh. "Do you believe in the prophecy?"

I pull a face. "I don't even know what the prophecy is." I'm not even sure I know what a prophecy is. "But I like the idea of someone in another world writing a story about me." He grins. "What?" I should really pay attention to the road. But it's not like I'm going to come across another driver. "Seriously, what?"

"You sound like Ella." He smirks. "It's like you're sisters or something."

"Why's that so funny?"

He falls back in his seat while pulling out his book. "I never paid attention in history class. But I know the prophecy involved twin siblings, and one was trapped on Earth."

Earth. The place where nothing good grows. Biack. The place where apparently nothing bad grows, until recently at least. Every minute longer I spend on this world, I fall more in love with the distance between me and Earth. I'm finally starting to admit that even though I'm probably billions of miles from my house, I've never felt more at home.

What if all these years this girl I was dreaming about was important? Not just to her world and her people, but to me. Sisters? I have a sibling and I'm not looking to replace him, but I've grown up with Ella's life in my head, and she's grown up with mine. I've barely spoken to her, but I think I know her more than anyone else.

I think cynical Jess died the moment she woke in that alley. Since then I've been living a lie, pretending I don't feel the ways I feel, telling myself how badly I want to return to Earth and denying how alive I've suddenly become. Maybe other worlds exist. And maybe prophecies are a thing. Maybe Ella has powers, and maybe I do too.

"Anyway, if you want to know more about this prophecy, you should ask Ella."

"Okay, I will." He immediately looks up from the pages of his book. "I'll go with you. But first I have some questions about what'll happen to me when I do."

"What do you want to know?" he returns.

Everything. "Will they interrogate me? Hurt me?"

"No," he replies like a dart. "Ella can stop that. You'll probably need to answer the same questions still, but she can be the one asking. And she won't hold you in a cell if you go willingly."

"And what about the people I killed? What happens to me because of that?"

He thinks. "Ella will protect you."

Okay. "And can you help me control this…power?"

"Yes, we can teach you how to control your gift," he responds.

"Just like you taught Ella to control her 'gift.'" It looks like he wants to add something but fights it back. "What do you need my help with?"

"I don't know." How would he? Stupid question.

I raise an eyebrow. "Do you think it'll be dangerous?"

He grins. "I hope."

"So then," I say, "how do we contact the future queen?"

How do I go home?

❖❖❖

The car runs out of gas outside a petrol station. But it's ironic because the station is in ruins, so even if there's fuel inside the storage tanks, we're unable to retrieve it. We continue our journey on foot, hands brushing against the wind while it blows our hair everywhere. It's not far till the nearest city—they seem to appear out of nowhere—and as it's now their rush hour, it doesn't take us long to find our method of contact.

"Can I borrow your hexagon?" Will asks a passerby.

The man, smartly dressed and neatly groomed, hands us a smartphone-like tablet. After Will hits buttons on the screen, I can hear a distant ring, although it's more like a repetitive beep, but I'm assuming that's the dial tone here.

"Ella?" He sounds so relieved to hear her voice. "Yeah, it's me. I actually have someone here who wants to speak to you."

His arm stretches out as the phone moves closer. I hesitate

before accepting his offering and even then I just place it next to my ear and stand frozen. Ella's voice rings excitedly. I guess she likes surprises. I'm the one who asked for this, so why am I now regretting everything? *Enough. Jessica Durand, you're many things, but you're not a coward.*

I speak. "We'll be waiting at an abandoned petrol station near this city." Will points to a sign. "The city of Castrum. Don't bring soldiers." I press the big end button on screen.

Receiving the phone, Will hands it back to the man. While they engage in pleasantries, I examine the city around us. If I'm making a mistake, then this could be the last time I'm free. So what do I do with this freedom?

"Tell me about Castrum," I say.

"I've never been here before. I don't know anything about it."

I frown. "Well then, we need to ask someone about it." He has this weird expression on his face, maybe confusion? "I need to know where the best restaurants are or if there are any land-marks we need to visit."

"But we need to leave? Ella will be looking for us at the petrol station?"

"I know, but...what if I never come back here? What if I never get to explore your world again? I need to make this visit count."

He laughs. "You'll get to explore our world again, but I can't promise you'll ever come back here."

"Why not?"

"Because The Cities are the most boring part of Biack." He

starts the journey back to the car, and I reluctantly follow.

"So, if I could go anywhere on Biack, where would I go?" I've barely seen England.

He thinks for a while before answering. "I think you'd start with The Old World and try to understand where we came from. Then maybe The Sparse? To understand why." He pauses. "You'd have to visit The Plains and The Tribelands, but you'd want to see the Illuminated Forest and Dragon Isle." He laughs to himself. "Also you'd need to climb Vici Peak and come face to face with a giant."

"What about ride a unicorn?"

"Yeah, you can do that in The Plains." He misses the joke somehow. "There's so much to see, Jess, and so much to do."

I say, "Well, write this down, make me a plan and one day we'll do it all."

The rest of the journey back to the car is accompanied with silent thought.

I think meeting at an abandoned petrol station is a good idea; it's isolated, so I know whoever turns up has to be Ella. Who else would go there? And it's also surrounded by woods, just in case I decide last minute not to go with her. Must be prepared.

At the petrol station, we sit on the curb for ages, which was to be expected. Ella does have to travel here by conventional means, after all. Will's occupied by his book. Good for him. Meanwhile, I have to sit and occupy myself with my thoughts, and that'd be okay if we only had to wait an hour or so. At least two hours must pass before I interrupt his reading.

"Are you more than a page in now?" I ask.

He replies, "Nope, it's a long page." I playfully nudge his arm. "I'm almost done. You can read it after me if you want?"

"I don't really read."

His interest peaks. "Why?"

"I don't know," I state. "I do like movies, though." He turns to me. "Not the kind with happy endings but the tragic ones, the ones that make you ache after they're over because—"

"You can't stop thinking about them," he interrupts.

"Yeah. I mean, no one remembers the happy endings."

"Of course. They don't feel real." We pause. He says, "You know, you get that with books too, but it's better."

"Yeah, well…" I fall away from the seriousness. "None of it compares to a good cup of tea."

Another hour passes before we speak again; the early morning is creeping upon us. This time, Will breaks the silence.

"Someone's coming." He doesn't seem happy. "It's too quiet."

"What do you mean?"

Abruptly, he stands up. "It's not Ella. Someone else has found us first."

Out behind the trees, I can see subtle movement, although it could just as easily be the wind blowing the leaves or small animals running around their home. Will seems convinced it's not as he peers closer, following a particular breeze. Not willing to take chances, I find the gun within my rucksack and, after some thought, exchange a few of the bullets with the spare one and pass it to Will. He immediately turns to thank me but before he can speak, something stops him.

The Unbreakable Boy pushes me down, his body falling protectively over mine. I don't need protecting. I try to make this clear as I push him off me. He falls to the floor dramatically. I take aim but, unable to find a target, I begin to doubt there ever was an enemy.

And then I realise I was wrong—I do need protecting. There is an enemy.

And how wrong I was to call him The Unbreakable Boy, because as the hole in his chest floods red, I finally see him as human.

"Will!" Falling to my knees, I try to stop the bleeding with my hands. "No, no, no, no, no," I mumble as the warm liquid leaks through my fingers. "No, you can't." I can hear footsteps approaching but I'm unable to leave his side. "You're going to be fine."

"I know." His words are strained but his veins, his veins are glowing green.

What?

He fires at the monsters approaching in suits of red. Pushing me off, he reveals the wound in his chest has almost disappeared. I'm still as I witness the remaining hole healing before my eyes.

How? No. That's not possible. I saw the blood. I felt the hole. I saw it. I saw everything.

"Come on, get up." Will grabs me by my arm. "Are you blind?"

Am I blind? Have I lost my sight? Would that explain this?

"Jess!" Will pushes me back as another bullet flies into his arm in place of me. I fall onto the floor. His arm glows green and before my eyes the wound disappears. What's wrong with me?

Is any of this real?

The Red Suits are gaining on us; I watch as they move and bullets fly. But they can't hurt me; none of this can hurt me. This isn't real. None of this is real. I'm dreaming, yes, I'm dreaming.

"What's wrong with you?" After dragging me behind a pump, he shakes me. "Why are you just standing there?" My fingers stroke the holes in his top. He finally realises. "I thought —" A Red Suit interrupts him but shortly receives a death sentence. "I thought you knew."

I don't have any words as my fingers play with the holes. Are the holes proof?

Will's getting desperate as the monsters keep coming. Soon he runs out of ammo and snatches my gun out of my clasp. I don't resist. Several shots later, he falls back behind the petrol pump. Counting ammo, he bangs his head back against the concrete.

"One shot." He sighs. "I need you, Jess." Why? He's a much better shot than me. I'd probably waste it.

The Red Suits are all within meters as Will tries to drag me towards the woods, somehow managing to escape their sight; maybe they can't see so well through their red covers. They're all in the station. The petrol station. Where, with some luck, that storage tank contains fuel, flammable fuel. And if a bullet is fired from a great enough distance, it'll pick up heat from air resistance and ignite. Will tries to resist as I grab the gun and fire, but when the station explodes into flames, and with it all the Red Suits, he lets the gun fall completely into my grasp. Science. And a bit of luck.

Flames fly out at us and Will shields me again. He doesn't bother to put out the fires that are spreading across his back, at least until we reach the safety of the woods. And that's when I finally find words.

"What the hell?" I start. "How did you do that. I saw you. I saw the bullet hole. How?"

"I thought you knew," he replies.

I laugh. "Well, clearly I don't, so why don't you tell me."

"You aren't the only person with a gift." He's still patting down the flames. "You saw Ella stop that bullet. A bullet you shot at me because you knew it couldn't harm me."

This is ridiculous. "If I knew bullets couldn't harm you, why would I take you hostage and threaten you with a gun?"

"I thought you were bluffing!" His voice rises to match mine. "I thought you were just trying to learn from me."

"Like you were trying to learn from me?" I shout. "If you could escape at any time, were you just using me?"

"Don't act all high and mighty. You used me too. If you didn't know about my gift, why did you keep me around? You seem to be a pretty capable killer," he shouts. "And if you did know about my gift, why did you take me with you in the first place if you knew a gun was useless against me?" He continues. "You did it to gain information. We're both guilty here."

Was everything an act?

"Don't." He notices my eyes planning an escape. "You've come so far. Don't turn back now."

"I travelled planets. Space, maybe even time. I don't know." My voice is breaking. "Just to learn you can't trust people any-where."

"I never lied." He tries to grab me, but I pull away. "I never lied about anything; it was all real."

"This—" I point to the faint black of my veins, "—this isn't real. This doesn't happen to real people. This doesn't happen." I stagger backwards.

"I'm real. You're real. This is really happening. You're just like us, Jess. We're the same."

"No. I don't know what I am, and I don't know what you are. But we're not the same." I want to get away, but the black is disappearing from my arms. Why isn't it working this time?

Noticing my arms, he smiles. "You don't want to leave."

"But I do!" I shout. "I hated my life on Earth. I hated being home and I hated going to school. I hated my friends and I hat-ed my boyfriend. The only thing I didn't hate was my brother, and he was forced to leave me. But despite all that, I'd rather be there than trapped in this world."

"Then go!"

I try but I can't. Why is this stupid ability working against me? I storm off into the woods. For several seconds, Will watch-es before beginning to chase after me. Why won't he let me go? Why won't this world let me go? I don't belong here, in this world of unbreakable boys and—wait, does that mean Fire Boy can control fire?

This is mad.

Chapter Twenty

Ella

Biack 27/01/2014

I thought I'd feel different, but I feel the same.

I try to focus on something other than myself as I rush into Ben's lab. "Ben, you'll never guess who called."

Stopping immediately, I realise he has company. Council member Adams stands in the centre of the room, disapproving of everything. I mean, I assume that's what he's doing from the look on his face. My presence certainly doesn't help.

"Who called?" he asks.

Ben's eyes yell warnings.

"No one important," I reply. "How can I help you, council member?"

He turns up his nose. "I was curious about your little trip yesterday, especially since there was no evidence showing the fugitive girl was there. So why did you visit the castle?"

"Just a hunch." I shrug. What if Adams is working for the Rose? He's taken a very keen interest in Jess and he could easily keep track of our movements, as he's just shown. But that would mean the Rose has people in the highest of places; above the council, it's only my father. That's a worrying thought.

"A hunch?" he says.

I decide it's best not to tell him anything, just in case. "I want to find Jess more than anyone else. But there's no information right now. All we have to act on is hunches."

He laughs. "Is that so?"

Out of his suit jacket, he reveals a folder. After he slides it across the table towards me, I find it contains numerous tip-offs and leads on Jess's whereabouts, including pictures from that drone. The protectors didn't have any of this. He's been running his own investigation.

"We don't need you to do our job for us," I state as the anger in my voice shows.

"It's not your job. You were never tasked with this." He heads for the exit. "But I expect that the next time you return from one of your little outings, you'll have the freak in your custody."

Ben grabs my arm to prevent me from doing something I'd regret. *Freak*. If he thinks that of her, he thinks that of us. There must be a way I can change his opinion of us; maybe bringing Jess here is that way.

Once he's out of hearing range, Ben speaks. "Who called? And please let it be someone who's going to piss him off."

I grin. "Who's the one person who could do that right now?"

"No." As I nod, he starts to laugh. "She wants us to come get her. Will did his job."

"I'll go book a stealth. Are you going to find the others?"

"Yeah," I say, "but can I ask you something before we go?"

With full seriousness, he turns to me. "Okay, what?"

"Do you think Adams could be working for the Rose?" I whisper. "It can't be Damien—she's still receiving information, and he's locked up."

He thinks for a while before answering. "Let's not tell anyone where we're going. Just to be safe." He smiles to himself. "You're starting to open your eyes."

✵✵✵

It wasn't the centuries that finally brought down the petrol station, it was flames from the very substance it stored. As it comes into view farther down the overgrown road, we're stunned by the charred remains of something that was once so important, although for a while now it's been obsolete. Several flames are still fighting when we arrive, but it doesn't take long for Aiden to kill them.

"What happened here?" he asks as we slowly move around the remains.

And then we notice the real remains.

Burnt bodies lie across the ground; judging from their positions, their final moments must've been a struggle. I try to contain the acid stirring in my stomach but I can't as it bursts out into a nearby bush. Jia rushes over to pat my back while the rest of the sick departs.

"It's okay." Her words are soft. "It's okay."

"It's not them," Ben shouts over. "They're all men."

"Last time I checked, Will was a man," Aiden replies.

"And last time I checked, his gift would prevent him from burning to death," Ben responds. "His body would heal faster than the flames could burn."

"Okay." I return to the graveyard. "How do we know if they were here?"

Ben searches around for signs. "Any clue would've perished in the flames. But someone had to light this place up."

"So, what, they were here waiting when these guys attacked?" Aiden asks.

Ben's voice rises, "How would I know? I wasn't here."

Will's absence hasn't gone unnoticed. Aiden and Ben have always had a fiery relationship, with every action somehow angering the other. But Will has always prevented their digs turning into anything serious. His brotherly friendship with Aiden and the mutual respect he shares with Ben put him in a different position to the rest of us. A position that's safe in the middle of them.

"Ben." I stop them before they can get into another argument. "Are there any signs showing where they went?"

His eyes dart around. "Well, if they were here, to start with, my guess is they're somewhere in there." He points into the woods.

"I think these were Red Suits," Jia says as she crouches next to the bodies.

Aiden replies, "Who else would it be?"

"But…" She seems confused. "Where's the rose?"

"It probably burnt to a crisp," Aiden answers.

Shaking her head, she starts to search around. "No. The roses found at the sites of fires were always untouched." Her head turns to us. "They were placed there afterwards."

The Red Suits are going to come back.

It's then, before anyone can reply to Jia, that I notice a tiny object flying through the air. So graceful and small, one blink and you could miss it entirely. Luckily for Jia, whom it's flying towards, my mind works faster than any bullet. Before any harm can come to my friends, I'm able to stop it in its tracks.

"They're here!" I yell as we all fall under cover.

I think there's five, dressed in suits and concealed under covers of red. Why red? If you wanted to hide in plain sight, black would be a much more suitable colour, so why didn't they just go all black? Unless there's something else they're trying to hide in plain sight. Does blood even show up against the red?

"Aiden, be careful with your flames and prepare to contain any fire that starts. We don't know how much stored fuel is left," I shout. "I don't want this place blowing up again, especially not with us in it."

Ben adds, "Any fuel will have burned out in the previous fire."

"Be prepared for Ben to be wrong," Aiden yells. "Got it."

If looks could kill, Jia would've won this fight the moment it started. Rain pours from the sky and she uses her gift to direct it at them; her veins light up blue. The waterdrops manage to distract their eyesight. It throws off their aim and destroys any energy blasts, but their ammunition seems never ending.

Aiden's entire body glows red as he struggles to work; any fire immediately fizzles out. But Jia's created gaps in the ocean to allow his flames to thrive. So, in a combined effort, she distracts them and he lights them up. And I think it's working.

Then Ben jumps into the mix. In a flash of green, his appearance changes to that of a wolf. Darting between the bullets I try to turn away, he charges straight towards the Red Suits. Saliva drools from his mouth, a growls escape through his teeth. While he runs, his claws change shape to become sharper and deadlier.

Ben approaches the Red Suits, they all turn their attention to him. Meaning we turn our attention to protecting him. And it proves to be no easy task, the rain no longer distracts their aim due to Ben's proximity. The perfect partnership between Jia and Aiden starts to fall apart as her attempts to blind the enemies kills his attempt to burn them.

A gut-wrenching scream roars through the air when Ben digs his teeth into one of the Red Suit's legs. In their moment of weakness, I rip the gun from their hands. Ben jumps to the next victim, again just trying to disable them. We repeat our previous actions. It's working.

But our luck runs out as Jia and Aiden's teamwork abruptly ends.

"Your water keeps putting out my fire!" Aiden turns on her.

The rain loses any hold she has over it. "*I'm* trying to distract them! What's your fire doing?"

"Nothing! Because the rain's getting in its way!" They move towards each other.

"That's because the rain's more important right now!" she fights.

He fights back. "Fire's always more important!"

"Not if you can't control it." She laughs. "Do you know how much focus it takes for me to do this?" Rain shoots directly at Aiden's face.

"Not as much as this." Both his arms light up. Wow, he can do it.

"Guys, stop it!" I join in. "Ben's going to get hurt!"

It's as if the universe heard me, because as soon as the last word slips from my lips, a painful cry screeches through the wind. And there, across from us, Ben falls to the floor in his human form. A pool of blood grows underneath his body that once again causes my stomach to stir. This is the price you pay when you lose your focus.

You lose control.

Chapter Twenty-One

Jess

"Stop following me!" I yell at him, but nothing changes.

"If you want me to leave you alone, why don't you go back to Earth?" he shouts back.

Because I can't. "What's your problem? Are you obsessed with me or something?"

"You're not that special, Jess." He laughs.

I'm sick of this now. Stopping in my tracks, I pick up a fallen branch and wield it like a baseball bat. My hands crumble under the weight, but I force myself to keep it together. "So why won't you leave me alone, then?" I breathlessly yell.

He can tell I'm struggling; he gestures to my ridiculous bat. "Are you serious?" I try to form a response but I'm dying under this branch. I can't even wipe the rain from my face. "Look, you're going to hurt yourself before you even get close to hurting me, so just put it down."

"No." I strain. "Leave me alone."

Stepping forward, one of his hands grasps the side of the branch, preventing me from swinging it into him. I admit defeat and let him take it, throwing it onto the nearby ground. What does he want from me?.

"Are you done running now?"

"Don't you know who I am?" His hand on my wrist prevents me disappearing into the overgrowth. "Are we really back to this? Are you going to force me to come with you?" I say as I shake his hand off. "You know that friendship we spent a week building? Yeah, you're kinda burying it right now."

His eyes rage. "Friendship? Is that all we are to each other?"

It was just sex. "What else would we be?"

Before he can respond, our petty squabble is interrupted by the distant sound of guns. We killed them all, didn't we?

"I thought they were all dead." Will takes the words out my mouth.

We race back through the forest towards the site where the ending began; smoke is still seeping around the trees. The air becomes thick with the smell of things that should never be burned as the sound of gunfire increases.

When we arrive in sight of the station, we discover its new inhabitants—more Red Suits and those meddling kids. While the Red Suits take cover in the trees to one side, Ella and her friends hide behind the ruins of the station to our other side. Her pastel-blonde hair sticks to the rain on her face, but somehow she still looks perfect. It's as if she was made for battle.

"We need to help." Will begins to move towards them, but I grab him by his wrist.

"No. We need to stay out of sight," I demand, and reluctantly he obliges.

It turns out Fire Boy really can control fire, and The Girl of Oceans is really "The Girl of Oceans." They look like fools waving their arms around, but I now know they're the cause behind the weird movement of the rain and the flames sparking from the ground. It's just like it's always been in my dreams, so why is it so hard to accept as reality?

Darting across the gap between the two groups, a wolf that isn't really a wolf prepares to attack. The Invisible Boy, ironically named, digs his teeth into one of the Red Suit's legs. And slowly, one by one, each of the Red Suits start to fall victim to his assault. There are only two left when the rain returns to normal and the fire disappears, and with a gut-wrenching cry, Ben falls to the floor in perfect timing of a roaring gunshot.

"No!" Will jumps up from our hiding spot.

I grab his arm as he starts to move. "You can't! They can't know we're here!"

"For life's sake, Jess!" He yanks his arm back. "For once, can it not be about you?" He starts to leave. "I won't tell them you're here, but I'm going to help my friends. And if you care at all for anyone other than yourself, maybe you'll help too."

"And what? Sentence myself to death? Because that's what that is!" I half shout, but it's not loud enough for him to hear over the rain as he runs off.

Sprinting out from the cover of the forest, The Unbreakable Boy shrugs off the gunfire as his body wraps around The Invisible Boy. Taking enough damage to kill twenty men, I think, he carries Ben to safety with the others. After a chorus of hugs and relief, the group gathers around Ben engaged in unknown conversation; their backs block their actions.

I turn to leave, planning a journey that'll take me far away from this scene, but I can't go. What's wrong with me? I don't know these people and I don't owe them anything. This isn't my world and this isn't my fight. Still, I can't walk away. I try, but my legs won't obey.

"Why are you doing this?" I shout to the sky, to the universe.

No response.

I continue, "How can you expect that of me? How can you force me to help, to be good?"

Nothing.

I fall to my knees. "This is cruel!"

The rain pelts at my face.

"You made me like this! You made me cold! You let all those bad things happen to me—you caused all that hurt. Why?"

As lightning strikes behind me, I spin around. The sky roars.

I tell myself I don't care about them because I'm not someone who cares.

And I tell myself to not think about them because I'm all that matters.

And I tell myself I'll get myself killed. Because this isn't my war. And this isn't my home.

But oh, dammit. I know I'm just going to do it anyway.

What a stupid idea, I think as I pick up another fallen branch. Why has the universe burdened me so? I wonder as I sneak towards the remaining two Red Suits under the cover of gunfire and rain. And if there is a God, why oh why did he make me so bad, only to make me so good?

No one notices me until with strength I didn't know I had, I knock one of the monsters to the floor.

Then they all notice.

Oh, shit.

I turn to the last remaining Red Suit, who's raising their gun to face me, when the branch I'm barely clutching flies from my hands and straight into their mummified head. Just like their companion, they too fall to the floor unconscious.

With a smile, Ella looks straight at me.

You know how sometimes in movies the spotlight shines on someone and the clouds part and it's incredible cliché? Well, the clouds do part, and the sun does shine, and she just stands there, in the middle of all the chaos, under a shining light, and it is cliché. But it's also real.

I start to walk towards her. Despite the abundance of deadly weapons and abilities, this fight's had a very different outcome to any I've previously been involved in. Mainly, no one's dead. Yet.

I get as close to them as I can before I find myself incapable of stepping any further. This'll have to do.

"Is he okay?" I say. Somehow I lack the strength to shout.

They're all staring.

Ella speaks first. "Are you?"

And Will said I wasn't special.

But as I look down, I realise he was right. Without another

word, I meet the same fate as the Red Suits. I fall to the floor.

✿✿✿✿

When I open my eyes, the sun's shining down on me. Wait. No, it's just a ceiling light.

"Hi," Ella whispers from my bedside.

I whisper back, "Hi."

For several moments, we watch each other in silence. I'm still trying to decide if this is real when she finally speaks again. "Shh, you're okay."

"Where am I?" I don't think it's a cell, so that's a start; it seems like a hospital room, but where are the windows? Maybe it's a hospital cell? "And how long have I been out?"

"A day. And you're at the BCD, in a treatment room. You're fine, by the way. Look." She gestures to my stomach, which is decorated in bandages, but there's no pain or discomfort. "That's just a precaution; the treatment you've received will allow you to operate at ninety-eight percent of your normal functions."

I pinch myself; this is real. "You're making it sound like I'm a robot." I pull myself up. "So what's the two percent I can't do?"

"I don't know." She doesn't have my humour. "The healer didn't say."

"You can't make any more bad jokes about tea." The Unbreakable Boy speaks from across the room. I didn't even notice he was here; he unfolds from an uncomfortable nap in his chair.

I hide a smile. "Did you say tea?"

"I'll go get you some." He rolls his eyes. "By the way, it's nice to know you can think about someone other than yourself. For a moment there, I didn't think it was possible."

"I'm a girl of many talents," I say. "Hey, question. Where are my clothes?" I tug at the awful white scrubs they've put on me—deja vu. "And who undressed me?"

Ella turns around to reveal a neatly folded stack of garments. Obviously, she's put that together. "That's your original clothing recovered from The Capital General Treatment Centre. It's been cleaned, and so has your jacket."

"At least you didn't clean the colour away." I still don't think she gets my humour. "So, what have I missed?"

"We unmasked the Red Suits you took down." I can't take all the credit.

"What was underneath?"

"People. Just ordinary people." She looks disappointed. "I don't know why they tried so hard to hide who they were from us. There are no links between any of them. They're all from completely different places on Biack. It wasn't…" She hesitates. "It wasn't the big discovery I thought it'd be."

"Yes, it is," I say. "You shattered their illusion. Until now, they were monsters, they were no one. Now you know they're just ordinary people. They have faces."

The biggest smile breaks out across her face. "You're right."

I reply. "I know. This is the first step. You guys have somewhere to start. You just need to figure out how they were recruited." She nods. Seriously, why is her hair so perfect? Not a strand out of place. And how has she kept her pink dress so clean? And why is she always in pink? "So…what about me? What happens to me now?"

"There's something I need to show you," she states.

"Is it dangerous? Apparently I have a thing for danger."

"I suppose there are minor hazards?" One day she'll get my comedy.

"I'll take it."

Chapter Twenty-Two

Ella

It's kind of poetic how the cracks in her skin match the crumbling buildings before us. Meanwhile, plant life breaks through the already fractured windows and wraps itself around the exterior, just like her hair around her face. There's something beautiful about ruins. Maybe it's knowing that once there was life in the empty. And maybe there can be life again.

"On Earth, we're somewhere in Brazil. It's a country in the continent of South America." Jess's stare is fixed on the wreckage as we walk through the old city. "The pilot showed me a map," she explains. "Although Brazil has a lot more people." She searches the city with her eyes. "In fact, it actually has people."

"This is one of the old cities. From the old world," I say.

"Old world?"

"Before people were forced underground," I answer. "Before the Dome, this continent was full of cities. But there were many earthquakes, and then came the scorching sun, and very quickly the cities became too dangerous, so people were forced to abandon them." In the distance before us, the side of a skyscraper topples to the ground with a thunderous crash. "None of these buildings can be fixed. To repopulate this area, you'd need to start fresh; scrap everything and rebuild."

"So, why don't you?"

"We don't need to. We have enough space in the new world. So, this place has become a monument to the life left behind."

What must it be like to see this world with fresh eyes? Untainted by the knowledge of all the threats and the history of disaster, with a blank canvas laid before you to make this world what you see. Because behind the damage, this place is beautiful.

"Why did you bring me here?"

I gesture around us. "To show you what happened to our world. It was magnificent, and then it crumbled. But we knew it was going to happen; all of this was predicted millennia ago."

"The prophecy?"

I nod. "It's more than a prophecy; it's our history," I begin. "Over two thousand years ago, Biack didn't exist. And neither did Earth."

"Okay, no." She starts laughing. "For a second, you guys really had me believing all this prophecy shit."

"It's true. There weren't two worlds, there was one—Biackearth. And it all began with the First Tree."

She shakes her head. "That sounds ridiculous. A tree? And what kind of a name even is *Biackearth*?"

"What kind of a name is Earth?" I reply. "It starts with a

vowel. Isn't that suspicious at all?"

She doesn't have an answer.

I continue. "Before anything, there was the First Tree, and from its roots grew the Throne of All. The tree was rumoured to have special abilities that helped create the world of Biackearth and ensured its survival. These abilities were said to be hidden within six gems that decorated its bark.

"Biackearth was ruled by a long line of kings who all sat on the Throne of All. The first of them was said to have carved it himself. They were just and fair rulers the people adored. They built a thriving world that grew at an alarming rate, but nevertheless they made it work. At least until the Last King—the first evil.

"He had all the power in the world, but it wasn't enough. The people followed his orders, but they still had free will. And so the fear that they could turn against him drove him mad. He ripped the six gems from the First Tree, along with its bark, and crafted a crown with the power to do anything. With this crown, he turned the people into mindless drones whose only purpose was to follow his every order. He created a world of suffering.

"But he didn't know that when he tore those gems from the First Tree, six protectors would be born to the world. These six protectors were legendary figures with abilities that matched the six gems. They were the world's salvation.

"There were the protectors of the planet—one of water with the ability to manipulate the very atoms that create the oceans. And one of fire, who could burn and alight anything in their reach. Then the protectors of the mind, one of deception who could change their form and manipulate how you saw them. And one of control who could move anything without a touch. Then finally the protectors of survival. One of health with the ability to heal themselves and others from any injury. And one of escape who could transport themselves and others across any distance with a single step.

"The stories tell that two of the six were twin brother and sister, who upon realising their gifts began the search for the other four. And together they started the journey that'd fuel legends. They rebelled from the king's control and fought for the will of the unknowing people. They battled his armies of drones and survived his attacks of nature. They saved cities from his rage and children from his vengeance. And then they saved each other, for they knew it'd only be possible to defeat him as six.

"They dedicated their lives to freedom, eventually breaking into his palace where he sat on his corrupted Throne of All. Legend has it, the First Tree was burning behind him as it struggled against the evil. And then the great fight began, and it lasted days.

"The palace was shielded by this bright light, so no one knows how it went down, but finally, when it was over, the Last King fell to his knees before them. But with his last few breaths, as he relinquished the throne, he cast his final act of ultimate evil.

"He split the world into two, Biack and Earth, and with it he split all the people. Families were broken in half, and partners were separated. Including the twins—one was trapped on Earth, while the other with the rest of the protectors remained on Biack. And instead of staying to meet a certain death, the Last King too disappeared to Earth, leaving behind only an empty, stoneless crown.

"They were devastated by the loss and the knowledge the world would never have its justice, and for a moment they thought the king had stolen with him the six gems. But as they looked down at their hands, they found the gems in their palms. They decided to hide each one out of reach, as they couldn't allow anyone ever again to possess the unlimited power found in the completed crown. When they were done, they hid the crown too.

"With all parts lost to the world, they set about repairing Biack but noticed it was as if nature itself had turned against them. Biack was plagued by natural disasters, and the protectors were unable to prevent them. All they could do was pick up the pieces afterwards. They soon realised the king hadn't just split up the worlds, but he'd doomed them both to a lifetime of suffering.

"It was said Earth was cursed with the evil of people, while Biack was cursed with the evil of nature. And the only way to defeat both evils was to reunite the six. But the lost twin was the one with the ability to travel worlds, so their only choice was to wait for her return, which never came.

"The other twin was named the new King of Biack, and without any crown, he began his own line of kings. It's said that on his deathbed, he talked of hearing his lost sisters' voice; she warned of another person who'd one day destroy everything he built, because from total loss, evil is inevitable. But she said that once again, in the time of ultimate peril, the six would rise.

"Two thousand years later, that brings us to now." I turn to her. "I don't think your presence here is an accident."

After a while of silence, Jess states, "You think the Rose is the person the lost twin warned of."

I nod. "The Last King swore that one day our world would erupt in flames of rage. And just over a hundred years ago, Biack was lit on fire."

"Your sun," Jess says.

"The only way to save our world is by reuniting the six."

She turns. "And me being here, I reunite the six?"

A further nod. We walk for a while longer; I think she's processing all I just said. The city continues to crumble around us— every few minutes, another grand crash occurs nearby. We stay in the middle of the old roads and weave in between the abandoned cars. As we pass every one, Jess peers inside, searching for signs of life. On her world, they still use cars; it must be so strange for her here.

She finds a resting spot on top of one of the vehicles. Together, we sit back and watch the city as it slowly decays.

"You realise how insane all this is for me, right?" She speaks. "Two weeks ago, I was living a normal life; I had normal friends, a normal boyfriend. I was normal."

"Jessica Durand," I say, "your life has never been anything ordinary." She hides a smile. "And," I continue, "the most extraordinary part is only just beginning."

Unable to take any form of compliment despite her clear enjoyment of them, she changes the subject. "So what's the plan, princess?"

"I think the Rose wants those gems. I think she's trying to restore the crown," I answer.

"Does she know where they are?"

"No one does. Before you arrived here, she kidnapped some of the scientists working on a project dedicated to researching the crown and its missing gems. I think she was trying to find out their location from the scientists."

"But they didn't know," she states.

I shrug. "I think her next plan was to use you to locate them."

"And now *you're* going to steal that plan and use me instead? I don't know where they are."

"I know," I reply. "But the original six hid them somewhere ordinary people wouldn't find. I think they meant for us to use our gifts to locate them. They planned for all of this."

"You know..." She pulls herself off the car. "All I wanted was your tea." What? "And somehow I've been roped into saving the planet, and it's not even my planet." She pauses. "That Last King, he did this? Indirectly?" Her hands gesture to the ruins around us. I nod. She tuts. "He must've fitted right in on Earth."

We head back to the stealth. "When we get to the BCD, you're going to have to answer a lot of questions," I inform her.

"Okay, but I don't have a lot of answers," she replies.

"That's fine. Just tell us as much as you can."

Jess asks, "Will I be in trouble?" She shrinks in on herself. "For those men I killed?" She did distort the dream.

"No, because you didn't kill them." She's shocked. "You're a terrible aim, you know." I laugh. "You didn't hurt anyone, at least not any of our people." I remember the blood stains in the castle. "So you're not in any trouble. You were never in any trouble to start with, but then you escaped."

"You mean everything that's happened these past weeks could've been avoided?" I nod. She exhales. "Okay, so what do you want to know?"

"Originally, where you came from, but now people have generally accepted Earth. So more importantly, we need to know how you escaped the BCD and everything you can tell us about the Rose and the Red Suits. And the person who helped you escape."

"Well, he was kind of attractive. But I think he's in love with that Rose."

"He?" It's a guy? "Was his name Damien, or was it Donald? Donald Adams?"

She shakes her head. "No. I think it was Scott."

Chapter Twenty-Three

Jess

Biack 29/01/2014

"Are you sure?" Ben keeps asking me over and over.

Yes, I'm pretty damn sure, as I've already said a hundred times.

I've told them everything I know. Ben even filmed it for their database—which I think is like the internet but with fewer memes—but they're stuck in disbelief at that guy's name. Ella left as soon as we returned to the BCD; she was silent the entire journey. Who was he to them? I can't place him in any of the dreams.

I can see Jia's mind racing. "Can someone please tell me who he is?" I ask.

Will's as confused as me. Leaning back against a table at the far end of the lab, I think he might be Italian. He definitely looks it with the white top tucked into his belted jeans. Right now, he fits every Italian stereotype movies taught me. No, I'm wrong. Damn, I really can't place him.

"Ella's been dating him recently," Jia answers before dramatically turning to Ben. "Oh my life, was he just using her to gain information? Ben, he knew we were going to that castle! What else did Ella tell him?"

"He's in the perfect position. Assistant to the king and in a relationship with the princess." Ben's getting agitated. "We need to tell someone!"

I say, "Ella's probably gone to do just that."

"She must've," Jia says. "We have to leave her to deal with this. Maybe she wants to confront him first?"

"No! We need to stop him now!" He starts pacing. "Every minute we let him continue, he might relay more information."

"Ella won't let him," Jia defends. "Besides, maybe we can use him the way he's used us."

"What if he tampers with something? He's inside the most secure and secretive and important complex on Biack. He could do untold damage!" Ben's still panicking.

"Stop!" I yell and like I asked, they both freeze and turn to stare at me. "If I know anything about Ella, and I like to think a lifetime of dreams count, it's that she knows what she's doing."

Ben relaxes into a chair. "You're right. She's always got a plan. This won't be any different."

"See?" I pull up a chair. "So, is she always that intense? All that talk of saving the world and other seriousness."

Jia smiles. "No one cares about this world more than Ella. One day she's going to be the queen, and I think that weight's constantly sitting on her shoulders."

"I like to joke that if she trips over, she might die under the weight." Aiden grins. He's found a seat on the table Will's leaning against, unusually quiet.

"You guys must have a lot of pressure on you too," I say. "I mean, you're the *protectors*."

"Actually, there are a lot of protectors," Ben corrects but soon realises from the look on my face I need more information. "We've always given the name of protector to anyone who defends and protects the people of Biack. So currently there are over a hundred protectors."

"Over a hundred?"

"Yep, we have twenty-six teams of varying sizes. And a few other protectors who aren't assigned to specific teams," he replies. "Each team is named after a letter in the alphabet, hence there being twenty-six. We're the S team."

"Aiden likes to nickname us the Supers," Jia adds. "He's the least creative person I know." A tiny spark narrowly misses her.

"Hey!" Ben yells as he points towards a very official-looking sign on the wall. "Remember the sign!" *No fire allowed.*

They're just like in my dreams. "I gave you all nicknames." They glance between each other. "Okay, look, until recently you were all characters in my dreams. Besides, I was young when I came up with them, and at the time they felt right."

Aiden's face lights up. "Please tell me I was the *King of Fire*."

"Fire Boy."

He bursts out in laughter.

"You're just as creative as Aiden," Ben states.

"What about the rest of us?" Jia pulls her seat next to me before adjusting the oversized, and probably useless, clear frames around her eyes that accompany a golden chain around her neck. She matches Will in a white T-shirt, although hers stretches down to her knees and is decorated in foreign words. There's a deep slit down the side of the T-shirt, and through it I can see her denim skirt.

"The Girl of Oceans." She smiles. "And you're The Invisible Boy." I gesture to Ben, he tilts his head.

Jia asks, "What about Ella?"

"I've always called her The Girl, but I'm starting to like this First-Queen thing," I say.

"And you're The Girl from Far Away," Ben adds. "Creative."

I shrug. "I like the Supers."

"Fire Boy, pew pew!" Ironically, he's pretending to shoot fireballs from his fingers as he runs around the room. "I'm just your friendly world-saving hero." He gasps. "No, superhero! Get it, because of the Supers?" He pulls me out of my seat.

"And I'm The Girl from Far Away." I strike a pose. "Hero to multiple worlds, but in debt to none."

"I'm friends with morons," Ben mutters under his breath as he resumes tapping on his screen.

Aiden winks at me as he pulls a crumpled-up ball of clothing out of one of the boxes around the room. He launches it at Ben.

"Hey!" Ben reacts by following suit but this time with a book from the nearest table.

Within seconds, all chaos unleashes as Jia, Will and I join in. Books, clothing, a pot of some kind, shoes, even a tablet, pillows, bags, a water bottle and more launches across the room. We've formed teams, Aiden and I against the others. We wrap blankets around ourselves pretending they're capes as we climb over the tables and hide behind chairs. Is this what friendship is?

I'm on Aiden's shoulders as a man dressed in a suit enters the room.

"Um, sorry to interrupt." We all fall silent. Some kind of sticky food falls from the ceiling. "The king has requested the girl —" he stops to think of my name, "—Jess, returns to the palace for the night."

I find myself looking to Will.

"I'll take you," he states.

The man nods to Will before leaving, trying to hide the disgust on his face at the mess we've made of this lab.

"I'll miss you, best friend. We'll have to save the world tomorrow." Aiden blows kisses.

I blow kisses back as Will leads me out the lab. *"Au revoir, mon amie!"*

"What in life did she just say?" I faintly hear him ask behind us.

Ben's voice is raised enough. "Don't you dare leave without clearing this up like last time!"

The Unbreakable Boy directs me down plain hallways.

"How do you know where you're going? Everywhere looks the same."

"I spend my life here," he replies.

He's taken me to some sort of lift thing. It reminds me of the carriages on the London eye, not that I've ever been on them. The rounded walls are formed of glass with a metal bench lining the inside for seating. Next to the sliding door is what I'd call a control pad. They probably call it a screen. How flawed is their naming system? I think this is a *pod*.

Will taps instruction in. "Aiden likes you." We lean against opposite sides of the pod.

"Yeah, I think I had him at *Fire Boy*." The pod thing shakes to life then rushes down a tunnel. It's like the underground, I guess? "I'm still working on Ben and Jia though. Any tips?"

"They like you."

I shake my head. "No I'm pretty sure Ben hates me."

"Ben hates everyone. It's not personal." He shrugs.

"He likes you. And Ella, and Jia," I reply. "Maybe not Aiden, though."

Will smirks. "Yeah, maybe not Aiden."

"So, what do I need to do?"

"I think you're overthinking this," he says.

How did I befriend Will? Held him hostage, shared food, robbed places, shared stories, killed people, played in the sand, ran through a minefield, jumped off a cliff, tried to teach him to drive, cried and yelled, had sex, fought off the Red Suits, yelled more then helped him. Okay. Now how do I condense that into one conversation or action?

"I just want to be a part of your group," I admit.

He sighs. "Let Jia dress you, and challenge Ben. That's all it takes." Changing the subject, he continues. "So, what's my nickname?"

"The Unbreakable Boy."

He laughs and looks away. "And you really didn't know." Is he still mad at me?

The lift-pod thing comes to a stop before changing direction and moving up; the ground above us parts to reveal the Dome. When it stops again moments later, we're in front of Day Palace. It's even bigger than it appeared in my dreams.

Think French chateau. Then imagine it much, much bigger.

"Welcome to Day Palace," Will announces.

Before us, two guards, maybe protectors, stand in front of the gigantic metal gates safeguarding the grounds. With a quick wave of some ID badge from Will, they allow us safe passage through the barrier. We follow the long road towards the grand entrance. The path's lined with well-maintained shrubbery, blooming trees and several fountains.

Why does it feel so French? I thought we were in England. Okay, I know neither of those places exist in Biack; everything seems to be combined into one multicultural, but predominantly British, country. At least from what I've seen so far.

We have to climb stone stairs to even enter the building. What house has their own grand stairway just to get to the front door? A front door that's hidden behind stone pillars and reaches up so high I have to tilt my head to see the end.

And oh my God, the inside is grand. Marble decorates the floor surrounding a further marble staircase, while the white walls are intricately embellished with detailed mouldings, and crystal chandeliers hang from the ceiling. Is Buckingham Palace this great? What about the White House?

"You're staying in my old room," Will states after returning from speaking to a nearby housekeeper—or maid, or guard. I really can't tell their role.

I remember. "You lived here."

"I still do, kind of. But a couple of years ago, they offered me a room in the BCD, and I'm not really...*this*." He gestures.

We climb the staircase. "So you have two homes?"

"This was never my home," he says. He directs me to a room at the end of one of the halls. This place is a maze, which is to be expected; it's huge.

I stop and turn to him, hesitating before speaking. "Are you going to stay?"

His eyes squint as he creases his brow. "We're just *friends*, remember?" He's mad. "What else would we be?"

I watch him walk away. He doesn't look back. Inside the bedroom is a four-poster bed complete with noble blue curtains. He was right, this place is...*this*. I drag my fingers along the chest of drawers, there's no dust, and testing the floorboards, there's no creaks.

I swing open the wardrobe doors to find a mixture of suits and expensive-looking jumpers. Flicking through them, I pull out a plain black T-shirt hidden in the mix. I quickly swap it for my over-worn Earth top. It smells like him.

I fall flat on my back and discover how comfy the bed is. Did they make this out of clouds? Can they make clouds inside the Dome? I can't even begin to understand the technology of this world. If stories are to be believed, in two thousand years they've well advanced us in every way. I guess it's hard to evolve when your world's consumed in war. Or it was the dark ages— that was a pretty wasted period.

There's something small written on one of the bed posts, mostly hidden behind the curtains.

Wilhelm was here.

Is that his real name? It might be. Does Ella know? I don't think she does. Why did he write that? Surely he knew someone would find it. Maybe he didn't think anyone would. But then, why did he write it? Maybe he's just as a human as the rest of us, desperately wanting to leave some mark on the world. On this world. On Biack.

I throw myself out of bed. How am I meant to sleep when there's a whole palace to explore behind the door? Out the window I can see vast gardens trapped within a great wall, and behind that lies the city of The Capital. It's so bright and alive and somehow comforting to know that despite the emptiness of Day palace, a city of people lies beyond.

Back out in the hall, I stroll past the high walls and regal pictures. There's a painting of a young Ella; she was so cute with her blond hair tied up in bows. A few doors down, a light shines from underneath, is this Ella's room? Twisting the door handle, I peer inside. She's awake, lying curled up in bed. Our eyes meet.

"I couldn't sleep," I say.

She moves the covers, and I climb in next to her.

I think this is the first time she's appeared imperfect. Her eyes are red, while her hair is strayed and messy instead of in its pristine form. And she's still in her previous pink dress, but now it's creased. In her hands she grasps a toy bird, I think called Alaria. She says nothing as I lie next to her; for minutes we stay

JENNIFER AUSTIN

in silence.

"Let's make a blanket fort," I whisper.

"What?" She sniffs.

"Let's make a blanket fort," I repeat.

She watches me as I rearrange her room, moving the corner lamp to centre stage, straining under the weight of chairs, opening drawers just the right amount, and then I struggle when searching for blankets. After failing to find any, I turn to her, and after a few more seconds she pulls herself up and travels to the end of her bed, opening a chest to reveal lengths of warm covers. Together, we throw them over the furniture. I climb onto the windowsill to unwrap the fairy lights from around her curtain pole before passing them to her to decorate the inside of the fort. Finally, I grab cushions from her bed and throw them under the blankets. When it's complete, she follows me inside.

She's trying to smooth out the creases of her dress when I start. "Hi, I'm Jessica Durand."

She seems so confused. "What?"

"Just trust me, okay?" I continue, "I'm Jess, I'm seventeen and I'm scared every time I close my eyes that I'll wake up on Earth again. But I'm also scared of what'll happen to me if I stay here." She's listening. "I'm scared of those monsters with the face bandages and why they need them. I'm scared of your stories and this role you want me to play. I'm scared I'm going to disappoint you all." She goes to speak but I continue. "I've never wanted to be special or save the world. I've just wanted my own little bubble." I hug a nearby cushion. "But I like this feeling of being wanted. I like being a part of something. And I like your friends and you. I want to stay, and that's the scariest thing."

I think she's trying to figure out what to say as her eyes search mine. "I thought you were fearless."

"Everyone's scared of something," I reply. "Okay, I'm scared and you're sad, and now it's your turn."

She takes a deep breath. "Hi." I nod. "I'm Ella Day. I'm seventeen and I'm sad that...that it was all a lie." Her voice fades. "I'm sad that he used me and stole from me and..." She stops as her gaze falls to the floor. "I thought my first love would be beautiful and poetic. But instead I feel...shattered."

I can see emotion filling her eyes. I try to distract her. "I had sex with Will." It works—the expression upon her face completely changes as she looks up at me. "We're just friends, though." I mutter under my breath, "What else would we be?"

"No. I'm just friends with Will." I think she's also mad. "Aiden's just friends with Will. Jia and Ben too." She pauses. "He's never been with anyone before. In any way."

"What?" But in the dreams, he always had girls after him. "No, I did *not* get that impression." My joke falls flat.

She mumbles, "I didn't think he was into, well, anyone."

"He's definitely not into me anymore." She seems confused. "And it's okay, because I'm not into him." She creases her brow. "I'm messy. And so is he. We need people who'll fix us, and you can't fix someone if you're broken." My arms tighten around the cushion in my lap. "I thought Chris was going to fix me. But Scarlett ruined that."

"He ruined it too," she adds. I must look confused because

she continues. "You can't blame her entirely for it. He's just as responsible."

I guess she's right. Why am I so determined to defend him? I always thought he was going to be this prince who rode in on a white horse to rescue me, but what did he actually do? Did he ever really listen to me? Was I ever able to tell him how I felt about anything? I can tell Will anything. He always listens.

She takes another deep breath. "I think I'm broken now."

"Why?"

She turns away. "Before, if I was ever sad, I knew what to do. I knew who to go to and how to ask for help."

"But this time you don't," I state.

Emotion is welling in her eyes. This isn't the girl I thought I knew so well. Her confidence has crumpled with her dress while her blind faith has revealed its true face as naivety. Her perfection has melted with her mascara, and her control has slipped through her grasp. But the person left behind is real; that's something I can believe in.

"Ella, one day you'll be the queen, and this entire planet will bow to you." She looks up at me. "Do you know how impossible it'd be to have the whole of Earth listen to one person? That's why we have hundreds of countries and so many wars." God, Earth's a mess. "And you're going to do incredible things that'll *literally* save the world. So don't you dare let one tiny person get to you. He's a blip in your life, a speck on your painting." I let go of the cushion to squeeze her arm. "He's an asteroid, but Ella, you're the sun."

This is so much more than a dream.

I tell her about my stepdad and the things he does; she tells me about the council and how they use her for the cameras. I talk about my time with Will; she talks about how after telling her dad, they found Scott had already disappeared. We talk about our favourite memories and our worst, and then, when the light starts to break through the window and our eyes start to finally give in, I want to relive it all again.

This is so much more than a dream, I tell myself as under the rising sun we finally drift off. And then, as if I willed it myself, I have another dream.

Chapter Twenty-Four

Ella

"Are you sure it's a good idea to give me a gun?" Jess stands with it dangling from her finger like it's dirty hosiery. "I'm not complaining. I'm just saying."

"She makes a valid point," Ben states.

"Jess, do you promise not to shoot us?" I ask.

She looks between us and the gun. "Maybe?"

Ben doesn't seem convinced.

"That's good enough for me," I say.

It was Jia's idea to do this, although I think Jess planted it. We're around my dressing room as they search through the rails. Ben's waiting next to me on the sofa while Aiden prods around my tiara collection and Will leans against a wall with his head in a book. When they first arrived, they all tried to fit next to me on the sofa; it took a while to convince them I'm fine. Because I am.

"This?" Jia suggests.

Jess shakes her head. "Ella, do you own anything that isn't pink?" She adds before I can reply, "Or white, or yellow, or any other bright colour. Where's your black and green?"

Aiden interrupts her. "Why do you have so many of these? They all look the same."

"It's a princess thing," Jess answers for me.

"How much longer is this going to take?" Ben complains. "It's been an hour. An hour of you looking at clothes. Why do I need to be here to suffer this?"

Jess replies, "You said you needed me to do something?"

"Yes, but at the BCD." He sighs.

She grins, playing with him. "So why did you come here then?"

"Because you were here!" He's getting frustrated.

"I found something!" Jia jumps with excitement as she reveals a pair of black combat boots.

"These are perfect." Jess shares her excitement.

Jia turns to study Jess; she's wearing a plain black top half tucked into her dark skinny jeans, and next to us on the sofa lays her old jacket that I think I've seen her brother wearing in my dreams, which makes sense, because it's definitely too big for her. Suddenly Jia moves towards her and rips the neck of her top before tugging it down so it hangs off one shoulder.

"I guess that'll do." She doesn't sound happy. "But it's okay, I'll go shopping and find more options for you."

"Are we done now?" Ben interrupts to ask. I'm impressed he's still here.

Jess checks with Jia before responding, "Yeah. So, what was it you wanted me to do?"

Will shuts his book. "Is that my top?"

Ben lets out a loud sigh. "Right now, anything but this."

✺✺✺

The BCD is made up of one hundred and ten floors. Within that there's a whole floor dedicated to the cafeteria, another for the medical centre, several floors of living quarters, another few of offices and meeting rooms, and mixed amongst the rest are gyms and labs. But then there's floor zero.

We must travel past multiple security barriers, each guarded by couple protectors. We're subjected to several searches and scans and have to hand over every weapon in our possession. But finally, we're allowed to enter the biggest laboratory in the BCD. Finally, we're a high enough rank.

"After the New Year Ball attack, the Last King project was moved here," Ben holds out his arms. "Before the attack, I'd never heard of it. It was just a history project."

The lab appears to have been cleared of personnel for our visit, but everything they were working on remains. Lab benches and screens decorate the room with various books and scrolls on show. Some vases and ancient items are displayed on shelves while in the middle of the room, on a stand of its own, rests a hologram of the crown.

Jess waves her hand through the hologram. "So, what's the Last King project?"

Ben replies, "Like I said, it was just a history project. They were studying the crown and collecting information about the possible whereabouts of it and the gems."

"But they didn't find them." Jess remembers our previous

conversation.

He nods. "Yes. It wasn't a complete waste of time, though; they did find clues in old relics."

"What clues?" I ask while I trace the holes in the crown.

The screen in the centre of the room jumps to life as Ben taps something on his control pad. "So we know the gems were meant to be found by us."

"If you believe the stories," Will says.

"Which you do." I glance at Aiden. "He told me."

"Lies!" Aiden rages. "She read your journal too!"

"Anyway," Ben shouts over us as he flicks a drawing on to the display. "Jess is the answer."

"Hey, that's me!" she exclaims.

We examine the drawing; it does look like her.

"I think you're supposed to know where we need to go," Ben says.

"I'm what now?"

"Have you seen any strange places in your dreams lately or any random flashes of images?"

"Well..." She hesitates. "I had a weird dream last night. But it didn't involve any gems or hidden locations."

"What if you look at the crown?" He pulls her towards the hologram. "Do you see anything?"

We're all watching as Ben positions her in front of it, and after a moment of silence she speaks again. "Are you guys seeing this?"

"What?" I let excitement claim its hold on me. "What do you see?"

"Well…" Her words are slow.

Aiden interrupts. "What? What is it?"

"I see…" she drags.

"What?" Ben asks.

She replies, "Some old crown." Will smirks as she erupts in laughter. "I don't know what you want from me, but this is stupid. Now, where's the nearest kitchen area? I need tea."

Ben gives in. "I'll go get some food." Jess pulls herself up to join him. "No, stay. I need space from you."

"There's six of us. You'll need some help," Jia joins.

Jess turns to us after they've left. "I think he likes me."

"Same." Aiden grins.

In the corner, Will's busy reading through scrolls. I walk over while Aiden and Jess giggle at some vase.

"Jess told me." I catch his attention.

"What did she say?" he asks with wide eyes.

"That you're just friends," I reply.

He pauses while the information sinks in. "I was trying to win her trust."

"Will." I wrap my hand around his. "I know you. You're my brother. And that, that is a lie."

"We're *just* friends." He yanks his hand free. "And even that's debatable. She can't be trusted, Ella. She barely cares about anyone other than herself, and what do you think will happen when she has to make a call? Herself or us? What do you think will happen?"

"You don't know her like I do then."

"Oh, stop being so naïve." Anger creeps through his words.

"She knew about Scott, and did she tell us? Who knows what she's still keeping from us?" His voice is starting to draw attention from Aiden and Jess. "She's killed people, and she tried to kill us. She can't be trusted, and you're a fool for thinking she can."

"Why are you being so mean?" Hurt breaks out as I think of Scott. But I'm fine.

"Yeah, you dick," Jess joins in. "And I only tried to kill *you*."

Will escapes to the other side of the lab, where he finds a quiet reading spot. Until Ben and Jia return, Jess distracts me by telling us how old the queen of her world is and about all the royal family's secret plots. Earth sounds like a dark place.

"It was a plan to get rid of her because she threatened them, and you can tell, because it's a bit suspicious how the other car was never found." Jess is still talking when the others return with noodles. "Yes! You guys have Chinese food!"

"Chinese?" I ask. "What's that, a type of vegetable?"

She laughs. "No, it's a type of people. It's what you call people from China, and they invented this food, so it's named after them."

Aiden shares my confusion. "You have different types of people?"

"But that's nice that you named food after them," I add.

"Yeah, there's hundreds of countries, and each country has a different type. There's French and American and Russian and Moroccan and Canadians—everyone loves the Canadians," she lists. "And the Chinese, they look like Jia."

Jia replies, "What, like, how I dress?"

"No, it's…" Jess hesitates; she seems nervous. "Never mind."

Ben says, "That's ridiculous. Are you not all humans? Why do you need to categorise everyone?"

Jess pauses again. I don't think she has an answer.

"Ah, Ella." My father enters the lab. "I see you've found the Last King project." His eyes spot Jess. "And you…" walking over, he holds out a hand, "…must be Jess."

Taking his hand, she says, "And you must be the king."

"Oh, please, call me your Highness." He smiles, but she seems unsure. Heading back over to me, he pulls me aside. "We're having another ball."

"What? But we had one ten days ago," I reply.

He nods. "Yes, well, I've been trying to control the damage Jess has caused, and I've managed to spin it into a celebration. But now we have to actually celebrate it."

"Okay. When?"

"Tonight."

"What?" I stumble. "Again?" The last one only worked because of Scott. Scott.

He sighs. "Yes, we're really not doing so well with the planning of these this year." His tone changes. "Oh well, as with the rest of them, it's just a show to win people over. And so, for Jess, we'll put on the very best show we can muster."

I glance at the others. I guess the crown will have to wait a day.

❊❊❊❊

We choose matching dresses. It just feels right.

Pink watercolour spreads across the tulle with far and few faded patches of white remaining. I untwist the thin straps around my shoulders as Jess bunches the blue of hers up to peer at her bare feet. She's deciding between several shoes, but each one fails to meet whatever expectations she's set. Jia holds up another pair of delicate white heels, which Jess tosses aside.

"I don't know, I feel silly." She looks between the blue tulle in her hands.

Jia holds up her combat boots from earlier. "So make it more you." The single white sleeve of her suit jacket contrasts with the oversized pinstripe grey. She paired it with tightly fitting pinstripe trousers and stand-out red heels.

Jess is much happier with the combat boots hidden beneath the layers of watercolour blue. I start to pin up her hair but struggle to brush out the tangles. She doesn't flinch as I accidentally yank.

"Doesn't this whole thing feel…" she pauses, "…patriarchal?"

"What does that mean?" I manage to free a further tangle.

She shrugs. "The boys downstairs waiting while we get ready. Like we're their puppets."

Jia laughs as she passes me a crystal hair decoration. "Surely it's the opposite." Jess turns to her, causing my hand to slip and half her hairstyle to fall apart. "They're waiting for us. They're our puppets. We have the control."

I hold Jess's head still as she replies. "Okay, I like that."

It doesn't take too much longer to finish getting ready, although I have to enlist Jia's help to get Jess to stay still. Finishing touches: Jess and I strap weapons to our thighs, concealed innocently under the tulle, and Jia hides hers underneath her suit jacket. We find our puppets waiting for us at the bottom of the grand staircase, just like every time before. In a suit of raging red, Aiden holds out his arms as Jia jumps into them, spinning around in a chorus of laughter. Ben checks the buttons of his waistcoat, while Will sits on maybe the fourth step with his gaze fixed on another book—no, one of his journals.

"Lovely people." My father's voice booms from across the entrance hall as everyone falls silent. "I'm over the Dome to introduce to you our guest of honour this evening, all the way from the land of legends, Earth." He's gesturing towards Jess as the others fall back into the crowd, leaving us exposed on the staircase. "Jessica Durand."

The room breaks into applause as predators escape from the crowd and find their way to us, recorders out and shouting questions. I squeeze her hand. She's not alone.

"I'm actually trying to make *The Girl from Far Away* a thing so…" They love her. The lights flash over the laughter and continued applause.

"Jessica." A single predator manages to break the sound barrier. "Why did you come here?"

"For that prophecy," she replies. "Turns out you're in desperate need of my help."

"Are you here to stay, or will you return to Earth?" another predator shouts.

"Undecided," she answers. "I left some pretty big things behind on Earth. Well, one thing."

"Is it true you've met the Red Suit's leader?" How did they know that? They're not meant to know.

Jess hesitates. "Yes, and I'm disappointed she didn't spread the word about *The Girl from Far Away.*"

"Is it true that originally you refused to help us?" another voice reaches.

Jess begins to stumble. "I…er…"

"And I have reports that you were seen attacking protectors in the middle of a city."

The original voice returns. "Yes, and I have reports you set a building on fire."

"It wasn't a building, it was a petrol station, and I was being attacked and—"

I interrupt. "I hope you'll excuse us. It's been a long few days, and we're here to celebrate."

I drag Jess through the crowds; I want to say it's nice to not be the one people are reaching after, but that'd be a lie. We find a space in the grand ballroom, lost amongst the crowd. Across the room I can see protectors stopping the predators from entering.

"I don't know how to dance," Jess says.

I reach for her hand. "I'll show you. It's pretty simple. Just follow my lead."

She's a bit unsteady as her feet try to copy mine; it should be far easier in the level of her boots compared to the rise of my heels. "Do I have to do that now?"

"Do what?" I try to guide her waist.

"Talk to the cameras like that." Cameras?

"I'll do what I can to keep you away from the predators but…"

She reads my face. "Predators," she repeats as she looks at the crowd around us. Her hand is placed across her stomach. "Do I have to do this?" she asks before answering her own question. "I'm going to go find Ben. I'm sure he's not dancing."

"Wait, Jess—" I lose her in the flocks of colour. Why do people keep leaving me?

"Do you need a partner?" A hand finds my shoulder.

Spinning around, I reply, "Oh, Ben. Jess was just going to look for you."

"Well, she can find me here." He takes my hand as our feet start to skip in time. "Look, Ella, I know I'm not the person you usually go to when you're sad but—"

"I'm not sad anymore. I took some time, I had a big cry and now I need to move on with my life," I can't look him in the eye. "It ended as quickly as it lasted."

His face scrunches as the music moves slow. "I'm not Aiden or Jia; I don't know anything about people like they do. I used to think I was like Will, but now he has this weird passive-aggressive thing with Jess where they look at each other too much. But I know I'm not like you, because where I see an average person talking average words, you see everything they could be and fall head over heels in love with all of it." He continues as I remain quiet. "You did it with all of us, Ella. And it's not a bad thing. In fact, it's something I envy greatly. You believe in people enough that they start to believe in themselves." There's sympathy in his eyes. "It must be a lonely thing, to believe in the dark." I push a loose strand of his hair back. "So, when you tell me you're not sad anymore, I know it's not true. And it's not because he lied to you or tricked you or used you; I know you bounce back from pain like that. No, it's because you believed in him, and when he stole that, he stole a piece of you."

I close my eyes to keep my emotions at bay. "So what do I do? Be sad forever?"

"I have no idea. But whatever happens, you won't have to do anything alone."

I'm not alone. I have my team. I have my Supers.

"Ella! Ben!" Aiden appears out of nowhere and grabs our hands. "You have to come quick. It's Jess—she's doing something!"

Chapter Twenty-Five

Jess

Biack 30/01/2014

I burst out onto the balcony, gasping for air in the tight dress. Throwing my head over the balcony, I stare at the gardens below. If I threw up, would it reach that fountain?

"Yeah, they're not really my thing, either."

I spin around to find Will sitting against one of the glass windows, book and pen in hand. "I was just—"

He interrupts me. "Escaping?" Yeah.

I find a seat beside him. The window vibrates against our back to the hum of the orchestra inside as our hands rest inches apart on the cold stone. I glance over at his book, and he doesn't hide it from me. His hand returns to the pages as he continues to write. I could read it but instead I lean my head back and close my eyes. I find my breath again. His fingers stroke mine.

"You did well," he states. "Even if it didn't feel like it."

"Really?" I turn to him. "But they brought things up and I-I…" I pause. "I wish I could go back in time and change things. Why did I ever run? If I'd just answered your questions from the start, they'd have nothing bad to say."

"They always have something bad to say." He turns the page. "That's their job." He continues writing. "Besides, if you hadn't run, we wouldn't be such great *friends*."

I trace his fingers with my eyes, not really focusing on the words they write. "You do that to remember." He doesn't respond but I guess I didn't ask. "What do you do when you want to forget?"

He stops writing to look at me. "I burn it."

I don't have to say anything for him to hand me his pen and tear a few blank pages from his book. They sit in my hands, but I don't know what to do with them. What do I really want to forget? Do I regret the time we spent together? What about the life I lived before all this, my friends and family and love life? Do I really want to forget all the things that made me, me?

"What do you want to forget?" I ask him.

He thinks before replying. "I want to remember everything that's happened to me: the good, the bad, the painful. And I don't regret the things I did or said. But the things I thought, the wrong judgements of myself and others. That's what I burn."

What I thought. That's what I'll burn.

I start to write. *I'm not enough. I'm not Scarlett. She's prettier, more interesting, and more attractive. She's everything I'm not. Maybe I was always her pawn. Maybe I wanted to be.* I glance back inside at the party through a gap in the curtains. *I'm all alone. I have no one. No one cares. How did that become my life? Apparently it's too much to be around me. I can't ignore it; I can barely see past it. They would experiment on me; they'd use me for the cameras. They were never my friends. Everywhere I looked I never ticked enough boxes.* I turn back back to Will.

Did he ever care about me? Was it always Scarlett? Did he ever love me? Maybe I'll kill him before then. Maybe he'll kill me. I take a deep breath. *Maybe this is my life. Maybe I'm not the leading lady. Maybe I'm just a minor character. Maybe the cameras have already moved past me.* I'm not who I thought was. *I belong on my own where I can't damage anyone else with my cracks. I belong far away, far away from everyone. Where no one else can leave me. The Girl from Far Away will never be far enough.* I'm going to build my own team. *I don't care about them because I'm not someone who cares. This isn't my war. And this isn't my home.* And I'm finally starting to feel free. *I'm trapped within my own mind. I'm crazy again. I'm still broken.*

"Okay." I stare at the paper. I'm finished. "Let's burn it."

He grins before disappearing back inside the palace. It takes several minutes for him to return; I begin to believe he's abandoned me to look a fool. Then I decide to write that thought down instead.

When Will returns, Aiden's at his side. "Okay, what do you need?" Aiden asks.

I hold up the paper. "Can you burn this?"

He laughs, his face lit up. "Okay, I *really* love you." Taking the paper from me, he turns to Will. "She's my favourite."

We watch as he lays the paper flat in his hand before flames reach around it. Slowly the ink starts to drip and melt away as the edges crinkle black and in. My nose scrunches under the smell, but Will was right. I feel free. And that's when I see it, dancing amongst the flames, trying to escape my mind, but I cling onto the remnants of my dream from last night.

I reach for a leftover rip of paper and against the balcony's edge, I start to trace the outlines of an image, without care for critics' opinions. My hand rushes across the page as Will and Aiden watch the picture form. Will realises what I'm drawing as he nudges Aiden, causing him to return back into the palace. I scribble in the shades to add definition and make it feel more physical.

Aiden returns with Ella, Jia and Ben.

"Okay." I stop and stare at my scribbles. "I don't know how I did that."

"I was right," Ben announces with a proud huff.

"Jess." Ella wraps her hand around mine. "Can you take us there?" She gestures to my drawing.

I hesitate. "I don't know how."

"I believe you do," she replies softly. "I believe in you." Maybe she's right.

With a nod, I give it my best shot. I'm staring at walls and the hidden entrance behind the trees as I pull myself up onto the balcony. They all reach to grab me, but I need to feel the risk as I push their hands away. With one hand grasping the pillar and another holding out the drawing, I fall back into my dream. I relive the sound of the wildlife, the smell of the forest, the taste of the stale air, the touch of gentle breeze and the sight of it all.

The wind blows the layers of my dress as I close my eyes. I don't need to see in order to feel the chill of my veins. For a moment I think the wind has blown me away; I believe I'm drifting through the clouds towards the place they so desperately want me to take them.

Then my stomach drops

and my hands rush to my head

as I scream in pain

I fall back into their arms.

"Quick—" My voice breaks.

Jia and Ben are the first through. They're shortly followed by Aiden, as Will and Ella help me through. I can barely see as my brain stretches in all directions against my skull. The gateway shuts behind us.

I did it, I think as Jia, Ben and Aiden rush ahead.

I did it, I think as Will and Ella drag me forward.

I did it, I think as my body falls limp.

I did it, I think as I fall apart.

❖❖❖

"Jess!"

"Jess, can you hear us?"

"Is she dead?"

"No. She has a pulse."

"Jess wake up!"

"Jess, please."

I splutter back to life with blood flying out of my mouth.

"What happened to her?" Will asks. He's crouched on the ground, holding me. Did I fall? Did he catch me?

"It hurt." I manage to form words.

There's blood on my face. I wipe it off with my sleeves. My sleeves? A suit jacket has been placed around me. I wipe more blood. It's come from my eyes. I didn't know that was possible. I thought that only happened to demons in the movies? Wait. Am I a demon? Is this a movie?

"You made a portal that transported six people. That must've required a lot of strength," Ella says. "It's harder for me to control bigger objects."

"I…" I spit further blood.

Ella hushes. "Take it easy."

"Guys," Ben yells from the distance. He's standing before the cave entrance. "You're going to want to see this."

Will wraps one of my arms around his neck and slowly lifts me to my feet. Taking our time, we make our way over to Ben while they try to support me; I keep almost tumbling to the ground.

There's blood on Ella's dress, not much but enough.

"Is she okay?" Ben asks as we finally arrive.

"I think we pushed her too far," Ella replies. She's noticed the stains on her dress but ignores them; that's strange of her.

Ben leads us inside to reveal a makeshift home hidden within the stone walls. The place is fit with rugs, a fireplace, a table and chairs, a comfy-looking bed and other varying items.

Jia's face drops when she sees Will half dragging me. "What happened?" she asks as she rushes over.

"Do you remember that time Aiden cried when he tried to end that house fire?" Ella says.

"You said you wouldn't talk about that anymore!" Aiden appears to our side.

"Let's lie her down on the bed," Ella instructs.

Aiden helps Will move me across the room, my feet dragging the whole way. I've completely lost my strength, and there's only one solution I can think of.

"Tea," I manage to whisper.

"What did she say?" Aiden asks.

Will hides a smile. "Tea."

"Okay," Aiden says as he begins to set me down on the bed. "We'll try find some— *What?*"

His confusion is valid, with a flash of light I tumble through the bed as it transforms into a pile of books. Seconds later, a curtain of fire sparks to life against one of the stone walls. What is this place?

"Did you all see that?" he asks.

"Interesting," Ben states. "It transformed."

"Ouch!" Jia yells as she yanks her finger back from a knife. "It was a kettle," she tells us, "and then when I touched it, it became a knife."

Ella's holding Jia's hand. "She's bleeding. Does anyone have something we can wrap around this?"

They all glance between them; Aiden's still holding me upright on the pile of books.

Ben speaks. "We're not prepared."

"Here" Will rips the sleeve off his shirt. "Use this."

While Ella's helping Jia wrap the fabric around the cut in her hand, Ben and Will walk around, studying the room. Aiden moves me so I'm resting against one of the walls. He tests it first with his hand to make sure it doesn't transform.

"It's a puzzle," Ben announces. "They have to make sure it's really us, right? And not someone who's happened to stumble upon this place." No response. "Will, you're the only person who can touch anything right now. You're the only one who can heal from any injury, and we don't know what these objects really are."

"That's great." He doesn't sound happy.

I whisper to Aiden, "Why isn't that great?"

"He heals, but he still feels the pain." I didn't know; he seemed to shrug off the bullets before so effortlessly.

Will walks around the room, trying to figure out what his best option is. "Do you think one of these things will become the crown or a stone? Do we even know what we're looking for? Should I only try the small objects?"

"I don't think size is relevant," Ben states.

Will doesn't seem encouraged. Nevertheless, he proceeds to start touching objects; first a table, which with a flash of light becomes a bowl. Next a chair that turns into mirror. And then an apple that becomes a beaker of acid. He yanks his hand away, shaking in pain while his veins glow green, healing.

With another hopeful try, he moves his fingers over a glass cup, only for his face to crease again in pain as a knife replaces the cup and slices across his hand. Within seconds, the only evidence that it ever happened lies in the blood drops across the dirt of the floor.

"Try the fireplace," Aiden suggests. "I can't move the flames."

Hesitant, Will still proceeds as instructed. In the spirit of getting it over with, he flings his hand at the flames that indeed turn out to be the very thing they were portraying. Green spreads across his hand as it repairs the new damage.

"Okay." I've recovered some strength. "Why has no one suggested..." I point at the curtain of fire, "...that?"

They know I'm right as they exchange glances. And as I suggested, Will walks over to the curtain of fire. It appeared out of nowhere earlier. It was a wall of stone, and with a spark, there was a doorway of fire. Will's hesitant again; I can only imagine the reluctance when you know the pain you can't avoid. But he doesn't disappoint as with a wave of an ever-healing hand, the wall changes once more to a wooden door. With a tug and a shove, he reveals it's locked.

"What now?" He turns to us.

Ella walks over to the entryway, peering through a small window amongst the wood. "There's a huge cavern on the other side. And right next to the door is this pedestal with I think, yes, a key. A gold key."

"Interesting," Ben says. "We used Will to reveal the objects' true selves, but with a bit of trial and error, anyone could've done that."

"Thanks." Will glares.

Ben continues, "But now, a locked door with a key beyond it. And conveniently enough, the door has a window so Ella can see inside and move the objects within." He smiles. "Interesting."

"Yeah, the place is booby trapped so only the six can collect whatever's hidden here," I say as I stagger to them by the door. My strength is returning. "It's not that hard to figure out."

Ben looks surprised as I push past him to lean against the

stone. I shoot a strained smile of reassurance towards Ella before she turns to face the key. With her face pressed to the glass and her skin starting to glow white, her eyes gloss over, and I can just make out the key on the other side slowly inching towards us. Soon enough, it's taken to the air and is ungracefully floating towards the lock. I've seen her control bullets before; why is this such a challenge? But her grasp of it is so weak it slips through the air and crashes onto the floor.

I place a hand on her shoulder. "You've got this, princess." I smile, and she returns the gesture.

Another attempt proves more successful as the key lifts up smoothly and without falter. It slides into the lock with ease and turn with little resistance so, with a gentle nudge from Ella, the door swings open to allow passage.

"Okay, what's next?" Aiden barges through the door.

Will wraps my arm around his neck as he helps me move further inside. I look up but I can't see the top; the cave walls continue into darkness. Across the cavern from us is a throne of stone and in between us and the throne lies an unlit brazier shielded in glass. The brazier's flames somehow find continuous air to thrive within the metal bowl on stilts. We're able to search our surroundings thanks to pools of fire that litter the ground around us.

"Let's assume there's six trials," Ben says. "Jess, Will and Ella have passed theirs, so now all that remains is us." He gestures to Jia and Aiden.

"I knew it!" Aiden cheers. "Fire's always the solution! What am I setting alight?"

I speak up. "I hate to point out the obvious, but…" I gesture to the brazier. "Well, that."

"Yes!" Aiden's enthusiasm is unmet.

"Let's think before we jump to actions," Ella says. "What if this is a trick?"

"We aren't supposed to light the brazier?" Jia asks.

"Well," Ella continues, "maybe the question is what can't we light?"

"Wait." Confusion rests on Aiden's face. "So I'm not lighting anything on fire? What do I do then?"

"I don't know yet," Ella replies. "let's just think."

For several moments, we stand in silence. I'm not sure if everyone else is thinking about this puzzle, but personally I'm more distracted thinking about if they're thinking about it. Yes, somehow I've found a way to procrastinate even the most basic task. But seriously, are they all thinking about this, or are they thinking about thinking about this? *Jess. Stop.*

Aiden interrupts the silence. "Okay, I'm bored now." Before anyone can say or do otherwise, he lights the brazier with a click of his fingers and a flash of glowing red around his hand.

But we barely see the light, because as quickly as it starts, it's over. The pools of fire fade to black, and we lose our sight. Next we lose our footing as the ground disappears beneath us; Will's shoulder under my arm slips from my grasp. I fall so hard it aches when I crash into the ground; my hands are the only barrier between my head and the stone.

Before me is a single candle. I reach out to stroke the wax; the only sound is the flickering of its flame. There's no other breathing, no one pulling themselves up or reaching out to help me. No one's questioning if we're okay or pondering what happened. I realise before I move my head that I'm alone.

When I do pull myself off the ground, I find my latest entrapment, a small cave with no entrance or exit, just walls everywhere. I can't see where I fell from, as the ceiling matches the floor. I'm alone with the candle, my only source of warmth, and light.

"Ella!" I shout with all my returning strength.

For a few seconds there's nothing, and I can feel my heart start to race.

But then, there's hope. "Jess!" Ella's voice travels from the other side of one of the walls.

I press my ear against it. "Ella! Where are you? Are you with the others?"

"No, I'm alone." Her voice isn't shaking like mine. "I'm in a room and there's this exit, but there are all these flying rocks blocking the way. I'm stuck. I can't hold even half of them still. But I'll keep trying."

I slide to the floor, my back to her. My once-blue dress has dirtied against the dirt and dust. "My room has no exit. I'm stuck."

After a pause, she replies. "No, you're not. You can create portals." Barely. "Create a portal to me."

"I can't see where you are, and I have to be able to picture where I want to go. Every time I've done it, I've dreamt of the place or been there myself. And it's more than seeing, it's hearing and feeling and touching and tasting. So when I create the portal, I'm continuing a memory." I can't create a portal to her, but I can create one somewhere else. But then I'd be abandoning her and the others.

"What if I describe it to you? Let me try."

I don't want to abandon her; I want to be the hero. "Okay." I close my eyes.

"Well, it's a cave, a little damp and cold." Just like where I am now. "But it'd make a great blanket fort. I'd hang the illuminators—" *illuminators?* "—from the ceiling but stick them to the walls, so it's as if the veins in the stone are lighting up like we do. And I'd lay several blankets across the ground to keep our feet warm; I think you could fit a mattress in the middle so we wouldn't hurt our spines." She stops. I wonder if she's smiling. "My dress is ruined. There's blood and dirt and somehow soot. But in our fort, it's perfect. And everyone's here, and we're drinking tea from that china set your mother has in the living room cupboard. We have the little food Aiden loves and he's laughing at something Jia said—no, something she did. Because she'd be dancing around the room under the illuminated light." I feel the chill spread across me as she describes something that isn't real. "I think we'd be dancing too. First, Jia would pull me into it and then after some hesitation I think you'd join. And you'd somehow manage to get Will involved—maybe you'd anger him into it." My shoulders start to sink under a new weight. "Aiden would already be spinning around, and after a while Ben would have to join in." My breath is being sucked away from me. "Life, it'd be beautiful. I wish you could see it." But I can; I believe it.

I open my eyes to see the darkness. And I pull myself through to find the light.

"Jess!" Ella's arms wrap around me. "You did it!"

I take deep breaths to calm my chest. "I think we did it." *Breathe.*

I made a portal. I knew exactly what I was doing, and I made a portal.

I can go home.

My eyes search but fail to find the image she painted. The cave is just like mine, even down to the candle on the floor. Although there's an exit, it's blocked by hundreds of tiny rocks shooting back and forth from tiny gaps in the wall. Beyond it, I think I can see ice, but the stones are moving too fast for my eyes to focus.

"I thought we did the trial," I say.

She replies, "I think it was just a warm-up, to prove it was us."

I gesture to the flying rocks. "And how is that possible?"

"How is any of this possible?" She shrugs. "The original protectors, the ones who must've created this, the stories sound as if they could do far more than us. I think they'd unlocked more of their gifts."

"So, maybe you're meant to stop the rocks?"

She hesitates. "I already tried."

Ella doesn't give up; she'll keep on trying till her final breath. But there are hundreds of the tiny rocks. I sigh. I don't think she's meant to stop them all.

"If you can hold as many still as possible, I'll try and create another portal."

Her hand rests on my shoulder. "Are you sure? You're—"

"Yes," I interrupt her. "We're going to get out of here together. But after we find the others."

I strain my eyes, trying to focus on the other side of the path; Ella's hand moves from my shoulder to interlock with my fingers. The warmth of her glow reaches me as several of the rocks stop in their tracks, shaking rapidly on the spot, trying to break free. The ice is more visible now; flakes of snow are being sucked into the whirlwind of the rocks.

It's much easier this time—I don't have to picture where I want to go. I can just look. Although, when the portal does appear, it accompanies pain; Ella has to guide me through as I clutch my head. I don't think the distance affects the strain, but the passengers do.

On the other side, it's cold. So cold I can see my breath freezing before me.

"Ella! Jess!" Aiden rushes over to us, holding out the flames across his hands to keep us warm, the veins on his arm glowing red. "I'm so glad you're both okay."

I think I get it now. I turn to Ella. "It's like you said. They had to work together to defeat him, and we have to work together to beat their puzzle."

"We have to work together," she repeats. She turns, shivering, to Aiden. "What's the next puzzle?"

He offers her his jacket before we follow him across the room, having to pause a flame as he removes each sleeve. "There's a boulder I can't move because if I stop the fire, we'll freeze." It's a heavy boulder, but yes, the freezing is the reason he can't move it.

"Okay, this is me." She shudders, wrapping Aiden's jacket tighter around her. I can't see the veins on her arms but for the first time I notice them across her neck and face. The boulder shudders like us as she creases her forehead, and soon enough it slides across the ice to reveal a gap in the wall, a gap that to my displeasure is far too small for any of us to squeeze through.

"Oh, thank life!" Jia's voice rings through the chilly breeze.

"Are y-you okay?" Ella asks, still shuddering.

Her voice is quick. "I'm fine, but you aren't. How can I help?"

"W-whats your r-room like?"

She looks around her. "There's a pool, but I can't see how deep it goes down." To her side, I can spot another candle. Only Aiden was left in the dark.

"S-stand b-back," I instruct. I hope this is the last time, but I somehow really doubt that.

On the other side I feel like I can finally breathe, despite falling to my knees exhausted. My head is screaming at me, but at least it's not cold. At least I won't freeze to death. I think I can die exhausted, and it'll probably be a relief.

"It's okay, I've got you." Ella's arm is around my waist, holding me off the floor. I have no energy to thank her. "This is the puzzle," she informs Jia. "And we have to work together at every stage to get out."

"We have to swim out," Aiden states.

"I can make air pockets!" Jia's face lights up. "I couldn't get out before because I couldn't see, but now you can use your fire to light the way." She stretches her arms. "I'll just need to make sure we have enough air for the flames."

"I've got you," Ella tells me as we all slip into the pool. The chill shocks me, but it's still nothing compared to Aiden's puzzle.

With Ella holding one side of me and Aiden holding the other, we drop further into the water. Jia's veins glow bright blue as she moves several air pockets around us while we descend; whenever Aiden's flame starts to die, she sacrifices another bubble. The deeper we go, the narrower the pool starts to get. Eventually, Aiden leaves my side to guide the flame into the abyss. When we reach the bottom, it's not over, as the pool continues along to the side; Aiden goes first, following the flame. Jia passes behind, guiding the air bubbles to us when she sees we need them. Then at the back, Ella drags me through. I start to recover some of my strength as I grab the cave around us to pull myself through the gaps.

When we finally do break free of the narrow tunnel, we rush upwards; Jia's down to her last air pockets, and they don't last long enough, as the flame dies first. Despite being in complete darkness, we continue rushing up. I use all the strength I have left—I don't want to drown. And I won't, because I can see it, I can see the light at the end of the tunnel. Literally.

We're out of air for the last few moments before we break the water's surface. Gasping like fish on land, the others pull themselves onto a nearby ledge. Ella waits and helps from the water as they pull me up.

"Will!" Jia exclaims.

He's still on the stone, lying on his side, soaking wet. Did he drop into the water? "I kept drowning," he whispers through deep breaths. They're at his side checking he's not hurt, but he's the Unbreakable Boy. "I'm fine, I just need a minute." He continues to heavy breathe.

I drag myself across the stone towards him, resting my head level with his. The others are searching around us. This room is the biggest so far. They take the candle to light their way and Will and I fall into the darkness it leaves. I find his hand, and he squeezes mine.

"Over here!" Ella shouts. I feel their footsteps as they rush to her. "Look, on the other side of the glass wall, it's Ben! He sees us!"

"We need Jess." Aiden's words are unintentionally painful.

I pull myself up into a sit. "I...I can try."

Ella shakes her head. "She's used all her strength."

With Aiden's hand, he picks me up and helps me over to the glass wall; I push them away and drop to my knees. I know what I need to do now—it's as clear before me as Ben is. But when I take deep breaths, I start to doubt myself, and I can't burn those thoughts.

I can't do this. I don't have enough energy left.

"No!" Aiden kicks the wall.

I give in.

Chapter Twenty-Six

Ella

"She needs more time," I say. I stroke her hair as her head rests in my lap; my dress is ruined anyway.

Aiden exhales, "It's been hours."

Jia and Aiden are using her heels to try to chip the glass, but it's so thick they've barely made a dent; on the other side, Ben scratches with claws that draw no marks, and across the room, Will's back to himself as he tries to dry his book near the candle's flame.

"Ben, it's not working!" Jia shouts.

Will replies, "He can't hear you." Tucking his book into his back pocket, he relieves me from Jess's weight. "We're missing something."

"Stand back," Aiden instructs before throwing balls of flames at the wall; they dissipate on impact.

"Okay, let's think about this." I start to pace the room, heels clicking against the stone. "We need Jess to get across to Ben, but she's too weak right now." Her body lies limp, chest barely lifting with each breath. "This is Will's room, but that's Jess's task. So what's Will's? And what do the rest of us do?"

"We need Ben." Jia's hand aligns with his through the glass.

"No, we need Jess." I go round in circles.

"And I need tea," Jess mumbles. She's so pale. We're all at her side quickly. "I need…" she stops to take a deep breath, "… water and food. I need more than sleep."

"That's it. This is where we die." Aiden falls back against the stone in the most dramatic fashion. "Well, except for you." He gestures to Will.

"I can heal, but I'll still starve." He kicks Aiden's leg.

"That's it." Jess takes long, gasping breaths. "We'll all die together." She tries to laugh but instead collapses on the floor.

Her body falls still.

"Jess" I shout.

I'm at her side, but Aiden's there faster. He shakes her, but it's no use, she's not sleeping. She's lost more than her energy. My mind is racing through the memories of any healing training I've had as I try to find her pulse. I can't tell if I'm doing it wrong or if she doesn't have one. I must be doing it wrong.

I claw at my head as I flash between Jess and Ben; he's shouting something, but we can't hear. What if he has the answer? This can't be how it ends. What do we do?

I glance across at Will, and our eyes meet. He can heal. And in the prophecy…

He shares my thoughts as he pushes Aiden out of the way to wrap his hands around Jess's face; it's not to stroke her cheek or find her pulse. Instead, his grasp is tight and pained. I know he's not trying to comfort her. No, he's trying to give her strength. Literal strength. My eyes widen as his veins glow green to heal her rather than himself. It's working.

She takes a deep breath. Droplets slide down my cheek; she's okay.

Aiden wraps himself around her. Through the floods pouring out of his eyes, he manages to say, "I thought you were going to die."

She pats him on the back, still breathing heavy.

"I called you a cold-hearted killer," Aiden continues through his sobs. "I'm so sorry."

She finds words. "That sounds like a compliment to me." Our eyes meet. I wipe a tear. She turns to Will. "You saved me." She smirks. "Guess you'd risk your life for me now, eh?"

"Oh, please, I just met you." He pulls her up onto her feet.

She wastes no time with her reborn strength as we walk over to the glass. Her hands rest on the barrier, her brow tense; with veins of tar and strength of Will, she opens another portal. Through the wall I watch the others run over to Ben. I hold her hand as we travel through. She's amazing.

"I didn't know you could do that," Ben says to Will.

He shrugs. "Me neither."

Aiden's already shooting fireballs around the room. "I need to get out of here." He's searching for the exit.

"Up there!" Jia points to a gaping hole in the ceiling, illuminated for brief moments as each fire reaches it.

"We have to work together." I take charge. "This is the real puzzle."

He nods; he knows what he has to do.

Within seconds, the Ben we know is long gone and in his place stands a creature with hard skin and long claws. Will collects his clothes. Ben's tail twists around us before lying to his side, acting as a step to his back. As we climb up, clinging to his scales, his head turns to watch us. He nudges Jess up with his nose. I can't place her expression.

"Ben can change his form," I explain.

"I know." She sits in front of me. "It's just…Everett would love this. His favourite part of *Game of Thrones* is the dragons."

What's a *Game of Thrones*?

Aiden lights the way as we take off, his flames float alongside us. Within the tunnel, rocks crumble, and I keep them away. After a short, while we reach a hurdle: a waterfall that rushes so fast, Ben recoils when he tries to pass through. Another try, and his leg, or hand, flinches away. He huffs.

Jia stands up on his back; Will and I hold her legs; her arms dance gracefully as she pulls the flow of water apart. She holds her breath to keep the water steady and Ben flies forward, wings narrowly missing the stream. Once we're through, she slips backwards. We catch her.

It'd be an understatement to say we're relieved when we finally touch down in the original cavern. Which is why we jump around celebrating while Ben returns to his normal form and re-dresses. As we laugh I almost forget why we were here in the first place.

"Okay, that *has* to be it," Aiden says. We start to search around. "We've more than proven ourselves."

"Especially me," Jess adds. "But I guess you learn by doing, right?" She walks towards the stone throne. "So I think I deserve a break. I'm sure you guys can handle the rest on your own."

"I don't understand," Ben says. "It should be obvious."

In the corners of my eyes, I notice that Jess takes a seat on the throne. I reply to Ben. "Maybe it's something to do with the brazier? That's how it started?"

"Hey, guys," Jess says.

"Or maybe it's back in the entrance?" Ben continues.

"Guys?" Jess tries again.

I ask, "Then why is this room so big?"

"Guys!" Jess shouts. We turn. "Do I have to do everything for you?"

In her lap, upon the throne, sits the crown.

So obvious.

"I actually don't know how we coped without you." Aiden laughs as we all rush over.

We did it. We actually did it. She passes me the crown. I'm holding it in my hands. "I'm going to go call for a stealth," I find myself saying.

Jess laughs. "Thank God, because I'm *not* creating another portal today."

I have to leave the cave to get a signal on my Hexagon. With one hand, I'm flicking through my contacts. No one can doubt us now. We did something no one else could. We started the prophecy. We started our story. It's all coming together, and everyone will see.

But as my gaze is fixed on the screen before me, I don't see.

Not until it's too late.

❊❊❊

"We have another problem," I shout.

Everything's going to be okay, I tell myself while the gun presses firmly into the grooves of my back. My veins are glowing white as I try to snatch it from their grasp, but since I'm unable to see it, nothing happens. And even if I was to free myself of their weapon, that doesn't solve the problem of the other five or so armed Red Suits, or the unknown more who could be hidden within their stealth behind me.

Jess is the first to appear and for a few moments she stands frozen at the cave entrance. Then she reaches for her weapon and takes aim—it's a bluff; our weapons are soaked and ineffective. She's as trapped as me. They don't know that.

"What's wrong?" Aiden asks from within. "Did her Hexagon get broken? I thought she had the waterproof model."

Just like Jess, once he emerges from the cave, he too is trapped. From the deep red of his veins I can see the internal battle he's suffering as he tries to fight the urge to erupt in violence. Somehow he understands this time that fire isn't the solution. What's different?

Shortly after, the others follow behind. The Red Suits turn their guns to them.

"How did you find us?" Ben's the first to speak.

"Funny you should ask." No. I know that voice. "Because it was you, after all, who taught us how to track Jess's ability."

"Scott," Aiden growls.

I can hear his smile as he moves closer. "Aiden."

"What do you want?" I search for control.

"Only whatever it is you've found," he says.

Jess replies, "What makes you think we've found something? We're just checking out the sights."

"The sights?" He stops in front of me. "You're in the middle of nowhere."

"Hey, don't mock my holiday destination."

"Oh, so you're on holiday now? I thought you were a little preoccupied trying to escape back to Earth."

She pauses. "Earth's overrated. Not enough caves."

"Put down the weapon, Jessica. You're outnumbered." He's done playing.

"Only people I dislike call me Jessica," she says, continuing to bluff. "So it's funny you should pick that over Jess."

He gives up on her, realising she'll never take anything he says seriously; what a useful defence. Instead, he stands before me, and his brown eyes lock with mine. Everything's changed but nothing has; my insides are fluttering. But I see it, that glimmer of hope hidden deep in his iris. There's still a light.

"Ella." His words fall so gently. "Make the right choice."

"Don't do this," I whisper. "There's good in you. I know it."

"Good?" he whispers back.

"Yes. I see it in your eyes. There's still hope." He moves closer while I speak. "You don't need to choose this life. Come back with us."

"Somehow I don't think the people at the BCD will welcome me back." His fingers grace my cheek.

I say, "We'll figure it out. Together."

"Together." He smiles.

Have I managed to convince him like I convinced Jess? The glimmer has turned into this beam, and it's shining down on me when he edges ever closer. His fingers find a place amongst mine as our hands intertwine. The fluttering in my chest increases; my heart tries to burst out my chest. And then it all falls apart. He slips away with the crown now in his possession.

He stole from me. Again.

Leaning in, he whispers in my ear, "Thank you."

"Okay," Aiden says, "you have what you want. Now let her go."

"Yeah, enjoy that useless thing," Jess joins in with another jibe.

The Red Suit holding their weapon to me turns to Scott, who's already started walking towards their stealth. How did they get a stealth? "What should we do with them?" It's a woman.

"Leave them. I know what little they're capable of. They're no threat," he replies.

Aiden laughs. "I'll show you a threat."

Will grabs him before he erupts in rage.

Scott smirks. "Bring that one, though." He gestures to me. "The Rose wants to meet her."

"No!" Jia yells but before she can act, Will grabs Jia and holds her in place alongside Aiden. He struggles to contain them both. "Ella!"

"We'll find you!" Ben shouts.

My last few glances are at Jess, who seems unusually calm.

What does she know that we don't? The doors are closing when I catch that glimmer in her eyes.

❖❖❖

They blindfold me the entire journey, which makes no sense, as inside the stealth I can't see where we're going anyway. When we finally land, they push me forward for what feels like forever, up and down steps. At one point we're in a pod and then finally, my eyes burn in the light as they toss me into a cell.

Am I above ground or below? I have no idea; the room has no windows and only one black door. Despite its great size, the only contents are the glass box cell in the centre. There's no bench or chair. Where do they expect me to sit? On the floor? Well, when the hours pass and my legs tire, that's where I end up.

After a great deal of time, the door opens. "Princess." Scott enters.

I don't have a response as he finds a place on the floor, facing me. Does he think by being on the floor that puts us on the same level? "Why are you here?" I ask.

"Together," he whispers.

I meant that. "I stand by what I said. You can come with me; I'll protect you."

He shakes his head. "I'm protecting you." How? "You were right, there is good in me. You don't understand yet, and that's okay, but we're the good guys."

"That's not true."

"You can't see it because the system's working in your favour," he argues. "Your father's the king. You were born with everything."

"So show me." *Let me talk you around.*

"Your father, the council, they're all corrupt." How? "No one votes for the king, so how is he meant to represent the choice of the people?"

"We vote for the council," I add.

"And it's rigged." He's so sure, even though he's wrong.

"Okay, so what instead?"

"That's it." His eyes light up. "The Rose, I choose her. She found me and told me about all this power I could have under her leadership, the wealth and land and respect. No more living in my father's shadow. I would have his success myself. So I choose her."

"It sounds like she just told you what you wanted to hear."

"Exactly! You get it!" He's animated. "She's our salvation, Ella. Under her leadership, you can have anything you want. She'll take from the corrupt to give to her believers."

"And what happens to the people who don't believe in her?"

He laughs. "Casualties of war."

"No." I shake my head. "This doesn't make any sense. You grew up with everything already. You have wealth and land and power—"

"But not respect," he interrupts.

Me neither. "That has to be earned."

"But what if it didn't? She can give you anything you

want." He pauses. "I don't understand how you can't see, Ella. We're the good guys. Under the Rose's leadership, we're going to get everything we deserve." Only her followers. "You have a choice to make. There's a war coming. Which side are you going to be on? The right or the wrong?"

This isn't the boy I grew up with; he was smart and caring and would stop to help passersby. This new man is power hungry. He has more than most, but it's not enough. And there's no affection for those who may suffer on his way, war casualties. But I still see hope. I always see hope.

"So, princess, what's it going to be?" he asks again.

I reply, "I'm on the side of good." His smile soon turns sour when I continue. "Long reign the king."

Chapter Twenty-Seven

Jess

Biack 31/01/2014

"What do we do? Ben, what do we do?" Aiden's freaking out.

"I don't know! Why are you always looking at me for answers?" he yells. He's mad.

"What if they hurt her?" Jia's worried.

And then there's Will, who's just done. "Enough!" he shouts. They fall silent. "We have to find Ella. Ben, do you have any way to track her?"

"No," he replies. "If she uses her gift, maybe? But that's how they tracked us here, so I doubt they'll give her that opportunity. They'll most likely lock her up in an empty room."

"Okay." Will paces. "We can't go back to the BCD. If they find out she's been taken, they'll send another more experienced team to rescue her."

I pipe up, "Would that be the worst thing?" They're all staring. "I mean, you just said they'd be more experienced, and I don't know anything about rescuing people."

"No one else is going after Ella in our place," Jia states. "She's our friend."

"And I'm sure she's their friend too. Everyone likes Ella," I say.

Ben frowns. "Do you know how hard she fought to be the person who went after you when you escaped?" What? "She was sure you'd listen to her over anyone else. She took on everyone for you."

"This is so different; there was only one of me! And I don't know how to fight. I mean, my brother showed me how to punch once, but I'm not even sure if that's right." My voice keeps on raising. "I care about her as much as you guys, but I don't know if we're what's best for her."

"Care?" *Oh no, Will, don't join in.* "The only person you care about is yourself. Ella would throw herself in front of a monorail for us." I think it's meant to be bus. "And we'd do the same. She's one of us." Aren't I? "Ella brought us together. She started this team. *We* care about Ella."

"*I* care about Ella," I return. "Did you not just see me in there? I could've run and left you all alone, but instead I chose to stay and it almost killed me!" I pause to get a hold of myself. "I care about Ella, but we're kids. We're not meant to run into burning buildings. This—" I gesture around us, "—was an adventure. But Ella now, that's enemy territory. So, I'm not going to let people hurt me again when there are better people for the job."

"You're so selfish," he utters.

I slam back, "I call it self-preserving. Life's about surviving, isn't it?"

"Why are you still here?" he asks. "Don't you have a world

to run away to?"

"Can you make up your mind already?" I'm yelling again. "One minute you want me to stay, the next you want me to go. What do you actually want?"

"Help. But it seems you're done for today."

"I got us out of there."

"And now when things get really tough, you want to run."

"Will, stop," Jia finally interjects. "This isn't helping."

"No," I mumble "No, it's not." And then I storm off into the woods. Deja vu.

❖❖❖

Not long later, while I'm sat resting against a tree, Jia comes to find me.

"I've never seen him like that before," she states. "And it doesn't make any sense to me. It's like sometimes he really dislikes you. But then at other times, it's quite the opposite."

"Well, I hate him too," I reply.

She raises a single eyebrow. "Sure." She sighs. "Jess, we need your help."

I don't respond.

"Ella told us some of the stories, you know. Because originally that's all they were, stories." She continues, "I know about your stepdad. And I know the pain's still there. It might never go. But if you're looking to escape it here, you can't. You'll probably get hurt again. It'll probably be worse. You may die."

"Is this supposed to make me want to help?"

I could sink into her eyes. "I'm sorry life dealt you this hand. It's not fair." It's not. "You have a choice to make. You can stay, and you'll probably get hurt, but you'll have us beside you every step of the way. You'll never be alone again. Or you can leave and spend your life running."

"Aren't you going to beg me to stay? What about all those prophecies?" I ask.

"I shouldn't have to beg you to do the right thing, especially not if you're one of the six. So stay or go. No one's forcing you to do either. This is your life, and you get to decide who you're going to be."

I laugh. "Do you know what you're asking me to do if I stay? It almost killed me. What will happen if next time there's enemies around and I can't stand?"

"I didn't say it'd be easy," she replies. "So, what's it going to be, Jess? Who are you going to be?"

I'm seventeen? How am I supposed to know who I want to be? I don't know how I want to spend the next eighty years of my life when I can only remember the past ten. I don't know what the right path is or what will make me happiest. All I know is how to stay alive another day. And every cell in my body is screaming at me to keep on surviving. But then, what am I surviving for?

And what will come of Everett if I don't return to Earth? Will he finally be free of the town we had to call home? Or will he spend the rest of his life searching for me? Can I bring him here, or is that a worse fate? What if I said goodbye? I don't even know if I could.

Maybe I need to fight my instincts; everything that's happened the past week goes against all I know to be true. What if I was born on Earth but made for somewhere else?

No. I don't need to decide this now. Or maybe ever. I can travel between the worlds—why do I need to pick one? I can stay to help Ella and be home for dinner. I can hang out in Ben's lab and still wait on the doorstep for Everett. I can help find these gems and graduate secondary school. But if I belong to two worlds, do I really exist in either?

Jia's already gotten up. I've been in thought a while. She's started to leave when I finally respond. "I think I know where Ella is."

❖❖❖

"You're back," Will states.

"There's no need to cry about it," I reply.

Aiden snickers. "Keep it in your pants, guys."

"Fight me, Aiden," I bark back.

Will continues, "I thought you were trying to run from death."

"I think it's time I changed my MO." He has no idea what I'm talking about.

Jia finds a space next to Ben on the floor. In the short time I was outside, he's managed to sketch a map of Earth—wait, no, Biack—across the cave floor. Where did he find the chalk? Several crosses decorate the continents; I'm assuming they're possible locations for Ella's imprisonment.

"Jess thinks she knows where Ella is," Jia says. "Do any of these places seem familiar?"

"I had a dream last night. It's how I knew about this place. I saw it. And I also saw Ella and I on the roof of this building, this underground building. I think they've taken her to an underground city," I say.

Aiden asks, "Can you do what you did before and draw it?"

"There are other ways to get there." Jia picks up on my hesitation. "Ben, how many underground cities are nearby?"

"I don't know. I have no idea where we are," he replies. "But there's only a few cities that are still habitable. We'd need to return to the BCD, and maybe I can see if the maintainers have picked up on any activity."

"If we return, we'll have to explain where Ella is, and then they'll hand this over to someone else." Pacing around the cave, Will is still returning objects to their original forms. "No one trusts us with the serious stuff."

"Maybe we can sneak back in," Ben says. "Jia, do you know anyone willing to pick us up and keep it quiet?"

Aiden laughs. "Awesome, we're really going to sneak into the most secure building in the world."

"I think I know someone." Jia pulls herself off the floor before heading towards the exit. "I'll go call him now."

Ben and Aiden follow Jia outside. Across the room, Will's found a quiet corner to sit and read. I swallow my pride.

"Can I sit here?" I gesture towards the empty beside him. "Or is that selfish?"

He responds with a roll of his sad blue eyes. I've been so

obsessed with the tragedy within me, but what of the tragedy of The Unbreakable Boy? It's easy to look at the scars and see them as victories, battles his body's survived, but they're also wounds he's suffered, pain he's felt. The Unbreakable Boy is broken.

"What does it feel like? To be shot."

He stares at me for a while before replying. "Bad."

"And yet, you always live. Are you immortal?"

"No." His gaze moves away.

At least he won't have to watch everyone he loves grow old and pass away. "What if you were blown up? Would you survive that?"

He turns back to me. "I don't know."

"What if you were beheaded?" I continue. "Would your head regrow, or would it somehow reattach to your body?"

"I don't know."

"What if your heart was ripped out? Would you need a new one?"

He shrugs. "Again, I don't know."

"What do you know?" I nudge him, defusing the last remnants of anger.

"That you're the most annoying person I've ever met. And I've spent years with Aiden."

"Aiden's an amateur," I say.

With fleeting smiles and quick glances, whatever was wrong between us becomes fixed. And I didn't have to apologise or talk about my feelings. That's a real win.

"Are you going to stay?" he asks.

"I'm here now, aren't I?"

He shakes his head. "No, I mean after this. Are you going back to Earth?"

I hesitate. Everett. "I don't know yet."

"And that's why I haven't made my mind up," Will states. Damn, I really thought I'd won. "I don't know if tomorrow you'll do the things you did today."

"I want to be the person Ella believes I am," I state.

"So does everyone. Okay, I'm going to go see what's taking the others so long."

As he leaves me alone in the cave, I return to my dream from last night. What hasn't happened yet? The images are fragmented; I remember being on the roof, but where were we before? I think we were in a cell—no, outside a cell. Ella's outside too. So who's in it?

My breathing's starting to feel heavier, and why are my legs aching? A quick tug of my dress reveals a darkness spreading across my whole body, across my veins. No, I wasn't trying to, I'm not ready yet, the others aren't here.

The portal appears in front of me.

"Guys!" I yell, but they can't hear me.

I lean against the wall. I can't sustain this for long.

I could hope that maybe Will could return my energy again, but what if he used up all of his last time? And even if everyone comes back before the portal ends, do I have the strength to take all of them? Oh God, where are they?

I can't do this alone. But I don't think I have a choice. I have to do this, for Ella.

I step through the portal.

✜✜✜

I've never seen an underground city before. Well I have, but not awake.

As I search around the cavern, lights guide me across the marathon of a bridge. And considering the unreachable sky, the street lamps and building lights make the city clear as day. Districts crowd over the underground mountains and surrounding cliffs, joined by further bridges arising from the pit of darkness below. Giant icicles of rock try to touch the city but are just out of reach above; I fear that if even one cracks off, everything will tumble into the below. I step over the cracks I don't miss. With thunderous applause, half of a nearby bridge collapses under the weight of abandonment. A colony of bats—I think they're bats—races out from underneath the bridge's remains, twisting around the nearest district. Within the centre, posters line the buildings in ode to the glory days; the inhabitants found something better. At the highest point, in the very centre of this massive underground cavern, lies a tower Rapunzel could call home. I gravitate towards the building from my dream.

I don't encounter any resistance on the way. How many Red Suits are there? Is it a new movement or decades in the making? Are there thousands of covert monsters hidden in plain sight, or a handful of delusional extremists living in the shadows?

This is where the clean ends; above, the world is so perfect, but underneath the trash lies decay and past.

I pick up an old bat, but really it's just a weirdly shaped stick. I cling to the dusty wood as I reach the building at the foot of the tower. The double doors creak as I peer inside—perhaps stupidly, but hindsight is golden. *Oh Jess, what are you doing, you foolish girl?*

Maybe this was the city hall, or the leader's house, or the headquarters of an all-powerful corporation. I tiptoe down hallway after hallway of this centre of control, hiding behind curtains when I twice run into patrolling Red Suits. My heart won't calm as I try to slow my breathing. I need to find Ella soon before my lungs give me away. Armchairs and side tables, benches and paintings litter the hallways. On the third floor I'm pressing my ear against every door. I don't know where I'm going. Then, from the room at the end of the hall, I hear a voice I vaguely remember.

"I'm protecting you." Is he speaking to Ella? "You were right, there is good in me. You don't understand yet, and that's okay, but we're the good guys."

If they're the good guys, why do they wear masks? Maybe it's to avoid prejudice. In superhero movies, the good guys always wear a mask.

"That's not true." I found her.

"You can't see it because the system's working in your favour. Your father's the king. You were born with everything."

It's true, she was born in a palace, and I've seen her closet— if you can even call it a closet. But surely if the system's working in her favour, she shouldn't have to fight for everything?

"So show me," she replies.

"Your father, the council, they're all corrupt." That's a big accusation. Is he going to elaborate on it? "No one votes for the king, so how is he meant to represent the choice of the people?" Isn't that why there's a council?

"We vote for the council." Exactly.

"And it's rigged." Another big accusation.

Ella asks, "Okay, so what instead?"

"That's just it. The Rose." Is that what she wants? To rule? "I choose her. She found me and told me about all this power I could have under her leadership, the wealth and land and respect. No more living in my father's shadow. I would have his success myself. So I choose her."

"It sounds like she just told you what you wanted to hear." Damn, Ella is good.

"Exactly! You get it! She's our salvation, Ella." The everyman's salvation. "Under her leadership, you can have anything you want. She'll take from the corrupt to give to her believers." Sounds like she's plagiarising Robin Hood.

"And what happens to the people who don't believe in her?"

"Casualties of war." That's a very human way to explain away murder.

"No. This doesn't make any sense. You grew up with everything already. You have wealth and land and power—"

"But not respect," he says as he interrupts her. Ironic.

She replies, "That has to be earned."

"But what if it didn't? She can give you anything you

want." I don't think respect is something you can take by force. "I don't understand how you can't see, Ella. We're the good guys. Under The Rose's leadership, we're going to get everything we deserve. You have a choice to make. There's a war coming. Which side are you going to be on? The right or the wrong?"

If thirteen years of history lessons have taught me anything, it's that Henry the Eighth had commitment issues, and there's no right side in war. But I guess there's usually a less bad side. Genghis Khan, for one, set the bar pretty low.

"So, princess, what's it going to be?"

"I'm on the side of good. Long reign the King." Oh damn, I wish I could see his face.

And I soon get that chance as footsteps approach the other side of the door; I hide behind an armchair in the corner, stuffing my ruined dress behind its shield and gripping my bat, prepared to fight if I need to. But I don't. He's completely oblivious to me as he locks the door and then waits outside. Why isn't he leaving? After too many minutes, a Red Suit appears. Are they one of the Red Suits I hid from earlier? There's no way to tell. They could be anyone.

"You took your time." Scott shoves a key into their hand. "I said give us a few minutes. Do you not know how to count or tell the time?" That's not fair, it's probably really hard to see clocks behind the bandages. "Just do your job." His face is disgusted as he walks away. I think he's just trying to hide his rage.

Scott leaves so quickly; it's quiet much too soon, and I struggle to control my breathing. Maybe they can't hear as well through the bandages? The person's back is to me as I peer around the armchair. There's only one of them. I can do this. I can take them, and even if I can't, I think I have to.

The only sounds are the whack of my bat against their padded head and the thud of their body against the floor, no scream or cry to give away their identity. I wait for a few seconds to see if they get back up. They don't. Stealing their keys and gun, I break into Ella's room.

"Jess! Are you okay?" She presses herself against this glass box she's being kept within.

I search for a way to open it. "A little shook. I knocked out this Red Suit outside, and I'm just hoping they're out for a bit."

She keeps watch of the door. "Are the others with you?"

"Funny that. I kind of fell here on my own." I mumble to myself, "I thought I was done with that."

"It's up to us then." As she replies, the bat flies out of my hands towards the glass box, repeating the motion several times until cracks start to form. It doesn't take long for it to give way, shattering across her in the process. Cuts garnish her arms while blood drips onto her dress, but weirdly she doesn't care.

She hands me back the bat; I hand her the gun. "What's up to us?"

"To recover the crown, defeat the Rose, rescue Scott, save the world," she lists casually.

"Nothing much then," I reply. "Should've asked the others to put the kettle on."

What the hell have you gotten yourself into, Jess?

Chapter Twenty-Eight

Ella

What in life have you gotten yourself into, Ella?

I'm trying to pretend I know where we're heading; every hallway looks the same, which is typical of buildings that had to appear quickly. As we slowly creep forward, I catch my foot in a crack in the tiles. The heel of my shoe snaps off. *They were so beautiful,* I think as I toss them aside.

"You don't know where you're going," Jess states.

I pause. "I don't know where I'm going." We stop in the middle of our nowhere.

"Well." She spins around, pretending to look for something. "Should I ask someone for directions?"

I'm smiling when I realise she might be on to something. "Yes."

"Wait."

I walk past her.

"You know I was joking, right?"

I think it takes us at least ten minutes before we find anyone; why were we being so careful before? Jess is storming down the corridor when I yank her back just before she can pass around the corner. Three voices—no, four—all men. They don't sound like they're on the move. Are they guarding something?

"Wait." I stop Jess again. "We don't want to attract more than we can handle."

"Okay, so how are we playing this? Should I make small talk first, or just straight-up ask them for directions?"

The bat. "Swap weapons with me."

Peering around the wall, I witness them in action, or non-action. There's nothing to guard. Maybe they're off duty. If it wasn't for the deep of their voices, I'd never know they were men. Their heights vary but their appearance is identical—the wrapping around their heads and hands, the deep red of their clothing.

We need to act fast before they discover us first. Holding up the bat, I slowly let it slip from my fingers and watch as it glides through the air towards them. My veins shine white. Suddenly, as if it's hit by lightning, it quickly strikes one red suit and knocks him to the floor. There's no time for them to react as the bat darts to the next victim and then the next. Only one remains.

"Freeze." Jess jumps into action and points her gun at the last man standing; he trips over the air and lands on the floor.

I collect the bat. "What's your name?"

"W-what?" he stutters.

"It's called small talk," Jess says. "It's supposed to break the tension."

He gulps. "Ninety-two."

Jess's face falls paler than before.

"Ninety-two." How odd. "We're looking for the crown that was stolen from us. Do you know where it's being kept?" I ask.

His hesitation is expected. "You-you can't kill me. I have a family."

"You're lying." Jess is quick to speak. "Tell her where the crown is."

Was she right? Quickly his mannerisms change as the shaking disappears, but a cold confidence takes its place. "The top of the tower. There's stairs that way." He gestures to another hallway. "They'll take you all the way up."

I place a hand on his arm. "Thank you, Ninety-two."

He meets the same fate as the others as Jess hits him across the head with her gun.

"I can't believe that worked," she says as for a few seconds she looks in disbelief at her own actions. Then she continues, "Let's go."

He was honest; we find the stairs where he gestured. The top is out of sight above. My feet ache from the cold of the stone and are dirty under its dust. Jess strides on ahead, fazed by nothing. Her hair sways in front of me as we pass by open windows. How does it do that when there's no wind?

Suddenly she stops. "I think there's something else we have to do first."

"What?" What could be more important?

I follow her onto a higher floor, then down further corridors. I don't know how she knows where she's going, but she does. She's so confident.

"Where are we going?" I ask.

She stops outside a set of double doors. She tries the handles, but nothing moves. Throwing her weight against them, she finally answers me. "We have to rescue these people. I saw it in a dream."

"Okay." I believe her. "Stand back."

She moves out the way. I stretch out my arms with no intention of reaching anything, at least physically. My veins light up their familiar white and the doors start to shake. I hold my breath as the hinges loosen their grip on the wood. Eventually one of the doors flies out of its frame. We only needed one.

"Princess!" A woman's voice.

We rush into the room to find another glass cell much like mine, but this time there are different people held inside, two men and a woman. I recognise them. That woman, that voice —she's from the New Year ball.

It's the scientists they kidnapped.

"We didn't tell them anything," one of the men says.

"Stand back," Jess commands. She aims her weapon at the glass. The scientists follow her instructions. The bullet pierces the glass, shattering it.

We're helping them out of the cell as I turn to Jess and say, "It's amazing you knew they were here."

"If I'm being honest," she replies, "I don't even know who they are."

We're checking if the scientists are alright when a siren rings through our ears; they've realised I escaped.

"Quick!" Jess shout over the noise.

With the scientists following between us, we sprint back to

the stairs and up the floors. My legs tire before my arms, but I don't stop. I can hear shouting below us. At the top, Jess shoves her way through the door's stiffness, and we fall out into the dark.

What a view. I was robbed of a chance to witness before, but this is a place of stories and tales I never considered I'd visit. Underground cities are mostly derelict, after all, due to their poor construction. But no, this place is beautiful. In the far distance I can barely see the end of the chasm, but the river flowing through the centre is as clear as day. And what lies within these buildings? Because I could easily mistake this void of a city for a home to many. Families could reside in the houses and workplaces in the offices, kids could play in the park while their parents shopped along the high streets. Life could exist here. Are we sure it doesn't?

In the centre of the rounded rooftop waits a single pedestal holding the crown. It was never intended to sit on stone, but it's the only safe place. I walk towards it, barefoot on the roof top, carving out the gaps on its surface with my eyes. It belongs with a protector. And yet, as I reach out to collect it, it fades before my eyes.

"Ella!" Jess yells from behind me.

I spin around to see Scott holding her in place, a gun to her back. Three other Red Suits stand around him with guns of their own aimed at the scientists. We're locked in a silent standoff until another player enters the game.

Slowly, from the shadows behind the entryway, a woman in all black emerges. With skin void of colour and strands of darkness falling from her head, she's adorned in a dress of black lace and lips of deep red that she pushes together in a smile. Upon her head rests the twisted bark of the crown. This time I believe it's real. There's a chill that fills the air as her presence becomes known.

"They said you were beautiful, but that word doesn't do you justice." The words slip from her lips so gently.

"W-who are you?" I try with all my might to stand strong.

"Darling, I'm the future. I'm the everyman's salvation. I'm the true queen and the destined ruler. I'm the start of the new age and the end of the old. I'm the bringer of justice and the destroyer of corruption. I'm the power this world's never seen before and the ultimate survivor of darkness." The edges of her mouth rise. "I'm the Rose."

I forget to breathe.

She continues, "And I'm going to give the people what they want, what they deserve."

I catch a glimpse of a single rose, the deepest red, held within her grasp. Does she plan to leave that behind? What will be left when this is all over? What story will they tell? No, I get to write it.

"You're twisting the anger people feel towards themselves and turning it on my father. You're playing on their hatred and rage, and nothing good can come of that."

I'm quick as I reach out and use my gift to snatch the crown from her head. She's quicker as she grasps it mid-air.

"Hate," she spits as we fight for control. "The strongest emotion."

Jess speaks. "You sound like seven billion people I know."

"And each and every one of them is welcome in the new world I'm going to build," she continues.

"I think they're a bit preoccupied destroying their own," she retorts. "So, this was fun. Nice to catch up. You're as creepy as ever, and I think it's time we left now."

Scott tightens his hold. "You're not going anywhere."

My eyes can't move from the body of the crown but my words say, "Scott, don't do this. This isn't you."

"This is what my parents have made me," he replies. "And this is what your dad has made you. You just don't see it yet."

The Rose continues. "Join me, Ella. Join us. Join the rebellion. Help us find the gems and rebuild the crown. Help me reclaim my throne."

How can she reclaim something she never had?

"I'm loyal to my father till the end." I stand firm; the crown shakes in her grasp.

"Your time will come. Soon he'll disappoint you too, and I'll be here with open arms."

I shake my head. "No, my father's the best person I know, an amazing leader. The people love him. You're building an army with false promises, and he's protecting a world with honesty."

"Honesty?" She releases an echoing laugh that reaches the far corners of the city, bouncing off the chasm walls and slicing through the streets. "You have a lot to learn, Ella Day."

"Nothing will change my loyalty," I state.

Her face turns sour. "Let go of the crown if you want your

friend to live."

Jess struggles, and I finally notice it, the black spreading through her veins across her neck. She has an escape plan.

"Scott, please don't do this," I distract as Jess closes her eyes. "I don't believe everything between us was a lie. I know you care for me. Do the right thing."

I still see the glimmer as he says, "I am doing the right thing."

Jess opens a portal to our side, we have to act quick. With my spare hand and spare thoughts, I fly the pedestal that once held the crown across the roof towards them. Scott and the Red Suits jump out the way, Jess breaks free. She yells at the scientists to run, and soon they've disappeared into the darkness. She's about to step through the portal herself when she notices I haven't moved. The crown still struggles in the Rose's grip.

"Ella, you have to let go!" Jess yells.

"I know you, Ella Day," the Rose shouts. "You don't want to be a queen. And you don't have to. When I rule Biack, you'll have the freedom to decide your own path." Freedom. "Let's work together. Let's help each other."

I want Freedom. It's all I've ever wanted. I want to decide my own life.

"She's just saying what you want to hear!" Jess grabs my arm. "You're stronger than that."

I move my gaze between her and the Rose. I know she's right. But what if…?

No.

I let go. But I don't give in.

Faintly, in the second before we step through the portal, leaving the crown in her grasp, I can hear her say, "This is just the beginning of our story, Ella Day."

Chapter Twenty-Nine

Jess

Biack 02/02/2014

"Jessica Durand?" Upon lifting my gaze, I discover a fair-haired protector standing above me.

"Actually, I've been trying to get *The Girl from Far Away* to catch on for a while now," I reply.

What an angelic smile. "It's a bit of a mouthful."

"I have a thing for long names."

He finds a seat beside me in the hall, which is circular, I might add. The building's comprised of circular layers; the first is the entrance, where security checks allow you to pass through to the layer I currently reside in. I think this is a waiting room? The floors above us are filled with offices, Ella said, so this is the business section. Beyond a set of double doors nearby me lies the grand chambers. That's where the council await and the ultimate politics happen. Or so I've been told.

"Do you want to be friends or something?" I try to decipher his intentions after giving him sufficient time to respond to my previous remarks.

Teeth flash through his grin. "If you insist."

"That wasn't what I meant." I pout. "Who are you, any-way?"

"Damien Griffin," he replies. "Unassigned Protector."

I state, "Just another solider then."

"But what if I'm not just another solider?" He shrugs. "What if I'm special?"

"And how are you special?"

That grin. "You saved my life. So I guess I'll be saving yours."

I have no idea what he's talking about.

"Jessica." A stern figure emerges from the grand chamber doors. "They're ready for you."

I turn to Damien. "Nice to meet you, *special solider.*"

"The feeling's mutual, *The Girl from Far Away.*" He waves.

Well, I guess all friends do start out as strangers.

❖❖❖

"Please state your name for the official record," the stern man orders.

"Jessica Durand." Am I nervous? "But I'm also known as *The Girl from Far Away.*" Apparently not that nervous.

No one seems impressed.

They sit on high pedestals around me, maybe twenty of them. But the seat in the dead centre before me belongs to none other than the King of Biack.

"Please state your place of origin," the man continues.

"Thirteen Acer Walk, Fairwater, England, United Kingdom." I almost forgot. "Oh, Earth!"

"Please state your date of birth." More instructions.

"The thirtieth of December, 1996," I answer. "For anyone who's bad at maths, that makes me seventeen."

God, these people need to lighten up. Are they capable of laughter? I'm on fire today.

"And now…" Liam Day, Ella's dad, the king, leans in. "In your own words, please explain to us the events of the last thirteen days."

Okay. "Right, well, where do I begin?" I start.

"Thirteen days ago," a woman answers from one of the high seats.

I roll my eyes; am I allowed to do that here? "I think to explain those thirteen days, I need to go back to the very start of my tragedy. I need to tell you how wonderful my early years were and then how out of nowhere everything changed. How my father took his own life and my mother remarried an abuser. How the only thing that kept me going were these dreams of another girl in another world doing things that seemed impossible. They kept me going.

"Then my only friend, my older brother Everett, was forced out of the house, and I caught my boyfriend with my best friend. And *then* somehow, in the chaos of it all, I kind of fell here. And got stuck here. Yeah.

"I remember waking up in a hospital, then a cell, then a locked room. I was a prisoner of this world. Even once I escaped the cages, I was chased, hunted. I was desperately trying to escape. But one of your own ended up on this journey with me. Originally he was my prisoner; I wanted to learn about this world from him, although it soon turned out he was using me for the same thing.

"We went to the beach, the cities, the towns and the ruins, and yet I'm pretty sure we never left this island. Somewhere along the way, Ella and he wore me down with their persistence, and that's how I think I signed my life away.

"I'm sure the others told you how we ended up in some cave where crazy shit happened, and then those pesky Red Suits showed up and stole Ella and that weird crown. Then by some accident I ended up in this underground city. It was impressive, I won't deny, but also filthy and falling apart. So long story short, I rescued Ella, but we lost the crown to the creepy lady who calls herself the Rose, and is probably the most dramatic person I've ever met.

"Did I miss anything?"

They're all exchanging annoyed looks, or maybe that's just their regular facial expressions.

"Jessica Durand," the king speaks. I think he's smiling. "As a consequence of losing the crown, you are now tasked with retrieving the six gems before the Red Suits can. Because this is a task also bestowed upon the S team, the only logical option is to assign you to the team and name you a protector."

What? "Wait," I hesitate. "I'm not in trouble?"

Another council member speaks, a much older one adorning a beard that dangles far below his seat. "In a way, you are. But in another much greater way, you're not."

What?

"So do you, Jessica Durand—" the king pauses, "—otherwise known as *The Girl from Far Away*, pledge to protect this world from all dangers that bestow it, at any cost it might take?"

My whole life, I've wanted to fit in, to find my home, my place of belonging. And all along, it was right before me whenever I closed my eyes. I may not know how this story will end, but I know what I have to do now. I know who I want to be.

"Yes." And I really mean it.

❖❖❖

I'm waiting outside in the hall for Ella when he appears behind me.

"Jessica, a word?" The king summons me to the corner.

He's taller than he seemed in the dreams, but nothing remarkable. In fact, with a glance, there would be nothing remarkable about him at all. He'd blend in on the streets of London or any commuter train. He's just a man in a smart suit. But then, he's also so much more.

"You'll be staying in Will's room in Day Palace until a room in the BCD is available," he says.

I nod. "Okay. Are there no spare rooms in the palace?"

"Oddly, no. But if you'd rather, I could arrange for one to be made available there, instead of in the BCD?" He's doing this thing where he straightens his clothes. Ella does that. I shake my head. "There's also another thing." Oh? "I wanted to thank you for rescuing Ella." It was kind of by accident. "But I need to ask something more of you." What more is there? "You see, Ella is my most important thing, my very most important thing. She's the best of all of us. And I never wanted her to have any of the responsibility she holds. When she was born a girl, I cried because of the weight placed upon her shoulders. And when she realised her powers, I cried again because I knew she'd give everything for this world. Even her life." He squeezes my arm. "So Jessica, Jess, I need you to promise me you'll keep her alive, no matter what's at stake. She's more than a prophecy, bigger than her destiny, but she is blind to it."

"Why are you asking me?" Why not one of the others?

"Because you're a survivor. And while I know Will is too, there's something about you. I believe you'll be the last person standing."

Maybe I'm starting to believe it too. "Okay. I promise."

❖❖❖

"One of us! One of us!" Aiden chants while slamming his fist into the wooden floorboards in rhythmic time.

"We're going to give this a makeover—" Jia gestures to my new uniform, "—and make it really you."

I spin around in my new clothes: soft cotton black trousers that fit tight against my legs with stretching fabric over the joints and pockets up and down; basic black T-shirt tucked into the webbed belt that ties together with a metal BCD logo; my previously worn black combat boots that I now consider a kind of lucky charm; and the coveted BCD jacket, complete with the golden logo on the side of the upper arm.

She untucks my T-shirt. "There, better already."

I replace the jacket with Everett's. There, better already.

Jia taps at the TV until some kind of electronic music starts blasting out of speakers around the walls. Dancing around the room, she pulls Ella up to join her; they hold hands as they sway, jump and twirl. Aiden joins in of his own accord. Ella extends a hand to me then yanks me up onto my feet. There's no unity in their dancing; they move however they feel. I reach out to Will and drag him up, him reluctant at first, but soon he sings along with Jia. And finally, we all grab Ben's hands and lift him to his feet too.

It feels like I've known them forever.

The evening continues as we lie about talking till the early hours. Aiden shows us how many of these cheese puff things he can catch in his mouth—I think Ella's just a good throw. Ben knocks over a wine glass that isn't a wine glass; we mop it up with blankets. Jia shows us her favourite songs as she recounts her first concert experience. It sounds very PG compared to concerts I've been to. Will and I recount our travels, and Ella and I describe the Rose for the hundredth time.

Eventually, they're all asleep. Ben and Ella lie in her bed with eye masks on, while Aiden sprawls out on one of the sofas. Jia lies across the floor with her head resting on a pillow in Will's lap. He pulls a blanket over to her to keep her warm and then starts writing in another book. I sit next to him and rest my head on his shoulder. For a while we don't say anything, and it's ever so comfortable.

Then he speaks. "You don't need to wait for me to fall

asleep."

I pause before replying, "I'll be back."

His lips touch my head as he whispers, "I know."

For a little bit longer, we sit here together and then eventually, as the night starts to brighten outside, I pull myself up and head towards the door.

I stop and turn around; our gaze meets for another moment that lasts too long. "Are we still friends?"

"Of course." He smiles.

And for me, that's all I need. "For what it's worth," I say, "I'd jump in front of a monorail for you too."

"Really?"

I grin. "Oh, please, I just met you."

❧❧❧

It's four a.m. and the palace is silent.

I tiptoe down the grand staircase, fingers sliding along the wooden banister. The stone walls are adorned with portraits of once-powerful kings. They all look like Liam Day. Every inch of the building carries intricate detail. No wall is simply bare and smooth even if decorated with paintings; the grooves carve out the location of the frames.

Lost in a minus level is an underground spa with gentle, mint-green water. Petals of flowers I've never seen before drift around the water, collecting in groups like in a schoolyard. Unlit candles wait around the sidelines, ready for the next guest. Loungers prepared with neatly folded towels sit in cut-away rooms to the sides. The lighting is dim.

At the far side of the ground floor hides a greenhouse dripping with plant life, from the railings of the second and third layers to the columns decorating the space. I imagine in the daylight rainbows gleam across the ponds as the light fragments from the glass, shielded only by the flowers living on the surface. Birds would sing and you'd lose yourself in the vegetation.

On the second floor I find the most important room, the grand library. Only two stories, distinguished by a balcony; there's no guide to find what you're searching for. You simply stumble upon it. Ladders of white lay against the mountains of colour. Gold detailing embellishes the bookcases. Single bookstands hold words of languages I don't recognise. Lone armchairs rest ready for the solitude of reading.

The ballroom is now vacant, as if hundreds of people never tried to fit inside, no trace of any occasion left behind. I walk across the middle, looking between each side at the paintings sitting in their grooves, from lone scenic views to celebrations of people. I twist around the columns and trace the faces of the sculptures with my fingertips. In the middle I lie down to witness the ceiling. It's like an out-of-body experience as I feel sucked into the art, the stars, the pictures. I run through the fields of crops and blend into the crowds; then I push through the branches of trees to drift among the gods of space.

I leave through one of the glass doorways; the sheer curtains blow into the room with the breeze. Outside, I to step down into the gardens. Hedges decorate walkways as I dance through the mazes, drawing water into the air as I circle the fountains, twirling along a path lined with arches of shrubbery mixed amongst fairy lights. Eventually, I find a rest upon a hill that looks across the lake and river to the sleepless city.

I want more. I need more. I've barely seen what this world has to offer.

A friend fills the space beside me. "Were you going to leave without saying goodbye?"

"It's not really a goodbye. More of a 'see you later,'" I reply. "Besides, we still have work to do."

We watch as in the distance, behind the hexagons of the dome, the sun starts to wake and the birds begin to sing. The fairy lights across the gardens dim, and the boats begin their days in the lake. Flowers bloom, and paths reveal themselves. And as I take my place on two feet, a known darkness forms in the space before me.

Ella says, "See you later."

And I will.

Earth

When I was five years old, I fell off my bike.

It was at the top of this hill that overlooks Fairwater. Everett ran home to get our parents, and while I cried all alone, this woman appeared to save me. She rocked me till the tears faded and the sobs softened. She told me about her own daughter, who was about my age. If she could've wished anything for her, it was that one day she'd be able to pick herself up when she fell.

I'm all alone again as I sit upon the very same hill, watching the town creep to life. But this time no one's coming to save me, and that's okay. Because this time when I fell, I picked myself up.

"Jess?" Clara climbs the path towards me. It's been a few weeks, but it feels like a lifetime since I last saw her across the canteen. "Oh my God, it is you." She finds a seat on the bench beside me. "Where have you been? Everyone's been talking—they said you ran away! Your parents went to the police, and there was this whole search party." Was Everett a part of it? "But they found nothing. It was like you disappeared in thin air." Something like that. "Are you okay? Where did you go?"

I sit in the silence.

"What happened?" she repeats.

I turn to her.

"Jess? It is you, right?"

More than ever before.

She asks again, "Jess?"

"Actually—" I finally speak, "—I'm trying to get something else to catch on."

"What?"

The Girl from Far Away.

Jennifer Austin

Jennifer has been daydreaming about Biack since she was five years old and writing about Ella since she was seven.

After growing up in Cardiff, Jennifer went on to graduate from King's College London with a degree in Chemistry with Bio-medicine before beginning a successful career in Finance. She has since lived and worked in London, Bristol and Dublin.

Jennifer is an overly obsessed dog mum to a goldendoodle named Rey, who was born on Star Wars day. When she isn't writing, she enjoys playing story-based video games, binge watching Netflix series and finding excuses to get out of social gatherings.

The Girl from Far Away is Jennifer's debut novel and the first book of *The Girl from Far Away* series.

To learn more about Jennifer and the next book in the series, go to www.jenniferaustinauthor.com. Subscribe to Jennifer's monthly newsletter to access *The Girl from Far Away Continued*, a collection of short stories set between the books.

You can also follow Jennifer on twitter, pinterest and instagram @imsonotjenny.